ACROSS TIME AND FOREVER

MICHAEL A. CRICHTON

RED LEAD PRESS
PITTSBURGH, PENNSYLVANIA 15222

The contents of this work including, but not limited to, the accuracy of events, people, and places depicted; opinions expressed; permission to use previously published materials included; and any advice given or actions advocated are solely the responsibility of the author, who assumes all liability for said work and indemnifies the publisher against any claims stemming from publication of the work.

ISBN: 978-1-4349-6025-2
Library of Congress Control Number: 2007942729
Printed in the United States of America

First Printing

For more information or to order additional books, please contact:
Red Lead Press
701 Smithfield Street
Third Floor
Pittsburgh, Pennsylvania 15222
U.S.A.
1-800-834-1803
www.redleadbooks.com

CHAPTER 1

 The heat was oppressive. His head felt as if it was being baked in his Stetson. The sun was at its highest point of the day. Every time that he looked at it, its rays blinded him. Flies buzzed incessantly around his sweating neck and ears. He really wished he had taken his coat off completely before getting into his position. His mouth was dry and his lips would soon crack. He fervently hoped that he would hear or see any snakes before they got too close.

As he lay on the hard ground, he looked over the sparse Texas terrain. He knew there were thousands of prairie dogs, snakes, lizards, rabbits, and birds out in front of him. For now, though, there was only silence, as all hid from the sun. He did not have any doubt that he would clearly hear the horse and rider as they made their approach. The approach would have to be made on the trail that hugged the side of the boulders; a trail like a snake's encircling tail.

In his left hand he held onto the forend of his Winchester rifle. It was a new model, the 1886, and it was chambered for the .45/90 cartridge; a big, heavy rifle and cartridge for serious work. He thought killing a United States deputy marshal was serious work. At least, this marshal was. He fully intended to empty the rifle into the man that had been tracking him for nearly a week.

This marshal had cost him dearly. First, the marshal interrupted the bank robbery. He didn't know how or when the marshal arrived in town, but he had and at the worst possible moment. He had known that someone was on his trail, but he never saw the person. Then he ran into Slim Wiley, an old buddy from east Texas and over a cold beer they decided to rob the local bank and head for California.

The robbery went off better than planned. He held onto the bag filled with the gold coins and Slim held onto a saddlebag filled with paper money. Slim went out the front door first and he followed. Just before he reached his horse, a shot rang out and struck the horse rail. He was so startled that he dropped the gold coins. He turned and saw the marshal with his rifle across the street. The rifle was being aimed directly at them. Slim hollered something at him and when he looked up, he saw Slim get shot straight through the heart by the marshal.

He had remembered the spurting blood as his partner fell out of the saddle. Through the screams, the horses, and the people shouting, the marshal's rifle could be heard above it all. This marshal had forced him to flee, lose sleep at night, and run before him like an animal. Well, this animal was through running.

Tommy Lang was 29 years old; a product of the wild environment that comprised the early west. His parents had settled in the eastern region of Texas. The youngest child of six, Tommy had no time for such boring activities as school. Neither did he take to the teachings of the local Methodist minister. What Tommy understood was having a good time. That usually involved theft, guns, and horses. A native son of Texas, he couldn't remember a time when he couldn't ride a horse. The fastest and wildest of ponies kept his interest. Maybe they were just like him.

Aside from his horses and guns, Tommy was a loner. He enjoyed the outdoors. As a youngster, he frequently would sleep on the ground, using the stars as a blanket. This love of the outdoors, and his abilities on horseback probably kept him alive as long as it had; more than anything else. He took up with some other young toughs in the region. When they robbed their first bank outside of Waco, they learned the value of fast horses and guns while trying to outdistance the local law.

Tommy was of average height and weight. He hadn't shaved in 10 days. It was that long since he had been in a whorehouse in Alexandria, Louisiana. It was that last morning that he shot that stranger for being loud and banging on one of the doors in the hallway. The incident was whiskey-clouded, but he remembered enough of it.

He was remembering too much, for he was almost lost in thought when he heard the horse's hoofs on the trail 60 yards out and slightly below his position. He slid the Winchester into place and slowly eased back the hammer; babying the trigger so that no metallic sound would be heard as it was set. He squinted over the sights. So intent on aligning the sights, he did not notice the intense heat emanating off the barrel from being baked by the midday sun. When the horse rounded the boulder, it took him a full heartbeat to realize it was rider less.

Tommy heard the heart-stopping sound of the cartridge carrier, bolt, and lever working together in another Winchester. The voice wasn't really that loud. It was rather calm and deliberate. "Drop that rifle. Don't turn around or I'll kill you as you lay, boy!" The voice was coming from behind him and slightly off to his right.

"I'm a deputy marshal, and you're under arrest." Thoughts flashed through Tommy's mind faster that any pony he had ever ridden as he lay still. "I'm through talking!" said the stranger.

Slowly, Tommy let his rifle slide out of his grasp. "All right, don't shoot, mister. I ain't armed, no more." Tommy was grabbed and turned over onto his back, so fast that he cried out in surprise. "Hey, what the sam hell..." Tommy stopped and squinted to keep the sun out of his eyes. He could feel the rifle barrel against his temple, while the stranger took the pistol from Tommy's waistband.

Finally up on his feet, this was Tommy's first good look at the man. He was of average build. He was wearing a black coat and Stetson. The once white, but now dingy, threadbare shirt was adorned with a long black tie. The face was clean-shaven and provided an unobstructed view of the features. Aged and tanned from years in the outdoors, and with sparse graying at the temples, Tommy guessed him to be in his forties. There was an old scar on one side of his face. With the addition of time, it seemed like someone years earlier had traced a line with a razor along the skin. The Winchester '73 was a rifle model with an octagon barrel. It looked well used. So, too, did the short-barreled Colt on his hip.

"Son, I'm taking you in for the murder of a federal judge and for bank robbing", the stranger said as he tied Tommy's hands together with a short piece of rope that looked like it had been cut just for this purpose.

"What judge? I ain't killed no judge, you damned fool."

The stranger backhanded Tommy across his face knocking him down. Tommy was startled and frightened by the stranger's quickness. As he tried to regain his footing, Tommy could taste blood in his mouth.

The stranger kicked Tommy's legs out from under him, causing him to fall onto his back. The stranger straddled Tommy Lang as he said, "The man you gunned down in that cat house in Alexandria was a federal judge." He leaned down further and shoved a finger into Tommy's chest before continuing, "And you had better watch your mouth around me, boy. I'm taking you back to Alexandria, but cause me any grief along the way and I'll take you in dead and tied across your saddle. You've had your warning."

The calm tone in the voice and the intensity of those coal-black eyes told Tommy that this man was serious. The words combined with the tone of voice and eyes had a chilling effect that while Tommy could not articulate, he certainly felt.

"What's your name, mister?" Tommy asked.

"Bob Forsythe" was the reply.

CHAPTER TWO

Robert Fairbairn Forsythe didn't look the part of an avenging angel or a demon. He was 43 years old and rather ordinary looking, except for those blazing coal black eyes of his. Marshal Forsythe also did not look wealthy, but a close examination of his clothing and equipment spoke of a man knowledgeable in the tools necessary and the means to obtain them.

The black Stetson hat on his head was a top quality 3x felt type. It was one of the slouch models worn by officers on both sides of the late war. It had a wide brim and the front and back ends were molded in a sweeping downward fashion to shield the sun off the face and neck of the wearer.

The leather holster was a top quality, tan rig riding high on the marshal's right hip. A full two dozen cartridge loops on the belt portion held the shining brass cases of Winchester .44 shells. Along the top of the holster was a leather thong looped and knotted which when draped over the pistol's hammer, provided a means of holding the pistol in the holster during riding or strenuous activity by the wearer. Tommy saw that the leather loop was not on the pistol, but hanging down the side of the holster.

The best quality western saddle held not only the scabbard for the Winchester rifle, but also one for a heavy Sharps buffalo rifle. The large, heavy leather saddlebags contained extra cartridges, a change of shirts, slab bacon wrapped in brown paper, coffee beans, and a fire-blackened coffee pot and skillet.

Robert Forsythe had been born in Summit County, Ohio. He was the only child of well to do parents and subsequently, he was pampered and indulged.

His father had been born in Canada to Scottish immigrants that had arrived looking for a fresh start from the harsh economic conditions found in their homeland. Wanting more than to be a farmer, Robert's father, Randolph, immigrated to America while still a young man. Determined and very intelligent, he studied to be a doctor. Dr. Forsythe struggled to make his place in the world and had settled in northeast Ohio. Of medium build, Dr. Forsythe possessed large, rough hands. His smile and heart were as big as his hands. He warmed his patients' spirits with his quiet charm and his practice flourished.

Quiet was one word that seldom fit into Clarise Boyd Forsythe's lifestyle. Clarise, Robert's mother, had also been an only child of a leading citizen in the Akron community. A dark-haired beauty, who was spoiled rotten, Clarise acted as if she were a princess and the small Ohio community, was her kingdom. She attended every civic affair, danced at all the balls and inaugurals, and teased and flirted with the local men folk.

That changed with the arrival of Randolph Forsythe. It hardly seemed as if the young doctor had put away his traveling valise before Clarise was aware of his presence. She boldly and brazenly made her way to the new doctor's office. Once there, Clarise had also fallen under the spell of the young Doctor Forsythe's charm. She found excuses for visits to the doctor's office. His gentle manner was the perfect foil to Clarise's bold and aggressive words and ways. Before too long, the doctor was finding excuses to bump into Clarise on her travels around town and eventually he began to call upon her at home.

Clarise's father referred to his daughter and her determined suitor as, "two sides of the same coin." After a proper courtship and betrothal, Randolph and Clarise were married. The casual observer may have concluded that the Forsythe marriage and relationship was as stormy as a churning sea against a backdrop of lightning. In reality, each admired and desired the other. The tempest that raged between their hearts and souls could not be kept hidden behind bedroom doors, yet they lived within the rigid structure of a more puritanical time in American society. That was the emotion that others saw.

Robert had been well educated, but he did not take to either of his parents' life styles. Dr. Forsythe wanted Robert to choose a career that would assist other people, as he firmly believed that people were placed in this world to make it a better place. His mother liked the social graces, moved in the correct social circles, and liked politics.

What Robert really liked was watching his uncle, Christopher Forsythe, make money. Uncle Chris was a banker by trade, but a rascal by choice. Uncle Chris had followed his older brother to Ohio in the hopes of making his fortune. Christopher Forsythe had fought in the Mexican War and returned back to Ohio in hopes of capitalizing on the nation's prosperity.

Uncle Chris made "friendly wagers" on fast horses, and was deadly serious about the gentlemen's game of draw poker. Uncle Chris had an infectious smile and a cutting wit. With his good looks and devilish ways, he could and did charm the petticoats off the pretty ladies. Uncle Chris also showed young Bob more than just the fundamentals in the use of firearms. While he never married or had children, Uncle Chris genuinely loved his nephew. While Robert's parents objected to Chris' influence on their son, they also knew that he loved Robert and no harm could come to him while under Chris' care.

Bob Forsythe was schooled in the art of "odds and probabilities", horses and horsemanship, and the use of guns. He spent his childhood running through the woods and streams of Ohio in the summer months. During the winters, he ice fished, snow shoed, and tobogganed. When the sap started to run in the maple trees, Robert rode on the horse-drawn sleds that carried the barrels of the clear liquid that would be boiled down into the sweet syrup. Regardless of the season, Robert always found time to ride horses. Robert loved horses!

The first horse that Robert ever sat atop of was an old Clydesdale that labored on a local farm when Robert was just a toddler. Big, slow, and ungainly next to the thoroughbred racehorses that Uncle Chris wagered upon, Robert thought the old farm horse was a winged steed. Its reddish-brown coat was offset by an almost blonde mane. He remembered that the horse stood taller than his father. The horse gave young Robert height and a vantage point. The horse's owner walked alongside with a hand on the bridle while the old plow horse carried Robert as far and as fast as he could have hoped to have gone in those early years. Horses, thereafter, were to play a major part in Robert's life.

So to, were firearms. Even as a small boy, Robert had been fascinated by the pistol that Uncle Chris carried in his coat. The pistol that caught Robert's young eyes was a Navy Colt .36 caliber cap and ball revolver. Long, sleek, lightweight, and richly blued, the steel sidearm was a valued treasure to men traveling in harm's way. Uncle Chris had learned the value of Colonel Colt's revolving pistols during his days as a soldier. He was never without one at his desk in the bank or in his coat at night as he gambled or escorted some lass about town.

As he grew older, Robert persuaded Uncle Chris to provide him with shooting lessons. Robert toiled at the day-to-day chores of disassembly and cleaning of the revolver. Though, he would rather spend his time shooting than cleaning the revolver, Robert was amazed at the genius behind the simplicity of the mechanism.

Robert spent countless hours learning to properly load and cap the revolver. He practiced the tasks of pouring the powder into the chambers, followed by the greased wad, and then the round ball. After some time,

Robert became rather fast and proficient at the regimen. Weeks and months went into the practice of pointing at and hitting targets with the old revolver. By the time that Robert was in his teenage years, he could hit all sorts of objects; running bunnies, copperhead snakes, and occasional targets tossed into the air.

The years passed and Robert continued to grow. He eventually was educated as an accountant. By the time he was eighteen, Robert had his mother's hair and eyes; her charm and poise and his father's facial features, determination, and intelligence. He also had his uncle's quick wit and love of adventure. There was also a war on.

The young Forsythe used his parents' influence to gain a commission in the 8th Ohio Cavalry. After some letter writing and a visit to the local congressman, his determination was rewarded and Second Lieutenant Robert Forsythe rode south and served in several major campaigns throughout the war. He once served under George Armstong Custer, another Ohio boy.

That scar on the left side of his face was from a Confederate colonel's saber. Even Robert could not now remember the name of the place where it happened. It was just another in a long series of skirmishes fought by desperate men. Southerners heroically trying to fend off Grant's relentless advances and Northerners trying desperately to punch a hole in Lee's line which would allow Sherman to take off through the heart of the South.

The day started out in what had become the norm: pitched battles between determined enemies in a repeated seesaw struggle for the same few yards of bloodied ground. The colonel had been quick, but he misjudged the distance to Robert's head. Just the tip of the blade made contact with Robert's face as Robert pulled back on the reins and using his pistol, shot over his horse's ears; hitting the colonel in the head. He does remember the fierce determination in those eyes. He also remembers thinking how much more the colonel looked like a schoolteacher rather than a soldier.

Major Forsythe came home and was welcomed like a conquering hero. He quickly married his sweetheart before the war, Miss Deborah Jensen. He really loved that girl!

Debbie Jensen was two years Robert's junior. Her eyes were the green of some polished gems. She had a good-natured laugh; soft, yet full and hearty. Slender of build and lively of step! And, oh, that long, silky blonde hair! It was long, but usually curled up on her head. Robert had taken it down the night he had tried to make love to her before he went to war, but she would have none of it. She was too prim and proper a young lady. What would she do with a baby if he didn't come back? Besides, she was Catholic and she told him he would have to marry her in the church.

The wedding was a social event in the community. It seemed that even the town caught the fever-pitched activity surrounding the wedding plans. Notices were sent out and there was more than one story in the local paper.

The day of the wedding, Randolph Forsythe was proud and beaming. Clarise complained that she had so little time to organize the affair, but the wedding turned out even better than she had hoped. The church was filled with guests and spectators. Clarise cried silently during the service and again that night after the newlyweds boarded the train for New York. Uncle Chris danced with Debbie and most of the single women in attendance, made toasts, and got drunk.

Robert resigned his commission, and after a honeymoon in New York City, the newlyweds settled down in Akron. Robert bought a nice, older three-story home for himself and Debbie. He went to work for his Uncle Chris at the bank. Within a very short time, Uncle Chris made Robert a partner in the bank. The nation and the local businesses prospered and both Chris and Robert were making money during the post war years. All went well for six years.

By 1871, Mr. and Mrs. Robert Forsythe had two sons and a daughter. They owned their own house and even bought some rental properties in town, as well as some acreage. Debbie had worked hard to make their house a home. She had the house interior wallpapered and planted a vegetable garden in the backyard. Debbie learned to put up with Robert's mother, whom she considered overbearing and pushy, mainly for Robert's sake. Debbie knew her place and kept peace in the family. Her good intentions did not go unnoticed as she was spoiled by Robert's father.

Debbie was a good mother, yet she retained that youthful innocence, and was at the same time womanly in her flirtations with Robert, which drove him mad with passion. It was all that she could do to keep from getting pregnant every year. She was as crazy about Robert as much as he was about her. She loved him mightily and she never really fought him off, but rather encouraged Robert's behavior. 1871 was also the year that Robert had to go out West on business for his uncle.

After stops in St. Louis, Kansas City, and Dallas; he ended up in Houston, Texas. Robert marveled at the wide-open countryside; a world apart from his wooded homeland. There and along the way, Robert saw the sights and sounds of big, riotous cities. Open gambling, cathouses that actually looked proper, saloons that never closed, fortunes made and lost in the blink of an eye, and violence! Men killing and getting killed over money and women. He also met rangers and marshals. The type of men bred by the tumultuous conditions of the frontier. Men whose words were few and actions that were deliberate and often times, violent.

One night, towards the end of his stay in town, Robert Forsythe bought dinner for a United States deputy marshal named Grant Moss. He had met Moss during a visit to the local courts and banks. U.S. Deputy Marshal Grant Moss was a quiet man in his late thirties. His eyes fixed upon you as you spoke to him or while he watched you. He sported a large handle bar moustache. He wore a white shirt adorned with a long ribbon black tie. Moss wore a black long coat over a vest. He sported a large Colt Dragoon revolver in a cross draw holster. He was an impressive sight.

During dinner and after-dinner drinks, Moss regaled young Robert with tales of the duties of the marshals. Blood-curdling stories of innocent victims, wild badmen ranging the frontier, the hunts and posses, and deadly shoot-outs. Before leaving town, Robert bought a parting drink for Moss and this time made inquiry into the selection process for deputy marshals.

On the trip home, Robert thought a great deal about life on the frontier and his own life at home. Robert slept very little on the train. In the early morning hours of the night, he looked out the train window. Actually, he stared out the window as if mesmerized by the landscape and fixtures that flew past. This trip out West had stirred something deep within him that he hadn't felt since wanting to go to war. After he arrived home, Debbie immediately noticed the change in Robert's mood. She, at first, suspected that he had an affair with some woman in Houston and confronted him about it.

After hearing Robert's explanation for his moodiness, Debbie wished it had been another woman. Women she knew and could fight. Fighting a man's dream was something that no girl learns from her mother. Debbie was desperately trying to salvage the life that she knew, and she was afraid that it was about to come to an end. She tried everything she could think of; she asked her mother-in-law to speak some sense to her son. She tried keeping him occupied with attending social events, parties, outings with the children, and frequent lovemaking. But nothing was to derail Robert when his mind was set. That strong will and determination were family traits etched into his spirit and forged by a war.

Debbie was beaten. She loved her husband and babies; and she knew that he loved them all dearly. Her options were few; divorce was out of the question. So a dutiful, but most unhappy and apprehensive wife boarded a train with her young family and United States Deputy Marshal Robert Forsythe when he was ordered to report for duty in the Oklahoma Territory in the spring of '73.

CHAPTER THREE

After delivering Tommy Lang to the jail at Alexandria, Robert busied himself with the necessary paperwork. Few people realize to this day the amount of paperwork that the early marshals had to perform to document their time and expense vouchers.

Robert didn't have any trouble learning the paperwork that went along with being a marshal. Actually, it was too easy. During the beginning of his tenure as a deputy marshal, Robert did not experience any problems with the complexities of dealing with the federal judges, the volumes of paperwork, the traveling by horseback or the tracking of wanted criminals. What bothered Robert the most were the constant traveling demands away from home and the killings; at least at first.

The traveling away from home started out slowly and for the most part, was overnight trips. These were either for serving papers on businesses or individuals or transporting wanted persons already in custody. Later, the trips were for the tracking of wanted persons on federal lands or those suspected of crimes in the Indian territories. The routine was simple; loaded with provisions and numerous warrants for named individuals and blank or "John Doe" warrants for circumstances that developed along the way, the marshals left on the hunt. They returned when they caught their quarries and turned them over to the federal judges for trials. After resting, the marshals repeated their routine. Often times, the marshals were brought in dead and tied across a prospector's mule or on the back of a stage.

Robert's war time experiences may have caused him to kill and view death, but it did not prepare the young marshal for the demands of facing each of the men that he killed. Riding and shooting into faceless and name-less massed troops in the heat of battle is entirely different than staring into the face of man that refuses to be arrested and is more than willing to kill you.

Robert soon learned that the men on the frontier who were wanted by the federal courts were men that were varied in their backgrounds and their criminal offenses. But they were similar in that they were determined not to be taken into custody and were more than prepared to kill or be killed, with-out hesitation. Federal law and the men charged with enforcing the law were of no consequence to these men!

Robert's skill with sidearms saved his life on more than one occasion during the first few years. As Robert gained expertise in the hunting of men and reading their eyes and mannerisms, he was sought out after by more judges for the difficult assignments. This necessitated more and longer trips away from family and home. While he was becoming more of a force to be feared on the plains, Robert was gradually becoming more of a stranger at home.

Many times Robert wanted to change things between himself and his family, but he couldn't. Something deep within him would not let the lawless go. He knew that he could catch them and he wanted to catch them as much as they wanted to remain free. Robert was becoming very good at what he chose to do; hunting men.

Expense vouchers! What a poor, pathetic business practice as Robert the accountant saw things. Depending upon the marshal in charge or the nature of the expense, the vouchers could be rejected and the deputy marshals were out the expenses and any money for meals that they fed their prisoners. Since the expense vouchers were the basis of the marshals' pay that also meant that occasionally, they were not paid for their "trouble". He was grateful that he had made sufficient monies to provide for a growing family before taking this job. At least he could visit his family and get a hot meal while in town.

Years earlier, Debbie refused to submit further to the primitive living and housing conditions she found on the frontier. That in addition to the months spent alone raising three small children, while her husband tracked outlaws and renegade Indians. After years of arguing, and Debbie and the children taking extended visits to his parents in Ohio, Robert agreed to buy a nice home for Debbie and the kids in Alexandria.

The house was a large, two-story structure. They bought it at a good price and it was relatively close to the Texas regions that Robert patrolled. There had been no other way. Debbie was just not going to subject herself and the children to the lack of schools, churches, good homes and the dis-eases, open vices, and poor living conditions found in the early frontier set-tlements. She had often said that she was through traipsing after her nomad husband.

After submitting the vouchers and his reports on the death of Wiley and the arrest of Lang, Robert put his horse away in the town's stable and took the horse-drawn trolley home. He sat quietly on the hard bench seat and stared out on the trip to his house; no, her house.

Deborah Lyn Jensen Forsythe had matured very regally with time. At 41, she looked several years younger. Her skin was still smooth (she attributed it to the climate and it was the only good thing she would say about the South's humidity), and her figure was more sensual than girlish.

She was the only girl out of the seven Jensen children. But she felt she had not been spoiled, as her parents had been as strict with her as they had with her brothers. While her father may have only given her stern looks, her mother disciplined her just as she did her brothers. Debbie's father had been a college professor. When she lived at home, he often entertained the family in the evenings by reading out loud the works of the ancient Greek writers, and once she remembered, he translated and read aloud one of the writings of Julius Caesar. It was no wonder that she found Robert Forsythe to be so dashing a character that Saturday when she first saw him.

Robert had entered a local horseracing contest, which was the liveliest of the events scheduled for a town celebration. On the ground, he was cultured and well bred. But astride that large bay stallion, he was a part of nature; something seething to burst loose! He had quite a smile and unlike the other boys his age, he could carry on a conversation with his elders and the women.

Debbie knew Robert was back in town. No one told her that Robert was back; she just knew. At an early age, Debbie had been very observant and noticed subtle little changes in people and their surroundings. Her ability to read people and her surroundings grew more acute with each passing year. Each of the children found out the hard way that their mother was no one to be taken lightly. She could sense things, good and bad, before they happened.

Debbie had the children cleaning the house and she was busying dressing for him. She selected the dark green satin dress. The white lace on the front of it and the large bow on the back accentuated her figure. From the kitchen, emanated the aroma of the cooked rabbits in the broiling pan with gravy. There was also the aroma of boiled okra on the stove and fresh biscuits in the oven. On the window ledge cooling was a pecan pie. Robert liked good food and he had a sweet tooth that knew no end.

In lighter moments, she thought that if the bandits and bullets could not dissuade him from marshaling, the love of good, hot food from the oven would have. It was one of the two things he dearly missed on the range. She was the other.

Robert looked the town over on the drive home. People were everywhere! It was definitely greener than the dirt dry area of the plains. He had to admit that the South had a pleasant look, as well as, nature to it. The people were usually friendly and the communities had a charm and sophistication that were lacking in other places.

It would be good to be home for a while. Tracking a hard case like Lang was getting harder with each passing year. Years spent in the saddle and sleeping on the hard ground were taking their toll. He was unaware of it, but there was still fire in those eyes of his.

As he walked the last blocks to the house, Debbie watched from her second-story perch. Robert still cut a good figure. He always shaved and washed whenever possible on the trail. In that black coat, Stetson, white shirt, and tie, he looked more like a preacher than a lawman. Though, she had to admit, she had never seen any preachers carrying Winchester rifles with their saddlebags. Even being Catholic, she would have settled for him being a preacher, rather than a marshal. At least they could live together in a civilized place.

Their daughter, Abigail, was first to greet Robert just as he approached the front yard. Almost seventeen, she could still afford to act the child. Debbie watched as Abbey ran and jumped into those strong arms. She noticed how her baby had grown and looked rather mature standing next to the man she was hanging onto. In addition to having filled out to womanly proportions, Abbey was only half a head shorter than Robert. Her hair was a light honey colored and she had the darkest blue eyes.

Debbie would have to tell Robert about the young man that has been rather steady company at the house since that summer church picnic. She was worried that it was rather serious and Abbey was just too young. Robert would not take this well. Still, Abbey looked the child as she peeked into his saddlebags, looking for any present that daddy may have brought his little girl. And as always, there was a wrapped package.

Jacob stood on the front porch. Jacob was the perfect blending of the best features of both his parents, but he was his mother's child. Serious in his studies and with a gentler demeanor than his older brother. "Quietly direct" was how Debbie described Jacob. During one of his frequent somber and thoughtful moods, Jacob would be teased by his father that he would make a fine priest someday. And he would, too. Jacob was too old for running and hugging. He approached his dad and shook his hand. Robert handed his rifle to Abbey and hugged him on the front porch; where anyone could see. Jacob was mortified; Abbey just giggled as she skipped into the house.

Christopher, the oldest, had been away for almost a year, now. He was studying to be a doctor in New York. Chris was Robert's favorite. Chris looked and acted more like his father than Debbie cared to admit. Early on, she recognized the fire in his eyes, as well. Debbie was determined that he would not grow up and follow in his father's footsteps. She was determined to break the man, rather than subject some other poor girl to such a life or fate has she had been forced into. Fortunately, for both of them, on one of those extended trips to Ohio, Chris had taken a keen interest in "Papa" Forsythe's profession.

Debbie stood at the bottom of the stairs as Robert entered. He took off his hat and just stood there, soaking up the sight of her like a thirsty man drinks a cold beer. He grabbed her and spun her around; kissing her the whole time. At least, their children were embarrassed for them.

Later that night, while everyone slept, Debbie stroked Robert's hair. He stirred ever so slightly. She knew he could afford the pleasure of deep slumber here in her bed. Laying naked next to each other, she could see and feel all of his numerous scars made by bullets, horse falling accidents, and the other hazards of life on the frontier. He was probably ten pounds lighter than the last time. Tears rolled down her cheeks as she realized that while he loved her greatly and she could keep his body in her bed, his soul and spirit belonged to no one; and he would soon leave on the hunt again. Long ago, Debbie had concluded it was too much like chasing thunder.

Robert slept, but it was not peaceful. As always when he did not have to sleep with one eye open, he dreamt. Probably having nightmares would be more accurate. Before him flashed thousands of images: faces of the men he had killed; mutilated corpses that were the victims of a wild, growing land; the crackling of campfires; the acrid smell of gunsmoke, the creaking of leather saddles; sounds of men and animals in their death throes; firing his Sharps rifle over his dead horse as Indians galloped towards him; and remembrances of pain suffered at the hands of those he pursued.

Seldom were there images of happier times: Uncle Chris explaining the finer points of the gamble; the sound of Debbie's laughter; the boys trying to rope a calf; or a little girl with pigtails playing with the shiny badge on his coat. He was only slightly aware of the fact that Debbie was holding his head to her breast and sobbing quietly.

CHAPTER FOUR

In silence, the riders and horses moved single file through the morning fog. The sun was just breaking over the horizon, and it was still cold and not quite light. There were five of them and they were in a foul mood. They had traveled throughout the night to reach their destination; and to avoid being seen for too long a period in the daylight. Too many of them were wanted by the law for too many offenses. Their destination was a small cabin on the Texas side of the Texas/Oklahoma border.

The leader of the group was G.W. Cooper. Gilbert William Cooper was 48 years old and he looked his age. He looked as if each and every one of those years had been harsh and cold. His hair was graying and his eyes were as cold as the morning air. Cooper was wanted for a variety of offenses in several territories and places on the Western frontier. He seemed to specialize in theft and murder, though.

A hard case from Pennsylvania, Cooper would later be referred to by Marshal Forsythe as "a stench in the nostrils of humanity". Cooper completed the fourth grade before his step-father put him to work full-time. His real father had been killed in a drunken brawl in Kentucky over a "soiled dove". His mother remarried to a miner that had no patience with what he saw as laziness and trouble in the young G. W.

Since G. W. could not be troubled with school and he only performed enough chores so that he could eat at the dinner table, his stepfather decided to put him to work.

Cooper's stepfather did not want to be around him at the mines and since he owed the local blacksmith money for shoeing his mule, he turned

G.W. over to the 'smith to square up his bill. Cooper worked as the apprentice of a blacksmith. It was more slavery than apprenticeship. Copper was given two meals a day, a place to sleep in the barn, and all the beatings he could endure for minor transgressions. While he hated his step-father and the blacksmith, he grew to love horses. To him, they seemed gentle and noble; unlike the people that surrounded him. Like his real father, Cooper would become an alcoholic; who had a short temper and no love for people.

By the time that the War Between the States broke out, Cooper was working at a blacksmith shop in central Pennsylvania. Enlisting in the Union Army, gave Cooper the chance to escape his drab existence. Up to that time, he spent most of his time, working, drinking, and spending the remainder of his money on two-dollar whores.

While his military career had been uneventful for the most part, Cooper was able to join a cavalry unit based largely on his blacksmithing skills more than anything else. Cooper had been exposed to numerous campaigns that were to be highlighted in the written annuls of the war. The war highlighted another of Cooper's talents — killing!

The act of taking human lives did not bother Cooper. He proved very adept at killing with either the sword or revolving pistol. Cavalry units, by their very nature, were usually well in front of the main fighting units; and therefore, in the thick of things without direct control of the established command structure. Oftentimes, their conduct was deplorable when viewed in the light of reason brought by peacetime.

Cooper was on the run from the law for a killing in Arkansas. While on a drunk, he killed a young whore for a laughing during sex; laughter that Cooper assumed was directed at him. The killing of the whore could have been explained, but Cooper compounded his troubles when he shot the whore's pimp; who burst into the room upon hearing the screams. Once again Cooper had acted without thinking; he just instinctively turned and shot. The pimp also happened to own the saloon as well as the seven whores. Both the girls and bar were major businesses in the town. Killing businessmen, even in small towns in Arkansas was a problem.

He was heading for Texas. He wanted to avoid any encounters with Indians and had gathered a group of misfits for protection from Indians, as well as his plans for riches.

His plans included robbing a stage. Cooper had been thinking about this robbery for some time. Everyone knew that Texas was being settled more with each passing day. It was safer for people to settle and for miners to roam the plains. A big mining outfit from the East had begun strip mining and was pulling out valuable ore; including gold. The stage was being used to haul goods and a payroll for a mining company. The driver and guard were old timers that knew their business and they were heavily armed. He would need help to pull off the robbery. The group consisted of Garth Davidson, Shorty

Thompson, Eli Harrison, and Jonathan Canby.

Garth Davidson was a big, dirty man who looked as if he seldom had many thoughts in his head at one time. He bathed fewer times than he had intelligent, sober thoughts. Davidson, like Cooper, was a veteran of the Union Army during the War Between the States. Unlike Cooper, he stayed in the Army. He liked not having to think for himself. In the Army, he was told when to sleep, when to get up, when to eat, when to shoot, and they paid him a regular wage. The army was the only real time that Davidson had a somewhat regular and normal life.

Wild and uneducated, Davidson was a runaway from a Pennsylvania reform school when he joined the infantry. Violence and murder were nothing new to him. Being out of a jail cell in the past few years was new. He fancied himself a gambler, but he was once beaten severely after having been found cheating in a card game in New Orleans. Davidson later went to Leavenworth for rape and attempted murder of a teenage girl. Davidson could handle a team of horses and he was a fair shot with either a Colt revolver or Winchester rifle.

Horace Thompson and Eli Harrison were cousins from Colorado. Both left home together and drifted around the plains states for a few years. Big and hard working muscular were their more endearing qualities. "Shorty" was a kid's nickname that stuck with Thompson since his early years when he started growing much sooner than his classmates. Both were over six feet tall and as strong as a team of oxen.

The cousins had struck a friendship as kids. They had attended school long enough to read and cipher some. Their muscles were more developed than their brains. Their carefree attitudes could conceal that they were lazy and thieves, to the casual observer. They were slow to anger, but they were fast and good with their guns and had killed several times, but they preferred cattle rustling, as there were no persons to have to face. 1886 found them with no money, wandering the plains states trying to avoid familiar faces and places where someone might remember that they were wanted for rustling and theft.

Jonathan Canby was a nineteen-year old kid, originally from New York City, who had deserted from the cavalry. Canby looked like a lanky, pimple-faced kid from next door. A tall, gangly youth who couldn't weigh more than one hundred and thirty-five pounds wearing wet clothes; Canby had his uses. He looked harmless enough, if not innocent; a quality that more than once had caused folks to drop their guard around him. But he was wild and crazy without having to drink. Behind that toothy grin hid the face of ruthless killer. Beaten by an alcoholic father and tormented by a selfish mother, he killed them both before enlisting in the cavalry under an assumed name.

Cooper had no way of knowing that at the moment he crossed over the border into Texas, his fate was decided. Cooper was to ignite a powder keg of violence that would span over 100 years and culminate in the strangest and most bizarre events in human history.

CHAPTER FIVE

 The time spent at home had been nice and quiet for Mr. and Mrs. Robert Forsythe. He and Debbie had not argued once. The children were on their best behavior, as well. Robert had caught up on his newspaper reading and had taken Debbie out on shopping trips as well as dining out in the more plush restaurants. He even enjoyed the semi-celebrity status in the community. This was due to newspaper articles over the years that had been written on a few of his more notable exploits on the frontier.

Lives of the early federal marshals were often cut short. While their duties of serving papers, levying against and auctioning property were boring; the marshals themselves were always in the thick of emotion-charged events and people. A practice that was not always conducive to long and healthy lives. Robert had been in the thick of things and had pushed his luck for more than thirteen years.

Within weeks, Robert had orders to ride shotgun on a mail car headed for Dallas. Once there, he was to levy the assets of a freighting company. It would be Dallas' proximity to the small cabin on the Texas/Oklahoma border that would place Robert on a collision course with Cooper and his men. Dallas would also be the place that would change forever Robert and his way of life.

Debbie was in her bedroom packing Robert's clothes in a valise for his trip to Dallas. Robert was there watching her as he stood eating a piece of pie. Her concluding ritual was to place his spare Colt .44 pistol and a box of Winchester cartridges on top of the clothing. Except for his Sharps rifle, Robert kept the same caliber in his weapons; ammunition interchangeability could be important to the lone man on the range.

She straightened up and looked at Robert as she took a deep breath before saying what was on her mind. As nice as the past weeks had been, there was something wrong. Debbie could not express why she felt or sensed the thoughts, but she knew that her time with Robert was drawing to a close and she had to speak her mind.

"Except for the first year of our marriage, these past weeks have been the best for me. I have always been home for your return. I have kept the house and raised the children. I feel as if I have been your beacon home; your security in an otherwise crazy world..."

"Honey, I know..."

"Don't interrupt me, Robert! Please allow me to finish this. It has taken too long for me to work up the courage to say it and I'm afraid of what may come, if I do not."   "All right."

"As I said, I have been here for your return. What am I to do if you do not come back for me? You are and always shall be the love of my life." Tears were rolling down her cheeks now. "Without you, I do not know what I would do or become; and I am deathly afraid that this time you will not return to me. I sense something dreadful. I want you to love me as I love you. I want..." There was no more, as she stood there and completely broke down sobbing loudly.

Robert dropped the plate on the floor, as he grabbed his wife and squeezed her against his chest. "Deborah Forsythe, you're imaging things! I have always returned home to you. I always will. Stop this foolishness, right now! They'll have to kill me to keep me from you."

Debbie looked up into those coal-black eyes, and she cried again. She could not explain it to him; it wasn't his dying she feared.

CHAPTER SIX

Robert had loaded his valise, saddle, and rifle scabbard onto the small buggy that he had Jacob get from the stable. Holding his hat to shield his eyes from the early morning sun, Robert looked about his house. He had said his good-bye to Debbie in the house. She never accompanied him to the train station or the stable when he left for work. She hated good-byes, and she thought public displays of affection were improper.

Abbey was already sitting on the bench seat for the ride to the train depot. Robert climbed onto the buggy and called out to the horse to get it moving. They were less than five minutes into their journey when Abbey spoke.

"Momma thinks you're not coming back", she said as she looked down at her feet.

Robert shifted the reins into his left hand, and with his right hand, cupped Abbey's chin and pulled it back and made her face him. "Did your momma say that?"

"No, but a woman knows."

"Your momma is having a hard time over something I cannot understand. I have always come back. I love you all very much and I will come back to you as soon as I'm through with my assignment. Do you understand that, girl?" His tone was that of Marshal Forsythe and not daddy.

Abbey nodded yes.

"Besides, who said you're a woman?" Laughter had returned to the eyes and the face of her father. "I thought you were daddy's girl."

"I always will be", she said and then curled her arm through his and placed her head on his shoulder. Everything was right again in her world.

"Your mother tells me that you're getting serious over that boy you met at the church picnic."

"He thinks he's in love with me. I can handle him. Don't worry, daddy, I'll make the right boy come and ask you for my hand in marriage. Momma, said any boy wanting to marry me would have to first ask you."

He put his arm around her, and kissed her on the forehead.

Leaning against Robert, Abbey thought to herself that her dad always started out smelling and looking good. She could smell the bay rum after-shave on the freshly shaved face. His shirt was ironed and stilled smelled of the fresh breeze that dried it just the day before. She and Jacob had polished his boots the night before and the sun glistened off the boot tips. The rest of the drive to the depot was in silence.

At the depot, he pulled along side the mail car where Freddie Cutler was standing with the sliding door open. Robert called out, "Freddie, you old horse thief! How have you been? It's been years since I last saw you. Why I would have thought they'd have buried your old carcass by now."

"Any time you feel lucky, come on over here, boy! I can take a belt to your backside any day of the week!"

The two shook hands. Freddie was an old postal employee who remembered the marshal when he was first appointed and working the Oklahoma Territory. Robert introduced his daughter to Freddie, and then loaded his gear into the mail car.

Robert was getting ready to say good-bye to Abigail, when he looked up and off the platform saw a black man driving a buckboard wagon who stopped it at the depot. It would have been ordinary except Debbie was sitting next to him! The driver helped her down and after she paid him, she reached into the back of the buggy and pulled out Robert's Sharps rifle and scabbard.

Robert ran to her and she started to walk rapidly to him. Robert caught up to her first and asked what she was doing.

"You may need this and you left it in the den", she said as she handed him the rifle.

Robert looked at the rifle, as if for the first time. It was a .45-100 Sharps Sporting Rifle Model of 1874, with a 30-inch octagon barrel, double triggers, and a Vernier sight. Handcrafted and meticulously assembled, the single-shot, breech-loading rifle was a work of art. It was designed for long-range hunting of large animals. The long, paper-patched lead bullets were the forerunners of jacketed ammunition of the twentieth century. The bullets and measured charges of gunpowder were capable of downing any animal on the continent.

At least in Robert's hands, it was still being used for hunting. He had used it on everything from wild animals to wild men. The farthest shot he made with it was just under eight hundred yards. It was the only firearm that

Debbie had ever purchased. Actually, it was Uncle Chris who instructed her on the rifle, caliber, and accessories. But it was her idea to have the barrel engraved with the words, "Straight and True". According to her, it described not only the way he shot, but also how he lived. Secretly, Debbie thought it best described their love for each other.

She bought it for Robert as a Christmas gift a few years after he was made a marshal. He had once been pinned down for hours by scalp hunters who fired at him from almost three hundred yards out, and he was unable to effectively return fire with his Winchester .44 from that distance. Robert was as deadly as sin with the Sharps. And like those he hunted, Robert possessed the willingness to use deadly force in the blink of an eye.

"Thanks, honey, but I'm riding shotgun in the mail car. I have my Winchester. I won't need this", Robert said handing the rifle and scabbard back to Debbie.

"I think you will. Take it for me, please, Robert", she said as she handed him his last four boxes of factory-made, paper-patched cartridges.

Debbie hugged him and kissed him in public view, and then she whispered in his ear, "I love you, Robert. Come back to me. I'll be waiting for you." She stepped back and flashed him a genuinely warm, yet, impish smile. It was the girl of his youth!

Robert kissed Abbey and watched as both his girls took the buggy home. Robert boarded the mail car, closed the sliding door; and with it, sealed his fate.

CHAPTER SEVEN

The ringing in his ears from the screaming was almost too much to bear for someone with a hangover. G.W. Cooper and his men had surprised the stage driver and his passengers as planned on a desolate stretch of land in Collin County, Texas.

Cooper and his men were dressed in long canvas coats and had neckerchiefs covering their faces. Cooper had done all the talking to the driver. He knew they had the right stage after watching the route and stage schedules for almost two weeks.

The driver had been reluctant to turn over the cash box, so Cooper killed him with a blast from his 10-gauge shotgun. Once the shooting had started, not even he could control his men. Three passengers were killed in addition to the driver and the man riding shotgun for the stage line. One of the passengers was a salesman for a St. Louis book company. He was shot right away. The others were a widow and her teenaged daughter traveling to visit relatives in El Paso.

They lived just a little longer than the others. Cooper was the only man who did not rape the women. They were violated on the ground next to where the dead had fallen. Davidson killed the widow with a pistol shot through her chest and Canby cut the throat on the girl, when they were through. Shorty Thompson had even shot the two lead horses.

This really angered Cooper, and he screamed, "Have you all gone mad? Why are you killing good horse flesh?" He was pointing the shotgun now at Shorty.

Davidson spoke up saying, "G.W., you know we can't let the horses go.

Why, they'll run back to the relay station and alert the wranglers. They gotta be kilt for our escape to be good."

Cooper agreed after thinking it over in his mind for a few moments, and said, "Hurry and be done with it. We gotta get out of here. We've been here too long as it is. Let's ride!"

The group rode back to the cabin belonging to Lester Kingsman and his common-law wife, Katy Walton. Cooper had decided to use Kingsman cabin as a base of operations while in Texas. Kingsman was a distant relative of Cooper's. Kingsman was a no-account that lived off Walton. Actually, he had killed Walton's husband in a dispute over her two years earlier. Katy's flaming red hair was all that was left of her once angelic beauty. Life on the frontier was hard. She was still a pretty picture compared to the women in cow towns that the cowboys amused themselves with.

It was because Mr. Walton was dead for over two years and no one had paid the taxes on the land, that the cabin site would come to the attention of the federal courts and marshals. It would turn out to be bad luck for the marshals and G.W., as well. In the aftermath of the robbery and killing, Cooper and his men stayed at the cabin and got drunk for three days. Later, when he sobered up enough to clean his shotgun, Cooper had decided that the cabin was close enough to hit several likely stages and mining lines. "Why" he thought to himself, "that he and the boys might even try train robbing, if they got good enough. Yeah, the Cooper gang. I like that."

The next day's stage came across the aftermath of the robbery. Even the old muleskinner of a driver had trouble keeping his breakfast down. Not even the flies and coyotes could cover up the savagery of the carnage.

Within two days, the news had traveled to the Dallas/Ft. Worth area. The notoriety appealed to Cooper the more he thought about it. But he really liked the idea of himself leading a gang that was the talk of the West.

CHAPTER EIGHT

Robert Forsythe was sitting at a dining room table by himself. It was seven in the morning, and he had a pot of coffee on the table before him as well as a plate of biscuits and strawberry preserves. He was reading the Dallas newspaper.

He lifted his eyes from the paper when he heard the door to the cafe open. In walked a woman who was well dressed, but definitely in a hurry judging from her quick pace. He had actually heard her walking on the wood planks while she was still outside. She spoke to the cafe owner, who in turn pointed towards Robert. He watched as this stranger turned and walked straight at him with the same rapid walk.

She stopped at his table and said, "You are an officer of the law, are you not?" Her tone was accusatory; she was not making an inquiry.

Robert stood up and said, "Ma'am, I'm Robert Forsythe. I'm a United States Deputy Marshal." He bowed politely, but he kept those black eyes of his on her the entire time. He noticed that she was flushed about her face and neck. There were slight beads of moisture the size of pinheads on her upper lip. He could not tell if she was hot from the weight of her coat and hat, the pace of her walk, or if she was really angry.

"I'm Amanda Weaver, sir. I don't think I've met a United States Marshal before. I run the local newspaper, and I want to know why you are sitting here instead of out trying to catch those murderers in Collin County that are roaming the countryside making it unsafe for decent, Christian women to travel?" She stopped and took in her first breath, as she looked him over.

"Are you referring to the stagecoach robbery that occurred a few days ago, ma'am?"

"You know full well that is exactly what I am referring to mister marshal. And stop calling me ma'am; you're older than I am."

"First, I believe I read in your newspaper that three Christian men, as well, as the women died. Secondly, Miss Weaver, robbing a private stage and killing the passengers are not federal crimes. I only enforce federal laws and court orders. I am empowered to investigate and arrest for violations of only those laws. I have no police powers per se in the state of Texas. This is a matter for the local authorities. Will you do me the honor of joining me for coffee?"

The eloquence of his speech caught her off guard. She was not used to such a vocabulary and the ability to articulate it in the Texas men that she knew. She found herself sitting almost by reflex. Robert obtained another cup and poured her some coffee. They were silent only for seconds, but in that time they scrutinized each other, closely.

She noticed that he was clean and freshly shaved. He wore his shirt collar buttoned and he was wearing a long black ribbon-style tie that was neatly tied. She also saw a Winchester rifle leaning on the wall behind him, and within easy reach. A man who lived on the edge of violence. It seemed rather exciting to her. She found him to be very handsome. His features were clearly defined. The straight nose and high cheekbones were the result of generations of Scots making up the Forsythe clan. Even more noticeable than the scar, were those eyes of his. Amanda thought to herself that if they were any brighter, there would be flames dancing in them. She was still flushed, but it had nothing to do with her temper or clothing.

Robert could not get over how pretty, no, how beautiful Amanda Weaver was as she sat across from him. She was probably in her mid-thirties. Her dark red hair had some curl to it; which he assumed was natural. She did not seem the type to wait around for a curling iron to get hot. Her skin was smooth, and her eyes were so clear, they sparkled. Her green velvet dress accentuated her eyes. It also defined her figure; slender, but full and womanly. She was actually smiling now. That smile made her look more the imp, than vixen or harsh boss of a newspaper.

She was the first to speak. "I really should go. I have a dozen things to do back at the paper. It was very nice to meet you. I have never met a U.S. marshal before. Will you be staying in town long?"

"I really do not know. My schedule is dependent upon the cooperation of others and the timeliness of the circuit judge. Please stay and finish your coffee."

"I drink tea; coffee's never agreed with me. I cannot image anyone not cooperating with you and that rifle of yours", she said as she nodded her head in the direction of the rifle leaning against the wall behind Robert.

"I have found that the frontier is still a wild and unsafe place to be at times", he said as his eyes fixed on hers. She could not see from where she sat, but there were slight rust spots on the left side of the rifle's frame. The rust was the result of the moisture on his hand and how he habitually carried the rifle in his left hand when off his horse.

"I must be going, now." She stood up and he immediately did so as well. "I do hope you will forgive me for being so rude to you initially. It's just that..."

"There is no need to apologize, Amanda Weaver, he interrupted. "On the contrary, it was my pleasure meeting you."

"Well, thank you again. Good-bye, Marshal Forsythe."

"Good-bye, Miss Weaver."

Probably no one in the cafe had ever heard of electricity before, but they would have been able to describe it if they had looked at the faces of either the marshal or the newspaperwoman.

CHAPTER NINE

Amanda Marie Weaver was 36 years old. Her beauty and youthful figure belied the years. She was of Irish descent and that temper of hers
fit the spitfire that was hidden under her heavy cotton clothing. Amanda
Weaver was slender and tiny. She had a demure little smile and a little girl
laugh about her. Amanda was quick-witted and enjoyed being spoiled. She
was also very determined and could be extremely hardheaded; depending
upon the circumstances.

She had only recently moved to the Dallas area. She told everyone that
she was a widow, but the truth of the matter was she was divorced. This
would have made for a scandalous situation, at that time. She figured that
being a businesswoman was enough of an obstacle to overcome.

Originally from New York, Amanda was a free spirit and she did as she
pleased. That alone was something of a novelty, considering the times for
women. Amanda met and lived with a man that owned a small freighting
business. They eventually married, but did not have any children; it just did
not fit into any of their plans at the time. They worked at trying to make the
business a success.

Success in the business world kept eluding, Timothy, her husband. The
freighting business began to crumble due to lack of sound management practices. As well as, his drinking and womanizing. Amanda thought she knew
better than her husband, and they argued about the business and finally
themselves, until she left him. Both were relieved as months of bitterness
came to an end.

Amanda continued to live in New York, and she found work at a newspaper and learned the trade. First, at menial tasks, then more complex skills from the types of equipment to the craft of journalism.

She left New York looking for adventure as well as a fresh start. Amanda had used her position on the paper to learn of other newspapers in need of a skilled manager. In Dallas, she found a paper in dire need of not only management, but an owner. With money that she had saved over the years, and some help from her parents, she found herself in Dallas only months ahead of the arrival of the first United States deputy marshal she ever saw.

The paper was basically very small, and was using very old equipment for the time. Everything about it was a struggle. She employed two others who primarily helped with the type set, ran the press, distributed the papers, swept the place, and in a pinch - were the reporters. Her hours were long, the work was hard, and there were few hours for anything she wanted to do. It worked out well, since she did not know what she really wanted out of life in 1886 Dallas.

Sometimes, late at night, Amanda would sit at the kitchen table too tired to cook. Looking at the ink on her hands and apron, she would start to cry. It seemed like another lifetime it was so long ago that she had been taken out to the theater and to dances in the spring and summer. Now, her evenings out were spent at the paper and there had been no dances and very little laughter in her life since her arrival in Dallas.

She originally shared a room with a schoolmarm, but found the lack of solitude completely unacceptable. Amanda had begun renting a house in town; a reluctant agreement due to her money situation. She really wanted a house and place she could call her own. She signed the rental agreement only after the addition of a clause allowing the option to purchase. Amanda Weaver was nothing, if not independent and resourceful.

For all of her worldly experiences, she had never met a man possessing her qualities before. She also was rather naive from the standpoint of those born or who had lived on the frontier. She had never seen anyone killed and she had never been involved in a physical struggle.

With the recent arrival of Marshal Forsythe, all that was about to change.

CHAPTER TEN

It didn't take long before they became the talk of the town. The marshal and newspaperwoman were seen together quite often. It started out innocently enough. Each week brought news of an additional stage robbery. Robert and Amanda continued to bump into one another in the course of their businesses. She asked him for an interview.

During it, Amanda asked personal questions of Robert, in addition to professional ones. Robert had surprised her by candidly answering them. Judging from the smirk on his face, Amanda thought Robert was teasing or flirting with her. He was and she did not mind. In fact, she enjoyed the newfound attention.

She joined him for dinner one night at a local restaurant and they had a long talk during dinner. He watched the tight curls on her head bounce each time that she laughed. She watched his eyes catch fire as he looked upon her. They had a long walk around town afterwards. As they continued to see each other and get to know one another better, Amanda learned that Robert had been schooled as an accountant. Amanda asked him about financial matters. They spoke of business practices. She needed help with her and the paper's finances. Record keeping had never been her strong suite. Since she spent most of her waking time working on the paper, there had been even less time spent in the tracking of monies.

Gently and thoroughly, Robert explained the banking and accounting concerns over morning coffee in the restaurant. At night, he would go over her books and ledgers. While he corrected errors discovered and balanced her books with her bank's financial statement, she watched his hands and ink-dipped pen smoothly enter the numbers in the proper columns. The books and ledgers were no longer something for her to dread. Amanda was thankful. Her smile and laughter were payment enough for Robert, who had become completely taken with her.

Robert had been carefully watching Amanda as she watched him. He noticed that she would hold her breath as she watched him enter the numbers. It seemed that only after he explained the method, would she release her breath. Robert watched too, as her chest rose and fell with each breath. He was beginning to lose his thoughts and composure being so close to this excitable and exciting woman.

Soon, there was no attempt at trying to hide their meetings and time together for interviews and legal matters. They made time to be with each other at every opportunity. They met for breakfast and dinner. They were seen around town laughing and hanging onto each other's words as they talked and walked. They genuinely liked each other; and maybe they needed something that only the other could provide. He was quiet, yet determined and knowledgeable. She was young, vivacious, and vulnerable.

The days were rapidly turning into weeks. The judge would soon be through with the auctioning of the freighting company's assets, and Robert's job would be over. While both thought and worried about the time remaining together, Amanda and Robert did not verbalize their concerns to each other. Neither could have known how little time they had left.

Robert had taken Amanda out on a Sunday drive in a buggy he rented just for the occasion. She made them a lunch and placed it a borrowed basket. Robert placed it in the back of the buggy along with his old rifle.

As Robert checked the harnesses, Amanda noticed how at ease Robert was with the horses. Horses frightened her somewhat. They were large, strong, and noisy. She saw that he skillfully moved his feet before the horses could step on them as he patted their necks and pushed them into their proper places. She marveled at how close he stood to the large creatures and yet, he seemed not afraid at all. On the contrary, he seemed almost comfortable.

During the drive, Amanda noticed how casually, yet expertly, Robert held the leather reins in his hands. His hands were rough and strong looking. The dark, moisture-stained leather pieces were laced among the fingers of both hands. He would occasionally slap the reins on the horses' rumps and at the same time, Robert would softly talk to the horses as if they could somehow understand the words he spoke.

His destination had been the edge of a small and quiet lake. Robert marveled at Amanda's beauty and her youthful naiveté. He observed that she could talk and ask questions as fast as she could wolf down food. Robert thought she could match many a hungry men. He wondered to himself how she could keep her slender figure with that amount of food. As they ate, they talked and laughed. How Robert thoroughly enjoyed the sound of Amanda's laughter.

Afterwards, they talked and they walked and they talked some more. Robert skipped rocks along the surface of the lake. Amanda took off her shoes and holding the hem of her dress in her hands, she walked along with Robert, but in the water. When they stopped walking and talking and started kissing, it seemed the most natural thing in the world.

Before the week was over, he had Uncle Chris' bank wire him money from an old account. He gave it to Amanda as a loan for the business and her house. Robert realized how brilliant, yet naive she was and he felt as if he had to protect her. She was enjoying his company and being spoiled too much to ask that it be stopped. She did not care that he was married; and he was acting as if he were not.

The last Saturday started out as any other. Robert and Amanda had breakfast together at the cafe. It was early in the morning and there was a chill in the air. As he was walking her to the newspaper office, they had to pass the photography studio. On the spur of the moment, Robert quickly talked Amanda into having their picture taken together. As they were leaving the studio, he stopped her and told her that he found himself falling in love with her. She said that she liked him and needed him, and started to tell him that she didn't know exactly how she felt about their situation, when they both saw and heard quite a commotion at the local sheriff's office. The marshal and the newspaperwoman rapidly walked over to find out what had happened.

Inside, they found the sheriff and U.S. Deputy Marshal Billy Hughes. Hughes was very young and just recently appointed a deputy marshal in a district other than Robert's. Hughes was badly wounded in the leg. His story was worse than the wound.

According to Hughes, he and another deputy named J.C. Coulter went to Collin County to serve papers on the owner of a cabin that hadn't paid taxes in over two years. The papers were for a Mr. and Mrs. Walton. When they approached just after noon yesterday, they found several men and a woman at the cabin. Once they announced who they were, they were shot at by the people. Coulter was shot off his horse almost immediately. Hughes thought he killed the woman, but could not get to Coulter due to the volume of gunfire. He left thinking Coulter had been killed. Hughes passed out from loss of blood and the strain of the nightlong journey to town. A doctor was sent for, while Robert turned into Marshal Forsythe and made inquiries of the sheriff.

No one yet made the connection to the group robbing stagecoaches and mining wagons. Robert just knew he had to get to the cabin, find Coulter, and deal with those responsible for shooting two deputy marshals.

Robert walked Amanda back to the paper. She was torn over trying to get a story for the newspaper and her concern for his safety. Robert's transformation had been sudden and complete. An ominous quiet settled about Robert and even his facial features looked darker. The fire seemed to die in those of eyes of his, while every muscle in his body flexed and tightened. While she wasn't afraid for herself, Amanda felt a certain combination of fear and awe as she looked upon him. At the office, he stopped at the front door, grabbed Amanda by her shoulders and kissed her on the mouth. He said good-bye and turned toward the hotel to pack his saddlebags. She didn't answer because her mouth was wide open in shock.

After packing, Robert sent two telegrams. One to his superior, informing him of the events; and the other, to Debbie telling her he would be delayed in Dallas due to local trouble. He went to the stables and obtained a good quarter horse. Years before, he had learned to appreciate their sure-footedness and speed. When given the choice, Robert always selected and rode quarter horses.

As he rode up the street, Amanda could see him clearly. She could sense the power and determination in the man. She opened the door and stood out on the steps to the office. Robert instinctively swung the horse closer. The mare snorted and shook her head as she carried Robert closer and closer to Amanda. Normally, Amanda would have been frightened by the proximity of the horse and her movements, but she wasn't afraid of anything as long as Robert was with her.

Amanda shocked herself, when she said in voice just loud enough for him to hear, "Robert, please be careful", and blew him a kiss.

Robert abruptly halted his horse, looked down at Amanda, and said, "I'll come back for you, Mandy."

As Robert rode out of town, Amanda's breathing was rapid and irregular due to more than just worry or surprise.

CHAPTER ELEVEN

The Walton cabin site had looked normal enough when Deputy Marshals Coulter and Hughes rode upon it. It was a simple structure nestled on a small slope. A small running stream ran across the back of the cabin. A small corral had been built along side a large barn.

Coulter and Hughes had seen smoke coming from the chimney as they approached. Katy Walton had coffee on the stove and was preparing food for the men. The men were in the barn putting away their horses and money taken from another mining company robbery they had committed the evening prior. It was a case of crooks caught with their loot that Coulter and Hughes rode into that day.

Katy Walton had stepped outside the cabin to call Lester Kingsman and the others to eat. Once outside, she saw the two riders, who were less than fifty yards from the cabin. She also spotted their badges. She sounded the alarm to the men in the barn. Cooper, Thompson, and Harrison fired their pistols from inside the barn. Hughes had fired wildly as his horse reared back. One of his bullets caught Walton in her stomach as she remained standing on the cabin steps. Coulter was knocked off his horse by two bullets that hit almost simultaneously; one in the lungs and the other in the shoulder. Kingsman, Davidson, and Canby joined the others as they ran outside the barn and continued firing at Hughes. It was during this volley of gunfire at such close range, that Hughes was wounded and fled.

Kingsman checked Walton, but she was dying from the wound and blood loss. Cooper and Davidson walked over to Coulter, who was still alive. "You, stinking sonofabitch. Trying to take the Cooper Gang by yourselves.

Well take this for your trouble", Cooper said as he looked upon the dying marshal. Coulter pleaded for mercy as Cooper put the barrel of his rifle to his head and pulled the trigger.

The men quickly grabbed provisions, resaddled the horses, and rode away from the cabin site within the hour.

Marshal Forsythe came upon the cabin site, just as the occupants had left it. He found the bodies where they fell. Together with the information that Hughes had provided and the death scene, it was easy to establish the sequence of events. He knew too, that someone would pay for blowing out the brains of the marshal who had begged for his life.

By reading the tracks left, Robert was able to determine the number of men and that their horses were tired. He thought he could catch up to the group if he wasn't delayed by caring for the dead. Under ordinary circumstances, he would have taken the bodies back to Dallas. This time, he settled for carrying both bodies into the cabin and covering them over with blankets. He would send someone for them after he caught up with the men he intended to kill.

CHAPTER TWELVE

The marshal watched the farmhouse for any signs of life. He had been intently watching it from his place of concealment for over an hour. The sun would be up soon and he would be able to make a better assessment of the situation. He had ridden throughout the night, when he came upon it. The tracks had led him here. Aside from the sounds of the horses in the barn, there had been no noise from the cabin.

The cabin had been built upon a level area in a clearing surrounded by woods on one side and a slow moving, six-foot wide stream on the other. As he studied the property, Robert figured the cabin was twenty feet by ten feet. It was made of cut lumber. It had a large stone chimney and at least two glass-paned windows. Across from the house were a corral and a barn. The horse corral was partially enclosed sheltering the horses from the extremes of Texas weather. Robert also noted that the corral was larger than the cabin. He surmised that the farmer was a man of many good horses that he wanted to keep in good condition to extract full service from them.

As sunlight started breaking over the horizon, Robert could make out the plowed fields adjacent to the property. The majority of the property was shaped in a wide and long rectangle. A section of the land had a jagged shape due to the path cut by the stream; still Robert noticed the straight furrows that had been plowed right to the edge of the stream. Such a farmer was an experienced and hard working individual. One that did not make a habit of laying in bed with the dawn breaking. Robert knew that there should have been a lamp lit and a fire going in the chimney, but there was nothing. Something was wrong!

With the sunrise, there still were no sounds or signs of activity. Robert knew that sooner or later, he'd have to go over for a look. He thought the sooner the better, especially if his quarry was asleep.

He loaded his spare pistol with six rounds and loaded the normally empty sixth chamber on the Colt on his hip. On the old Colt pistols, the hammer always rested on an empty chamber to avoid contact with a cartridge's primer to avoid an unwanted detonation. He didn't figure he would have time to reload.

Robert approached the house on foot. He couldn't get over the silence. Not even a dog barking. As he rounded a corner leading to the front of the house, he found out why. There in front of the house lay a large mongrel dog killed by gunshots. Peering in through a window, he saw the feet and legs of a woman laying on the floor next to the hearth.

Entering the house, he did not find anyone else, but the farmer's dead wife. She looked to be in her early thirties. Her throat had been cut. Her dress had been torn away and she must have been raped on floor and then killed where Robert found her. Even though he was a war veteran, Robert was sickened by the savagery of the gang's attack on the woman. In the Old West, women were usually safe from physical attacks by the professional outlaws. The molestation of women was a crime the early marshals had little experience in investigating.

Checking the barn, Robert found the farmer. He had been shot several times in the body and once in the back of the head. Inside the barn, he also found the very tired horses left by Cooper and his men. Apparently, they took fresh horses from the farmer. The tracks were leading towards Tarrant County.

Robert retrieved his horse and led it to the farmhouse. He carried the dead farmer's body into the house and placed it on the floor next to the woman's. He wrapped the woman's body with a blanket and then covered both the bodies with other blankets off of their bed. It was inside the house that Robert noticed for the first time, a child's bed.

Judging from the clothes, it belonged to a young girl; maybe five or six years old. Robert felt a twinge of panic and dread as he checked the house for another body. He couldn't find it; not even looking outside. He checked the privy and still nothing. It was outside the barn and corral area where the tracks led in a southwesterly direction, that he found a doll on the grass. Robert did not want to think about the reasons why a gang of murdering rapists would take along a child from one of their crime scenes. As he jumped into his saddle, he also didn't want to think about how much time he had wasted at the farmhouse.

It was a good cow pony, but it was tired and needed a rest. Robert caught up with the gang in less than five hours. As Robert swung off the saddle, he took out his field glasses. Sitting down, he scanned the countryside. He almost missed the riders, as they were moving slowly and were hugging a line of trees. They were also over four hundred yards out. He could see the back of the girl as she rode behind the saddle with Canby.

Robert's heart was racing as he pulled the Sharps rifle out of the scabbard and pulled a box of cartridges from his saddlebags. He decided he may not get another chance at saving the girl and he was not about to lose it simply because of distance. It was too risky trying to hit Canby without hitting the girl, so he chose to shoot the horse out from under them.

Robert quickly sat down and tore open a box that contained five factory-made cartridges. He placed three of them between the fingers of his left hand for quicker reloading. Next, he pulled open the lever, dropping the breechblock, which in turn exposed the cavernous chamber. Quickly dropping the fourth cartridge into the chamber, Robert closed the rifle's action, raised the Vernier sight, setting the sights for five hundred yards, cocked the hammer and steadied the rifle in his hands and rested his arms on his knees for support.

The buzzing of a large horsefly could be heard as Robert concentrated on aligning the rifle's sights on the horse. While allowing for windage and the horse's gait, it seemed an eternity before Robert pulled the trigger. The Sharps echoed across the silent distance like an oncoming freight train. Canby's horse fell dead. Both riders fell off and clear of the horse. The little girl started to get up, but Canby couldn't as the big Sharps' slug had gone through his left thigh before killing the horse.

Cooper and Davidson knew that sound and turned their horses to face this sudden threat. Cooper saw the marshal and the next cloud of smoke as the Sharps bellowed once more. This time the slug knocked Kingsman clean off the saddle. He was dead before his body started to move backwards. Two empty brass cartridge cases were on the ground in front of Robert as he was aiming his rifle for a third shot. Cooper leaned forward and spurred his horse back in the original direction of travel. The act of leaning forward saved him, as Robert had unleashed another 550-grain paper-patched bullet towards the lead rider. The bullet took Cooper's hat off. As the group moved out at a gallop, Shorty Thompson was the last to fall before they were out of Robert's line of sight.

The eight-year-old mare was a good horse, as she had stood rock still with the reins on the ground during the shooting. Robert jumped onto the saddle and rode forward at a gallop. He ejected the expended shell from the Sharps and holstered it on the run. As he approached the fallen criminals, Robert saw Canby still trying to stand. He also saw that he was trying to pull and cock his pistol.

Robert raced forward. The horse and rider were moving in rhythm with each other. The horse's rapid, rasping gulps of air were mixed with the deafening sounds of the hoofs beating the ground and then kicking out as they rose off it. Robert pulled his pistol and cocked it. His breathing seemed to match that of the horse and his heart was keeping time with the pounding hoof beats. He was leaning slightly forward and moving with the horse. The reins in his left hand were just a formality, as he was gripping the horse's mane and was one with her. As he spurred her on, the saddlebags and rifle scabbards slapped the horse's flanks as they moved in unison with horse and rider who were barely touching ground as they drove onward.

To Jonathan Canby, the horse and rider were moving in slow motion as he fired once. Robert must have appeared as an avenging angel as he continued onward, undeterred from his course by the sound of gunfire. Robert's shot did not miss as he rode up on the young Canby. Canby fell back dead, as Robert overran his position while trying to stop his horse. He turned the horse around to get a look at the downed riders to be sure they were dead. They were all definitely dead.

Robert heard and saw the little girl screaming hysterically. He dismounted and walked over to her. He picked her up and held her tightly against his chest as he let her cry. Much later, after she quieted down, Robert learned that her name was Melissa Peterson and she held up five fingers when asked her age.

Robert was forced for the first time since he began this journey, to consider returning to Dallas. He could not proceed after Cooper and his men with little Melissa. Since he had to go back, he loaded the dead onto their horses and tied them down. When he examined Canby's saddlebags, he found sacks of money belonging to the mining company. Prior to leaving the Walton's cabin, the money had been divided among the thieves in the event that they were forced to split while making their getaway.

After making his decision to return to town, Robert hurriedly reloaded his weapons and moved out as quickly as possible. He did not want to be caught in the open loaded down with a little girl, dead men, and tired horses in the event the others returned for the stolen money.

CHAPTER THIRTEEN

He rode throughout the night to get back to Dallas as fast as possible. He arrived just after 4 o'clock in the afternoon of the next day. Robert was just about asleep in the saddle as he rode into town. Little Melissa had a death-like grip on Robert's coat. She had to be pulled away from him to be taken off the saddle. Their arrival caused quite a stir in the community.

Amanda was there as much to look after Robert as to get a story for her newspaper. The townspeople were able to identify all the dead, except for Canby. The recovered gold amounted to over $8,500.00. Robert filed a quick report for the sheriff and informed him of the additional dead left behind at the farmhouse and cabin. The sheriff had the local doctor and his wife take Melissa home with them for the time being. He had someone take Robert's horse back to the livery stable.

As he was preparing to take his gear back to the hotel, Amanda stopped Robert and told him to accompany her home. He did and they talked all the way home. She confined her questions to the pursuit of the criminals. She found herself touching his arm as they walked. Amanda finally took his rifle and bedroll from him as they walked across town to her house.

Once inside her house, she helped him out of his coat and his boots. He looked done in and he said he felt like an old man, as he sat on her sofa. Amanda kissed him and said he was a real hero. Robert responded that for all of his experience, beneath the hero, usually beat the heart of a coward who felt honor-bound. Amanda stroked his hair once, before heading to the kitchen.

She placed kindling in the stove and lit it with a match. She started preparing him something to eat and had placed a pot of coffee on the stove when she told him that they must talk. When he did not answer, she walked back into the den and found him asleep. Amanda covered him with a blanket and whispered in his ear that she thought he was wonderful and kissed him on the cheek. As she watched his breathing, she felt jealousy and anger for Mrs. Forsythe.

Robert slept for over 12 hours, and when he awoke, he saw Amanda sitting in a chair across from him. She was asleep, as well. When he stirred, she awoke, instantly. Amanda walked over to Robert and kissed him. As he stirred, she told him to clean up and she would have something for him to eat.

When Robert sat down at the table, he still looked tired, but his eyes never lost that fire. She remembered how he looked with the child. She also remembered watching the man as he related his story to the sheriff of finding dead bodies, tracking killers, and in a matter of seconds killing three men and rescuing a little girl. It seemed strange to her the skills an otherwise quiet and gentle man had to learn; no, choose to learn. If she didn't know him as she did, Amanda would have been afraid of the man.

"Robert, I need to know just what your intentions are about us. I've spent a good deal of time and money trying to build a career and reputation as a businesswoman. You come here out of the blue and turn things around."

"Me, turn things around? I didn't come here to find you or fall in love with you. It just happened." Robert remained seated even though he felt completely vulnerable; he didn't know what else to do. Amanda moved closer and grabbed the back of one of the chairs at the table.

"What do you intend to do?" she fired back.

"It's more a question of what you intend to do? I've told you how I feel and I've stuck my head on the chopping block. I have a wife and family that I'm willing to leave for you. What do you have to say about us?" Robert stood up, but he did not move towards Amanda.

"I say that I don't know. I like you and I need you, but..."

In the instant that Amanda froze to gather her thoughts, Robert moved towards her and interrupted. "But what?" His eyes burned into her soul. She had to look down at the floor before answering.

"I don't know. Do we have to deal with this now?" She started moving towards Robert and her voice was pleading.

"Amanda, I hunt men for a living. I have to go back to catch the others. In my world, there isn't always time for the niceties or the social graces as I may not get a second chance to voice my thoughts."

She stood back away from the table now as she said, "Then don't go now. Stay, let's talk and work this through."

"I have to go after the others. I'll come back, but I want to know how you feel, now!" Robert replied moving towards her, but without touching Amanda.

"This is happening too fast." Amanda was almost desperate.

"Stand up for what you want. If you feel love for me, then stand up for it; us." "Please, don't leave now, Robert!" she pleaded. She was almost upon him.

"I have to go, there's killers on the loose."

"There's men you haven't killed, you mean. Then go! Go after the men. Go home, see if I care!" she said as she started to hit him on his chest with her fists. He grabbed her, hugged her, and let her cry. She stopped crying and started kissing his neck and face, when she caught herself and stopped.

"No, go on with you! Go on and get out! You have your career. You have a life and family. Get out and don't come back!"

"I hoped you would have loved me as much as I love you. I hoped you would have had more courage. There's nothing to be afraid of; I would have protected you. I'll miss you, and I'll always love you", he said as he left and she continued crying, standing in the kitchen.

CHAPTER FOURTEEN

Cooper and his men were huddled in a small group of trees. They did not light a fire, as they were not sure if the marshal would be returning with a posse of men. After running to safety following their encounter with the marshal, they regrouped to decide their next plan of action.

Davidson thought they should keep on going and head into Mexico. Harrison wanted to return to Colorado. The more that he thought about it, the more Cooper was for trailing the marshal in attempt to recover their stolen money. Initially, the others did not want to think of going after that marshal with the Sharps rifle. Cooper played on their greed and described what an easy target a lone man saddled down with a kid and dead men would be in the open country. They finally agreed to at least follow the marshal's trail, but they got such a late start, the marshal beat them into town by ten miles. The group remained there trying to figure out their next move and the marshal's.

What Cooper wasn't voicing to the others was his plan to kill that marshal who meddled in his affairs and cost him so much money. Besides, he felt he could never be free to enjoy what money he and the men had with such a relentless and killing individual on their trail. Cooper wanted them to stay and make sure they turned the tables on that no good, interfering marshal and kill him.

The local sheriff had formed a posse and started out after Cooper and his men while Robert slept. Their mistake was in heading in a direction that they thought would intercept Cooper with his last known direction of travel. No one counted on the group backtracking the marshal. So the posse and the bad men were half a Texas county apart when Robert saddled up his horse and rode out of town.

Over the years, Robert learned to backtrack himself; it often times saved him surprises. As Robert rode out following his own trail in, he continued to think of Amanda and his own life. He wasn't sure if he could or wanted to return to the life that he once knew. Robert hadn't cried in years; he was too old, but the steady gait of his horse jarred the tears from his eyes and down his face. It was being lost in thought that was the only reason that he failed to see the horse and rider's silhouettes at the edge of trees five miles out of town.

Amanda had cried for twenty minutes after Robert left. When she finally slowed down and caught her breath, she started thinking. The more she thought, the more she realized that he was a good, decent man; just the sort that could make her happy for the rest of her life. No, he was the man of her dreams that had been eluding her all these years.

She wanted to tell him that she didn't mean those things she had said. She wanted to tell him that she did love him and she needed and wanted him as much as he wanted her. She thought to herself that she could catch him and tell him that she would be here waiting for his return. She left heading for the stables. She knew what she had to do.

CHAPTER FIFTEEN

Amanda wasn't that experienced in riding horses. That's why she rented a two-horse buggy. She thought that with two horses, she would be sure to catch up with Robert before he was too far ahead. Her plan had worked well as she was only minutes behind him as he rode past the horse and rider in the trees.

Cooper was the rider hidden among the trees. He was holding back figuring to tighten the trap around the marshal. Davidson and Harrison were just up ahead and would open up on the marshal at a predetermined point. They would fire from two different directions and prevent him from successfully using that rifle of his on them.

Amanda spotted Robert just as he was about to top a small ridge. She stopped the horses, screamed his name, and waved to him. Robert wheeled his horse around in the direction of the shouting. Amanda whipped the horses towards him. Just as Robert turned to see her, Harrison panicked and fired his first shot at him. It missed and now Davidson, who had remained on horseback, joined in firing wildly at the marshal.

The horse Robert was riding wheeled about out of surprise at the number of gunshots being fired in her direction from different angles. As frightened as she was by the change in events, Amanda urged the horses on toward Robert's position. Harrison was too scared to expose himself, but Davidson charged straight at Robert. As Robert reached for his rifle, Davidson cleared the tree-lined cover and was almost upon Robert when Robert's horse spooked and reared up.

Abandoning his attempt to grab his rifle, Robert drew his pistol and fanned the hammer in rapid succession. Two of the three heavy slugs tore through Davidson and the last hit Davidson's horse. Both the rider and horse collapsed in a tumbling heap in front of Robert. Robert was fighting to remain on his horse and to get her under control with just his left hand as the right one still gripped his revolver which contained only two live shells now.

Harrison fired another shot at the marshal as he surveyed the scene to make sure that Davidson would not be getting up. Again, Harrison had not taken proper aim in his haste and nervousness and his shot was high and wide. Since Harrison was a farther target, Robert holstered his pistol and pulled his Winchester and fired back. Two of the marshal's bullets struck a tree next to Harrison's head. True to form, Harrison panicked and decided to clear out. As Harrison turned to run, he broke cover and Robert killed him as well. Robert turned and raced towards Amanda who by now had also passed Cooper, who was still in hiding.

"So, this is the marshal's woman", Cooper thought to himself. He spurred his horse out of hiding and raced towards the woman in the buggy. Amanda never heard or saw him as she was concentrating on reaching Robert. Robert saw Cooper at the same instant and realizing the danger, kicked his horse in the ribs to spur her on, and galloped towards Cooper at breakneck speed.

Racing forward, Robert practically stood up in the stirrups and levered another shell into his rifle. Not waiting to get closer, Robert fired the first volley from his rifle at Cooper in an attempt to turn him off Amanda's course. All of the shots struck wide as aiming from a galloping horse was an imprecise matter to begin with, and Robert was desperately trying to avoid hitting near Amanda.

Amanda halted her horses and stopped between them. Robert held his fire for fear of hitting Amanda, but continued towards her at a dead run. Cooper actually slowed his horse and continued to shoot several times at Robert with his rifle. One of the shots hit Robert's horse.

The next several seconds seemed to slow down and last an eternity for Amanda as she watched. At the horse's speed, both rider and horse tumbled and skidded several yards. Clouds of pale brown dust were kicked up. The legs of Robert's horse could be seen in the air and Robert's black coat and white shirt seemed to twirl around in the clouds of dust. The sounds of flesh hitting the ground mingled with the cries of the man and the horse drowning out whatever noise escaped Amanda's lips.

To Amanda, it looked very bad. The horse skidded on its side and in the dust, Amanda lost sight of Robert. The horse lay on its side dying. Raspy, coughing breaths choked the horse as it struggled for air. It kicked out with one leg trying in vain to free it from the reins. The saddle hanging loosely around the horse's stomach made for a pitiful sight. Robert was hurt severely. The horse had fallen on top of him during one of the tumbles. Robert was laying on his back. His Stetson was gone; as was his shirt collar and tie. His Winchester was on the ground at least fifty feet behind him. He was covered with a layer of fine dust. Robert was bleeding from his mouth, nose, and ears. His head hurt and he couldn't seem to gather his feet under him. He knew he was hurt badly from internal injuries, but he didn't know how badly.

Robert was aware of Amanda screaming his name. Before she could get to him, Cooper rode in between them. His rifle had jammed, so he dismounted, walked toward the downed marshal, and started to pull his pistol. Amanda jumped down off the buggy and ran at Cooper screaming and hitting him with her closed fists. Cooper punched Amanda on her jaw. She fell back, but got up again hitting and screaming at Cooper.

Desperately trying to think and move through his pain and disorientation, Robert found he could move his right hand and arm. He also found that his pistol was still in its holster in spite of the fall. Robert pulled and cocked it just as Cooper turned his pistol on Amanda.

Robert tried to aim, but his strength and vision were fading rapidly. The short barrel of his pistol almost completely covered the two struggling persons as he squinted over its length. He fired as the two people before him struggled for control of Cooper's pistol. Both persons were obliterated in the white smoke and the orange muzzle blast of the pistol shot. The pistol rose in recoil in the man's hand. By reflex, the strong hand held onto the pistol grip.

Amanda screamed again, and this time, so did Cooper. Robert's last shot to be fired, hit Amanda high on her back. The heavy lead .44 slug tore through her and exited striking Cooper in his right breast.

Startled and badly hurt, Cooper ran off. Amanda fell back onto the ground. Her heavy cotton clothing could not hide or stem the massive flow of blood from her chest wound. Stunned and almost unconscious from the pain of the wound, Amanda turned towards Robert. She started crawling to him, crying and saying his name. No matter how hard she tried to breathe, Amanda wasn't getting enough air. She called out that she was sorry and she really didn't mean what she said. She clawed her way through the dirt and clumps of wet grass.

She cried out that she loved him, but Robert never heard her words as he had died as he pulled the trigger. Robert lay face up with his eyes closed, his hand still holding onto the pistol. The early morning sun reflected off the shiny star still pinned to his vest. Amanda desperately wanted to touch him, to wipe away the blood from his face, and to hold onto Robert one more time. She hoped that by wiping away the blood from his face, she could make everything as it had been. Amanda needed that. From the mounting pressure and pain in her chest, she knew that she had to hurry. As she pulled herself along the ground, grass and dirt were buried under Amanda's fingernails. She scraped her knees as she pushed herself to Robert, but nothing compared to the growing pain in her chest.

She died trying to crawl to him. Amanda was five feet short of touching Robert when she died.

CHAPTER SIXTEEN

 "So that in a nutshell is the dream. It occurs more frequently now then it has in the past four or five years; though to be honest I have dreamed bits and pieces of this for as long as I can remember. It is more vivid with time as I see it in colors and hear all the sounds involved. I swear at times, I can even smell the damn horse. Well, Doc, am I crazy or what?"

Michael Stewart was talking on the telephone to Dr. Paul J. Paslosky, a psychiatrist in New York. The two had been Army buddies during the Vietnam War.

"Mike, I've known you for over twenty years. Hell, yes, I think you're crazy. But, it's over your actions in war that I witnessed and your chosen profession, not your dreams. How are you and Lynette getting along?" Paul dragged heavily on his briar pipe while waiting to hear Mike's response.

"I'd have to say very good. We're approaching our eighteenth anniversary soon; why?"

"Because love, unspoken feelings, and the conflict between duty and love seem to be prevalent throughout your dream. There's an internal struggle going on that is as powerful as the emotions displayed." Paul watched as the bluish-gray smoke fell off the pipe bowl before beginning its climb towards the ceiling. "Are you having an affair, Mike?"

"No, honest I'm not. Lyn has asked the same thing, but it's the bad hours I put in working vice and narcotics. Really, Paul, I'd tell you if I were, but I'm not."

"Does Lynette know about your dreams?"

"She thinks I'm having nightmares from the war and my job. I still have those occasionally, but I haven't told her about this one."

"Well, I wouldn't then. Most women are perceptive and smart enough to pick out the central theme in such a case. I think in the long run, you would frighten her or at least make her worry that there was a conflict over a loved one in your life."

"Ok, but what do I do in the meantime?"

"Look, buddy, I seldom diagnose over the phone. Besides, what about my fee?"

"Fee? I think you still owe me money from our `R and R' in Thailand. Paul, everything about this dream is unsettling. Right down to the scar on the guy's face; just like mine."

"Mike, think for a moment. You are the main character in your own dream; why shouldn't he look just like you. Your brother, Chris, is a Jesuit priest and you got that scar from falling across some concertina wire in `Nam when you got shot carrying me back to camp. You also recently bought a Sharps replica rifle because you're a gun enthusiast. In my professional opinion, you have been under too much stress recently, you're overdue for a vacation and are taking some mental relief out via your dreams."

"Ok, but how do you explain how I rode those horses so well on that trip to Arizona last year? I have never been on horseback before, and yet, I rode like a champ."

"Wait a minute!" Paul said as he took the pipe from his mouth and straightened up in his chair. "Are you trying to say that the dream represents a previous life for you?"

"No, it's just that ... Paul, I don't know what I mean. It's just that sometimes ..."

Pausing only for a moment, Paul replied, "Mike, you're tired. You've had a very dramatic incident occur. It's normal to be confused. Look, if it's any comfort for you mentally and emotionally, I remember that you took to machineguns and hand grenades, naturally. And you could chase the girls while on leave without any lessons. Maybe, you're just a natural on horseback, as well. My professional advice to you is to take some time off from work. Run away somewhere for a few days with Lyn. Better yet, get your ass out here and visit me. There, that'll be four hundred-fifty dollars please."

"Cute, Paul, cute. Though, I am scheduled to attend the next Western Region Vice Investigators' seminar in Houston, next month."

"Good. Just relax, Mike. You're ok. Send me something from Houston."

"Ok, buddy. Thanks for the help."

Lynette had overheard the end of the conversation with Paul as she stepped out of the shower. Wrapping herself in a towel, she walked into the bedroom drying her hair. Looking at Mike, she said, "Are we ok?"

"Angel, you're fantastic, and Paul says I'm ok."

Lyn sat on the bed next to him and let him hold her in his arms. She wasn't a doctor, but she knew it was too soon after this last shooting to be going back to work. This time she was really worried about Mike; he just wasn't himself lately.

CHAPTER SEVENTEEN

Michael and Lynette Stewart are friends and lovers. He is a detective with the Los Angeles Sheriff's Department and she's a cardiac care nurse at Daniel Freeman Hospital in Inglewood.

They met while in college. Even though he was older, they were in the same class year, as he had been away at war. He was handsome and fun to be with. He had returned home the hero; he had saved his buddy Paul and was awarded the Bronze Star. She found that the scar on his face could not detract from those shiny, black eyes that were the windows to the soul of a very gentle and quiet man. She fell in love with him on their first date.

She captivated him as well. That long auburn hair, those green eyes, and that gorgeous body. They drove him crazy then, and still do. The two of them dated each other exclusively; as there were no others in their world. After college, they were married. He went to work for the department when they returned home from their honeymoon. She continued with her nursing education and specialized in cardiac surgery.

Over the years, they were very happy. The only disappointment in their lives was that Lyn could not have children. She was crushed for years following the discovery. They were both Catholic and had anticipated raising a family. They supported each other through that crisis and threw themselves into their work. They actually grew closer in those early years. They stayed active in the different church groups, and kept a diverse group of friends. Lyn and Mike often took short, three or four-day weekends away just to spend time with one another. Everything seemed perfect in their world. Then, this last shooting occurred.

This was actually Mike's third on-duty shooting and killing. The first occurred while he was a patrol deputy. He came upon a robbery at a 7-11 store. The second was during a stakeout at a bank while he was on loan to the robbery detail. This last one involved a narcotics dealer who had set Mike up. It wasn't even Mike's case, but he is usually so good in undercover operations that no one ever "makes him as the man", and he was asked to stand in at the last minute. The shooting occurred in the crook's car. Everything went wrong, and Mike had to struggle with the crook when he pulled a gun. During the struggle, the crook fired twice, but Mike had control of his wrist, causing the weapon to be pointed away from Mike's stomach. Mike fought for several seconds before he could get to his own gun. It was over before his cover team could reach him.

The department said it was a good shooting and was preparing to send him back to work, but Lyn was sure that Mike's nightmares were the result of this shooting. Actually, ever since the honeymoon, she knew he had nightmares, but more so since the last shooting. He appeared to be more troubled; at least, more preoccupied in his thoughts. The call to Paul was the tip-off that something was on his mind that he couldn't say to her.

"Hey, wait a minute! I've got to get to work, Michael." Lyn said as he tried to pull her towel off. She quickly stood up and said, "Do we have anything planned for this Sunday, hon?"

"I don't, why, what did you have in mind, beautiful?"

"I thought I'd call Chris over for an early dinner. He hasn't been over in ages. I think it would do you both good to sit and visit."

"Sounds good to me, but just be sure to make two pies for dessert. That guy always ends up eating at least three pieces. To watch him eat, you'd think they fed him bread and water in the rectory."

"I think that sweet tooth thing must be in your family's blood. I honestly don't know how you guys can eat sweets the way you do and not gain any weight. Ok, I'll call and set it up. And one more thing: if you still feel like pulling towels off people tonight, wait up for me. I'll come straight home after shift."

"That's no way for a good Catholic girl to talk", Mike answered.

"You've got the good part right, detective. I'm damn good!" she said as she threw her towel at him and ran into the bathroom.

CHAPTER EIGHTEEN

The scene at the store was one of chaos. Numerous police portable radios were squawking incessantly and sheriff's cars were everywhere. The front glass windows of the market had been shot out. Groups of customers and on-lookers had gathered in different sections of the store and surrounding lot.

Uniformed deputies and plainclothes detectives were talking and writing. A few people were still in shock and more were crying or talking with tear-stained faces. Apparently, the big older man in the quick check out line had the shotgun under his arm and his coat. Until he pulled the weapon, no one had paid him any attention. He was unshaven, disheveled, but not out of the ordinary for the area.

When he pulled the shotgun and announced a robbery, his voice sounded gruff and guttural. He seemed as mean as a drunk being rudely awakened. The young checker was slow to react as she was in shock. The robber blew out the windows of the store with two shots. Thereafter, all the checkers complied with his demands for the monies in the cash registers. The entire episode lasted only seconds and he was gone; disappeared into the crowded night scene that is so typical of big cities.

The robber walked the several blocks back to his apartment building. It was typical of the downtown apartment buildings: ancient, cold, dilapidated and infested with vermin; the two-legged kind that doesn't have any identification and certainly would not give their right names, anyway.

Carl Payton Andrews was almost fifty years old. He was recently released from a California prison for armed robbery. When he got the chance, he drank too much and used cocaine occasionally. With his newfound wealth; he brought back a bottle of whiskey, a quarter gram of cocaine, and a street hooker.

Carl was born and raised in Parkersburg, West Virginia. His father was killed in the closing months of World War II by a German sniper. His mother married an iron factory worker. They had six more children by the time that Carl was a teenager. The family endured the financial hardships of the times and geographical location. The children had a roof over their heads and food in their stomachs. They went to the Word of God church and were sent to school.

By the time that he was a teenager, Carl was already skipping school more than attending it. He hung out some of the older town toughs. They taught the young Carl how to smoke, steal beer from the local stores, and shoot craps. He was eventually brought before the juvenile authorities and sent to a reform school for six months. While there, Carl usually fought or had to fight almost daily for his food tray and for cigarettes. He was sexually assaulted by the older detainees. It was a leaner and meaner Carl that was released back to his home.

Carl stayed long enough to get into a fight with his stepfather, who literally threw him out of the house. Back out on the streets and with no hope or thought of ever going back home again, Carl stole food and cigarettes from grocery stores. He slept in boarded up houses and buildings by day and roamed the streets looking for fun at night. He had several close calls with the law, but his luck was holding out, at least temporarily. The daily thefts added to his experience and served to fuel even further his appetite for taking others' belongings. From the daily food, cigarettes, and beer thefts; Carl graduated to joyriding in cars that were left parked with the keys in the ignition.

On night, Andrews was caught by the police as he broke into a gas station. Carl had intended to fill up the car's tank and leave, but he tried breaking into the cash register. Once again before the juvenile authorities, Carl was sent to reform school for the next two and half years for joyriding and breaking and entering. This time at the reformatory, it was Carl that was the detainee bully who stole, fought, and sexually assaulted the younger detainees.

Upon his release this time, his mother and step-father pleaded with the authorities to be relieved of their parental responsibilities as Carl was just too much to handle and he would a bad influence on their younger children. The court granted their request and released Carl to an uncle living in West Union. Carl's Uncle Stanley took it upon himself to reform Carl by trying to beat the very devil out of him. Carl stayed at his uncle's house for two days and slipped out in the middle of the second night.

Andrews left on the run from West Union where he thumbed his way to Clarksburg. Once in town, young Carl's presence in the big city went unnoticed. He panhandled and shoplifted for his sustenance. He got into fights with other youths and assorted street people. Some fights he won and others, he lost. Win or lose; Andrews' personality was being formed with a mean and violent bent.

Sleeping by day in abandoned buildings and wandering the streets by night was guaranteed to bring Andrews into more trouble. Stumbling across a crap game in the back room of a laundry one night, Carl was mesmerized by the green bills on the table. He decided to wait; he wanted that money. That money could buy him his freedom out of town and his miserable existence.

By two o'clock in the morning most of the players had begun to leave for their homes. Carl watched while the owner of the laundry finished playing and had a few parting drinks with his friends. Carl watched while they took turns drinking from a quart bottle of whiskey. By the time that the last of the players left, the owner was feeling no pain. Carl quickly made his move into the shop through the back door while the owner was turning off the lights. Seizing a Pepsi Cola bottle from the wood cases stacked in the back room, Carl waited for his opportunity.

When the owner came back into the room, Carl hit him over the head with the bottle, knocking him unconscious. Carl studied his victim for just a moment as he lay on the floor. The man's mouth was open and a small trickle of blood dropped onto the old linoleum floor pattern. Carl thought to himself that it had all been so easy. He wasn't nervous or frightened. Going through the man's pockets, Carl found over sixty-five dollars, cigarettes, a Zippo lighter, and a switchblade knife. Carl gathered up his loot and took the bottle of whiskey and ran into the night.

After making his way back to the deserted warehouse that he was calling home for now, Carl sat and counted his money, played with the switchblade, smoked cigarettes, and drank whiskey until he passed out. The next morning Carl woke up with the first of many hangovers. While sorting through the whiskey-clouded thoughts, Carl became nervous when he stopped to think that he never checked on his victim to see if he was breathing. Fearing the worse, Carl quickly made plans to leave town. Carl bought a ticket on a Greyhound bus headed for Los Angeles.

Los Angeles provided an entirely new and different environment for the young Andrews. Within days after his arrival, Carl turned eighteen. He also made friends with several neighborhood toughs. Carl soon had the first of many homemade tattoos. He quickly adapted to his new surroundings and soon was planning and leading his new friends in several street robberies. Sometimes they were of people just walking down the street for an evening stroll and others were gas stations and similar late night businesses. The money was always spent on booze, drugs, and women.

Before long, Andrews stole a gun during a burglary. With his newfound power, Andrews grew bolder in his crimes. He robbed small banks and liquor stores. He used the gun to kill a street thug who made fun of his West

Virginia accent. Soon there would be other killings. Andrews' life style brought him into regular contacts with law enforcement. Andrews started going to jail with regular frequency for assorted offenses. A robbery at a liquor store sent him to the state prison in Chino.

Once in prison, Andrews aligned himself with white supremacists; mostly to survive. Once released, Andrews returned to his life style and ended up back in prison within a relatively short time for violating his parole by getting stopped while in a stolen car. The last time that he went to prison, he ended up at Folsom after he stabbed a street hooker and almost killed her. Andrews was learning more each time that he stayed in prison, and in or out, he was becoming more violent. Andrews had been out of prison for twenty-three days this last time before he broke the law.

Before dawn, the homicide detectives would be called to the discovery of the body of the nude hooker left in a park adjacent to a school. Yes sir, Carl Andrews was a laugh a minute.

Andrews was moodier than usual and he drank more often to escape the nightmares he had been having. The nightmares were coming with greater frequency and in more detail; each greater than the last. It was the same each time; a pretty woman and lawman. His head hurt, so he drank more greedily from the bottle.

This time out of prison, he vowed he would not go back. He had made this vow at least three other times, but this time he knew he could keep it. This time he was like a man driven; he had a purpose he could not put into words.

Soon, no one would be laughing.

CHAPTER NINETEEN

Mike Stewart was heading for the elevator in the department's headquarters downtown. He had to sign additional papers as well as pick up his duty weapon from Internal Affairs. Stewart looked up in time to see Detective Sergeant Michael Cantrill exit one of the many doors along the hallway and start for the stairs.

"Cantrill! Mike Cantrill, it's me Stewart!"

Looking about for the sound, Cantrill caught sight of Stewart and stopped at the bottom of the stairs.

"Mike, it's good to see you. What brings you downtown?" an infectious smile appeared along Cantrill's mouth as he extended his hand out to Stewart.

Stewart saw that Mike Cantrill had changed very little over the years. They were about the same age, but you couldn't see a gray hair on his head, while Stewart had graying along the temples and was getting more than a few along the front now. Stewart noticed that Cantrill was wearing a sweater vest along with his coat and tie. Cantrill was still trim after all these years. Years ago when they had worked together on a case, Stewart met Mrs. Cantrill and attributed Mike having to stay in such good shape to his very pretty and shapely wife who looked younger than Cantrill.

Stewart really liked Cantrill. He knew that Cantrill was from a rich family in the community, but he never acted snobbish. Cantrill was quiet and unpretentious. Another reason was that Cantrill had worked to get where he was on the department; money never entered into it.

They hadn't seen each other in years.

"I had to take care of some business up here, but I'm working administrative vice. How about yourself?"

"I'm late for a meeting that my lieutenant couldn't make and is sending me to at the last minute. I hate to run, but I really can't stay and talk. How about if I call you later?"

"Sure, no problem. Why don't we do lunch some time?"

"Sounds good to me. I'll call you in the next couple of days", Cantrill said as he started up the stairs.

"Ok, I'll look forward to it, Mike. Take care."

"It was good seeing Cantrill again after all these years", Stewart thought to himself as he stepped into the elevator.

The offices of Internal Affairs seemed cold and drafty. No one is ever really friendly; just civil and sometimes, polite. The overhead lighting bounced off the plain and sparse furniture. The receptionist led Stewart to the sergeant's office. After a brief exchange of pleasantries, the sergeant returned Stewart's nine-millimeter pistol to him. The I.A. sergeant told Stewart he could load up and return to work.

Mike pulled the pistol's slide back and held it open by thumbing up the metal slide stop. He then took the loaded magazine and inserted it into the pistol grip and gave it a final slap with the heel of his hand. Pointing the pistol at the floor, Mike released the slide stop and the metal on metal sounded good as the slide slammed into battery after stripping a cartridge from the magazine. The pistol was loaded once again. After so many years of packing a gun, the pistol felt comfortable in Mike's hand.

For just a moment, pictures flashed before Mike's eyes. He could see another pistol in his hands. This time it a Colt single action army model; the type used over a hundred years ago. Mike could see just the hands and the pistol. The hands appeared to be his as they dropped the thick, lead-tipped cartridges in the richly blued cylinder as his fingers deftly rotated it, aligning the chambers with the loading gate. And then the mental pictures disappeared!

Mike quickly left the office and headed for the elevator that would take him to his office. He thought how good it would be to get back to work.

"Chris! Thanks for coming over. It's so good to see you", Lyn said as she kissed her brother-in-law's cheek and led him into the house.

"Lynette, you get better looking each time I see you. My little brother doesn't deserve you."

"Hush, now!" she said leading him into the living room. "You'll have to wait to get any fights going with Michael. I sent him to the store so I could talk to you alone."

This time her tone was different. Over the past years, Lyn and Chris talked and gossiped as old friends. Lyn felt comfortable around Chris. Chris enjoyed her company and really liked Lyn from the first time that they were introduced. He remembered the meeting clearly.

Mike had invited Chris to join them at a fancy Basque restaurant. Mike was going to tell Chris of his engagement to Lyn. He had already proposed and she had accepted. Mike desperately wanted the approval of his older brother. They met for the first time in the restaurant lobby. As they were seated at their table, Chris tried not to notice how good Lyn's perfume smelled on her. He fought internally not to pay any attention to Lyn's jiggling bosom over the top of the low-cut, sleeveless evening dress she wore that night.

Michael did most of the talking at first. Lyn was quiet and Chris could not tell if she was shy or just terribly nervous and ill at ease having dinner with a priest. As the appetizers were served along with the wine, Chris continued to watch Lyn and he would occasionally see her looking back at him. Mike poured the wine while he spoke rapidly to his older brother. She was definitely quiet and she wasn't touching her wine, Chris noticed.

"Michael, relax", Chris said interrupting Mike in mid-sentence. "Neither Lyn nor I will know if we like each other if you don't let us talk." Turning his eyes and attention back to her, Chris said, "Lyn, please drink up. I seriously doubt that anyone wearing that dress would be a teetotaler."

Lyn's face and neck turned red, but she broke into a smile, at least.

"Michael was so worried about breaking the news to me that you were a priest that he didn't tell me until he picked me up at my apartment tonight", she replied as she reached for her wine glass. After taking a sip, she said, "I wanted to just die when I found out. It was too late to change and he kept after me that we would be late if I changed dresses. I'm going to kill Michael later." The color was returning to her face and neck.

"Well, welcome to the Stewart family, then. Most of us have wanted to do the same thing, at one time or another", Chris replied as he poured more wine for her and himself. After that, both Mike and Lynette relaxed.

"What's up? Is something wrong?" Chris asked.

Lynette quickly told Chris about the past few weeks and the fact that Mike had spoken to Paul. Chris listened intently and as Lyn finished talking, Chris asked only a few questions; just a few, but they were logical and much too personal. Lyn answered every one of them. Chris sat quietly in the chair. Lyn watched while he scratched his chin and pushed back the hair on his head as he thought. Chris told her he would have a talk with Michael after dinner. He also told Lyn to relax. She stood up from her chair in the den and kissed her brother-in-law and went into the kitchen to prepare some coffee.

Dinner was nice; full of lively, if not good conversation. After dinner, instead of using the dishwasher, they all helped to do the dishes. Finally, Mike and Chris went into the den. Lynette brought in coffee and pie. She said it was good to see them together, kissed them both on their heads, and left to finish reading a medical journal.

While Chris poured coffee into the two cups, Michael remained standing and stared at his older brother. Finally, he said, "Ok, big brother! What did Lyn tell you?" "What makes you say that?" Chris Stewart wasn't trying to fake surprise; he was just making his brother work for the answers.

"She suggested this get-together, you're wearing your collar, and you haven't touched your pie."

"I'm glad to see that you're good at what you do for a living. What's troubling you, Michael?"

"Chris, what do you think about reincarnation?" Michael said without any introduction.

"You know what the Church has to say about it."

"I'm interested in hearing what my older, well-educated brother has to say about it. I don't want to hear the official, pre-printed version, but just hear me out first.

Christopher Stewart, the Church scholar listened intently to the dream sequence of his younger brother. Even Chris wasn't prepared for what Mike had to say next. "Chris, just suppose that my dream is real; and I lived it before, call it what you will. Is it possible for this to happen? I mean could God allow it?"

"Don't you dare bring God into this heathen talk! Have you taken leave of your senses, Michael?!"

"No, ..."

"Don't interrupt me! I listened to you without interruption! Listen to yourself! You and I were born in Bakersfield. I diapered you and on more than one occasion, I whipped your ass. Our father was a CPA and our mother was a seamstress. They're both gone, now, but we can trace our family's roots. What are you thinking?!"

"I'm searching for a logical explanation for my troubled soul."

"I think your soul would be significantly less troubled if you stopped reliving your dreams and continued to live according to God's plan", Chris said as he grabbed a coffee cup and sat down in one of the chairs in the den. He took a deep breath trying to compose himself.

"My point, exactly!" shouted Michael as he paced towards and around Chris' chair. "Just suppose that for whatever reason, God's plan wasn't carried out with the deaths of Marshal Forsythe and Amanda Weaver. Maybe, they were meant to be lovers. Maybe, their love was great enough to span time."

"God doesn't defy the laws of nature and man just to fulfill someone's sex drive, Mike."

"All right, maybe it wasn't the love between those two. What if their lives were cut short by an evil force that should have been destroyed and wasn't? What if in 1886 Texas, the wrong people were killed, upsetting God's plan?"

"I'm almost frightened, because for the first time in this discussion you may actually have a point. Though the Church does not believe in the theory of predestination, throughout the Bible and history, God has used individuals to carry out his plan; and on occasion, right a wrong. I still think you should proceed with your own life, Michael. Lynette loves and cares for you without question. Look to her for your great love that spans time."

"I'm looking for the truth here, Chris. I'm troubled and I'm beginning to believe that my dream means something.

"Truth is a philosophical search, Michael; like searching for the meaning of life." "All right, then, I'm looking for facts. Is love a tangible thing; a force? Is it something that is capable of spanning time between the right people?"

"All is possible in God's kingdom. He loves all of us, but it is not the kind of love that most men think of when they speak of it. It's total, complete, and without question. It surrounds and comforts; nourishes and thrives. His love is there for all time; for all of us. Similar to the love that Lynette has for you. She has given herself completely to you and it has nothing to do with sex. Similar to the love you talk about that the marshal's wife had for him in your dream. Don't you see, you already have that kind of love that you dream about? Can't you take comfort in the fact that you have your health and faculties, and you are loved by the people who care the most about you? Don't lose your focus on reality over a girl you fell in love with in your dreams."

"But, Chris, could I be right?"

"I'm the theologian; you're the cop. Bring me proof! In the meantime, don't talk about this to others. Promise me that you'll call me if you have to talk some more about this."

"I promise, Father Chris." It was the same mocking tone that Michael had used when Chris first announced to the family his intentions of joining the priesthood. The laughter had returned to their eyes and faces.

Upstairs, Lynette heard the laughter and breathed a sigh of relief.

CHAPTER TWENTY

Mike had a good time in Houston at the vice seminar. He learned a couple of things. One of those things was never try and keep up drinking with those cops from Jefferson Parish, Louisiana. They had a good time taking Mike around town. Mike had a good time, too; though, he wished Lyn had been able to accompany him. She had been scheduled for surgery duty the entire week he was gone.

At the Houston Airport, the Jefferson Parish cops presented to Mike a drinking tumbler. It was a gag gift with lines painted on it. A line near the mouth of the glass had the words, "Southern Boys", and one painted along the bottom said, "Yankees". The boys had painted with nail polish another line just a hair above the "Yankee" line, and wrote, "Mike from Calif." They all had a good laugh. After they boarded their plane, Mike sat alone waiting for his flight.

While reading a paper, an idea came to Mike and he got up and walked over to the airline counter. He inquired about Dallas, and learned it was an hour's flight away for $58.00. Mike sat back down to think. Actually, he was arguing with himself.

Mike thought back to what Chris had said. Mike could remember growing up in Bakersfield. He thought about his school days. He had played on the baseball team at Garces High School. There were those summer months of working in the carrot sheds in Wasco with his buddy, Dennis Sandusky.

That was the summer that he met Jodie Knopf, the blonde-haired farmer's daughter. The one whose father wouldn't let them date because of their religions; she was a Mennonite. Mike thought he had pushed back and locked up those memories. He remembered those stolen dates and times together. Years earlier, Mike had often wondered how much different his life would have been if he and Jodie had been allowed to see each other. Then, he thought back to his family. He had all those pictures and all those memories of those happy times spent together.

Then, Mike thought that all his memories of the marshal were just as vivid and real to him. Mike stood up, walked to the ticket counter and quickly rebooked his flight home via Dallas. He phoned Lynette, but she wasn't home, and he left a message on the answering machine. That was Friday morning.

By Friday night in California, Lynette was confused and bordering on irate as she spoke to Mike. "So, when will you be coming home, Michael?"

"I'm booked on the 10 PM flight tomorrow night, honey."

"Before you 'honey' me again mister, maybe you'll explain to me what you're doing in Dallas; we don't know anyone there."

"Lyn, I'm following up a lead; a hunch if you will. This is legit, angel. I'm on business."

"Ok, then. I'll pick you up at LAX tomorrow night. Be careful on whatever you're doing and hurry home."

"Thanks, angel. I love you."

Not far from Lyn at that moment, a Mercedes pulled into the driveway and into the garage. The area was a nice home in a very quiet neighborhood in Rancho Palos Verdes. The car following the Mercedes stopped outside on the street. Carl Andrews was driving the vehicle he took from a drug dealer. Andrews had killed him when he wouldn't give the cocaine to Andrews as Andrews was short the full amount of money.

Andrews had spotted the woman driving the Mercedes while he had been driving towards the beach. She looked rich and pretty. The young advertising executive never heard Andrews enter the house and she saw him too late. She struggled, but he held her throat as she was braced against the kitchen wall.

Her eyes were wide with fear. Andrews could see her face powder and the makeup in detail as he stared and sized her up. He saw the sweat beads forming along her hairline. He could smell her perfume; she looked good and she smelled good. She couldn't scream, but she continued to struggle. When she tried to knee him, Andrews stopped thinking and reacted. He plunged a knife between her ribs. He quickly ransacked the home for money and any small valuables.

Before leaving, he took his victim's weddings rings and jewelry. He couldn't help how he felt as he looked upon the still form on the floor; she was very pretty. Andrews sodomized the dead woman, before leaving with a bottle of brandy taken from one of the cabinets.

He left in the drug dealer's car. Before returning to his apartment, Andrews stopped on Pacific Coast Highway and picked up a streetwalker. He wanted another woman to celebrate the high he was on. The hooker would be found in the dumpster behind the motel in the morning. The young woman's family found her that night.

The sheriff's office was getting real busy.

CHAPTER TWENTY-ONE

"Paul, I'm glad I caught you at your office. Your housekeeper said I might find you there."

"What's up, Mike? Don't tell me you're at the airport?"

"I'm in Dallas at a drug store with a fax machine. I'll be sending you some copies in a minute. I played a hunch and flew to Dallas after my seminar in Houston. I've been busy as I promised Lyn I would fly home, tonight. You won't believe what I found."

The paper rolled out of the fax machine in Paul's office and Mike was right, Paul didn't believe what he saw. It was a picture from a scrapbook from the Dallas Chamber of Commerce celebrating the city's centennial. The picture was of a man and a pretty woman holding hands. The caption read, "Frontier marshal and wife". The man was the spitting image of Mike, right down to the scar on his face. By quick calculation, Paul figured Mike had been born six years *after* the centennial anniversary of Dallas.

The fax machine continued to spew out paper. This time it was a copy of the front page of a Dallas newspaper article. It read that the paper's owner, Amanda Weaver, and Marshal Forsythe had been found killed on a road outside of town. It appeared that the two had been killed following a gun battle with the Cooper Gang the marshal had been trailing. Besides Weaver and the marshal, two others from the gang were found dead; bodies and horses were found scattered for over a hundred yards. The article continued that the body of the marshal had been claimed by his wife, who left with it on a train bound for Alexandria, Louisiana. Miss Weaver had no known kin and she would be buried in town.

"What am I supposed to say, Mike? Better yet, what do you think of this information?"

"Paul, the woman in the picture is the same woman I've been seeing in my dreams! I've walked and driven around this town and so many places seem familiar. It's down right scary! And scary is just about the right word to use when you look at the things I'm digging up. There's the stuff from the newspaper and there's more!

I called a vice cop from Louisiana that I met at the seminar. I had him check and he told me that there was a property record of a Robert and Deborah Forsythe owning a house in Alexandria. Neither name is mentioned in the county records after 1886. According to the local newspaper archives, the marshal was gunned down and his wife claimed the body in Dallas. Upon her return home, she left and was never heard from again."

"This certainly is intriguing, Mike. Have you ever been in Dallas before?"

"Paul, I have never been in Texas before until this seminar. I have one more piece of information that you may find interesting. I found Amanda Weaver's grave here in Dallas. There is no date of birth, but the date of death is listed as Nov. 16, 1886.

Paul, I couldn't have dreamed all this up. I think that I'm onto something, but I'm starting to get scared."

"What do you mean scared?"

"I'm not really sure, but I believe that my dreams aren't dreams after all. Maybe they are real. Paul, I think I could be in trouble."

That was more than Paul needed to hear.

"I can be in L.A. on Wednesday, Mike. Will you be ok 'till then?"

"Me, no problem. Thanks, Paul."

What Mike didn't tell Paul was that it was his opinion that if his dream was reality, he was worried about the significance, if any, to the date. Amanda's tombstone said November 16, and this was October 19th. Things were coming together at a rapid pace. Was the one-man crime spree being committed by a present-day Cooper? Were the events on the same timetable? If there were issues to resolve, maybe they would have to occur in less than a month.

It occurred to Mike on the plane, that if he had been brought back to stop the wrong persons from dying, then Amanda had to be here as well, but where was she? Had he missed her in Dallas? Could he find her before Cooper did, if the nightmare had to be relived? Worse, would he still be in love with Amanda, and if so, what would happen to Lynette? What had become of Debbie? This was too much to think about. He had a drink and fell asleep somewhere over New Mexico.

As the stewardess woke him up for the landing, she handed him the xeroxed papers and the Polaroid photo of Amanda's grave that had fallen off his lap, so he knew he hadn't been dreaming that. Once inside the airport, he knew he had other troubles. There stood Lynette, who was frowning, and she was accompanied by his brother and his sergeant.

CHAPTER TWENTY-TWO

Mike hugged Lynette, but she was as rigid as a new recruit at boot camp. He shook hands with his brother and his sergeant, Ron Blakely. Blakely took Mike aside and said that Central Homicide wanted to see his ass downtown tomorrow morning at ten. Some nut had been working overtime killing street whores and they wanted some help in identifying them; and he was their pick from Vice. He had driven over to his house when he found Lyn and Chris leaving for the airport. Since this was important, he followed to talk directly to Mike. Before Mike could say anything, Blakely said he already talked with Lyn and there was nothing to worry about. Blakely left reminding Mike not to be late.

On the drive home, Chris drove; Lynette was in the front seat and Mike in the back. After leaving the airport lot, Lynette turned around to face Mike and said, "Michael Albert, just what in the hell is going on around here!" Mike knew he was in trouble when she called him by both his given names. Not even Chris was going to interrupt when she was this angry. "First, you go traipsing up to Dallas without an explanation and then the brass starts calling the house looking for you. What are you doing?" Her eyes were locked onto his.

"Lyn, I told you I flew to Dallas to check on a lead; no a hunch on an old murder case. As for Blakely, I only know what he told me: that Central Homicide has had several street prostitutes murdered and they're looking to vice for help in identifying them. I've been ordered to report at 10 AM tomorrow. That's all I know, honest."

Chris spoke up now. "Mike, Lyn called me as she is extremely upset and worried that you're in trouble. You scared her with your trip to Dallas. You do have obligations here. Are you ok, little brother?"

"I'm fine, Chris, and I'm sorry for worrying you, Lyn", Mike said as he patted her hand. Lyn turned back around and remained quiet the rest of the way home. In the darkness, no one saw that tears were rolling down her cheeks.

At home, Mike talked Chris into staying overnight as he was hoping to talk to him about what he found in Dallas. Upstairs in their room, Lynette was serious when she asked Mike if he was having an affair. She believed him when he said no, but she wasn't sure when he answered that he was not in trouble. She fell asleep in his arms.

Lynette woke Chris up early, so he would have time for coffee before heading to church to say Mass. She really wanted to talk with him about Mike. By the time that Chris dressed and walked into the kitchen, Lynette was standing at the sink waiting for the coffee to finish brewing.

Upon seeing Chris, Lynette started walking to him and said, "I don't think Mike is ready to be thrown into this hooker killer case, Chris. Can't you say something to someone?"

"Angel, I'd do anything for you and Mike, but I question interfering in Mike's professional business. He's very good at what he does. He's been troubled lately, but it's this last shooting. It was a pretty close call. And don't forget those nightmares of his. Right now, the only thing that's keeping him steady is your love; you're his balance in this crazy world of ours. He loves you dearly and he needs you.

I think he needs us both. With everything that Mike's been through, it's still harder to stand by and watch in silence than to actually do the fighting he's already done and the difficult jobs he must continue to do. You and I are that kind of tough; we don't carry guns or fight with our fists, but we endure silently and we are stronger each time because of it."

Chris closed the distance between himself and Lyn. He held her and brushed her hair back out of her eyes.

"Whatever his troubles and fate, remember that he loves you dearly. I told him on my last visit, that you were his one great love. At the time, he asked me a question I couldn't answer. After thinking about it, I'm convinced that true love is a force that can span time and space. Let him sort through his troubles, Mike will come back to you, I know it. Have faith, trust in him; I do."

"It seems I married the cute Stewart boy; the smart one was already taken. I trust that Mike will make the right choice, too. I just want him safe and sound; and I want him back because he wants me."

CHAPTER TWENTY-THREE

 Mike dropped Lyn off at home after attending church, before heading downtown. Before getting out of the car, Lyn asked, "How late will you be?"

"I really don't know. I don't think it will be very long, unless they have something in mind that I'm not aware of."

"I was thinking of visiting Annie, if you want to pick me up when you're through." Annie was Lynette's younger, married sister who lived in Torrance.

"Hon, every time you go over there, you end up crying after seeing her babies. Please don't subject yourself to that misery."

"I suppose it's better that I stay here and wait for you to return home when you're through playing cop?"

"Lyn, this wasn't my idea to work on Sunday. Have it your way. I'll swing by Annie's when I'm through."

The freeways were smooth sailing since it was a Sunday. Mike made good time into the downtown area. He flashed his badge to the deputy on guard duty at headquarters and pulled into the parking lot. Mike parked his car and after entering the building, he took the elevator to the fifth floor. The main receptionist's door was unlocked and inside the office people were waiting for him.

"Mike, it's good to see you! I haven't seen you since... when?"

"Since we worked patrol out of Lennox."

"Gosh, we're getting old."

The speaker was Lt. Tommy Delaney. Delaney was in charge of the Central Homicide Detail. Mike thought to himself that Delaney looked older. It was the stress of the job and the politics at his level. Lately, the rash of unsolved killings was really becoming burdensome.

They shook hands and Mike sat down at the small table provided. Also present was Sgt. T.J. Knox. "Mike, I'll get right to the point. There's been a string of hookers killed and dumped in areas from Central to Lennox to Carson. Most have been found dumped nude. All had their throats cut. We've ID'd only one so far, Libby Thompson." "I knew Libby. I busted her in '85 and '87 out of Lennox. She used to work around the main streets surrounding LAX."

"Well, I guess you and your old partner scared her farther south. She has been working PCH (Pacific Coast Highway) in Torrance. She was found in a dumpster behind a motel on Imperial Highway, yesterday morning. According to the autopsy performed yesterday, she was killed late Friday night."

"Ok, what do you want from me?"

"I'm putting a task force together before we get another hooker killed; so far, there's been seven. I want you from Vice. You'll report here starting tomorrow at 0800 hours. Before you go, T.J. has a packet on those killed that we'll be looking at. Included, you'll find are all the reports, initial, supplementals, and autopsy; as well as photos. These packets are numbered and are to be considered confidential. At this point, we do not want the press sticking their noses into this and broadcasting our only clues. Any questions, Mike?"

"Who else do you have on the team?"

"You, me, T.J., Paul Dougherty, and Kenny Baxter."

Stewart knew of Sgt. T.J. Knox from his reputation. He was a sharp individual in his late thirties who was politically correct and probably politically connected. Mike knew he had a reputation as a hard-ass while assigned as tac officer at the old academy at the Biscailuz Center. He was "by-the-book" and didn't hesitate to climb to the top over the backs of the dead bodies of colleagues he knifed in the back. Judging from his hairstyle, Mike guessed that Knox spent as much money on hairspray in a month as Mike spent on shoes for a whole year. Mike figured that Knox would be the ramrod on this operation.

Mike knew and had worked with Dougherty and Baxter over the years. Dougherty and Baxter were detectives back "when Christ was a corporal". They had been detectives going back to the time of the East LA riots. Over the years, both had worked on several high-profile cases.

Dougherty looked like a retired marine drill instructor and Baxter had the jowls and bushy eyebrows that immediately made one think of bulldogs. Dougherty would have cracked a joke in the Vatican, while Baxter was the type that wouldn't crack a smile if his life depended on it. Stewart knew of their work; they were ruthless and dogged in their investigations. They were very good at talking with people and interrogating suspects. You didn't want them on your trail.

"Sounds good. I'll see you tomorrow, Tom."

"Thanks, Mike."

Mike pulled into the driveway at Annie's house before she could serve an early dinner. Annie's husband, Dave, was watching football games on TV, and the girls were in the kitchen. Lyn was holding the youngest, two month-old Jason, while Annie was at the stove. "Hi, honey, come here and look at the baby", Lyn said. Dutifully, Mike walked over kissed Lyn and little Jason. This is how it always began; Lyn playing with the babies and then going home and crying herself to sleep.

Carl Andrews was waking up with a hangover at the same time that Mike was sitting down to dinner. Andrews' head was splitting from the whiskey, but not even the whiskey had stopped the nightmares. Lately, it was the same picture of the same woman in his head. He saw the red-haired woman even when he closed his eyes. Andrews couldn't explain the images he saw or why he felt so much hatred, but he wanted the nightmares to end. He drank some more whiskey and passed out again.

Over dinner, Annie asked Mike what the Sheriff's Department was doing about the rape and murder of the young woman in Rancho Palos Verdes. When Mike asked what murder, Annie showed him the copy of the newspaper. Mike quickly skimmed the article before setting the folded newspaper alongside his plate.

After dinner, Mike sat in the den where he carefully read the article. By the time that Annie served the coffee and dessert, Mike had read the newspaper story twice. Mike was intrigued by the use of a knife and the proximity in time and distance to the murder of Libby Thompson, but gave it no more thought for the moment.

Later in the evening, Mike found Lynette in Annie's bedroom changing Jason's diaper. She was kissing his forehead when Mike walked into the room. Standing just inside the doorway, Mike said, "The older I get, the more unsure of things I become. But I know that I love you and I know that you would have been a fine mother." He walked up behind her and hugged her and whispered in her ear, "I need you, Lynette. Don't fall apart on me. If we had babies, they would have been beautiful, but we don't need babies to prove our love. We have each other. Let's excuse ourselves and go home, now."

When the Stewarts arrived home, Mike checked the answering machine for messages and saw the flashing red light indicating a message left on the tape. Mike pressed the playback button.

"Mike, it's Mike Cantrill. I hate to call you at home, but I'm afraid I'm going to have to cancel lunch this week. It seems that someone is on a one-man crime spree committing robberies from Central to Lennox to Carson. Maybe we can get together for lunch or drinks after work one evening before the holidays. I'll talk with you later. Take care."

"'...from Central to Lennox to Carson' were Delaney's exact words about the murders.", thought Mike as he whispered to himself. Mike picked up his phone and started dialing.

Mike phoned the Lennox Station watch commander to get Tom Delaney's number.

"Tom, it's Mike Stewart. I'm sorry to bother you at home, but I have an idea about the case."

"No bother. Go ahead, Mike."

"Last Friday, there was a rape-murder of a young woman in Rancho P.V. The weapon used was a knife and the paper said she was robbed as well. This is pretty close to Libby Thompson's murder as far as time and distance are concerned. What if there's a connection?"

"You tell me the connection, Mike."

"What if they're related incidents? What if the killer picks up and then kills a hooker after committing each one of his robberies; maybe like a high or ritual?"

"Sounds as if you're stretching things a bit, Mike. Don't forget that he sodomized the woman in her house."

"Tom, I know it sounds thin until you put everything together. Mike Cantrill described a one-man robbery spree using your same words 'from Central to Lennox to Carson'. Do the other stations have recent unsolved 187's in which a knife was used?" "There have been several recently, but how would we go about sorting through them all?"

"Well, how about Mike Cantrill? Isn't he working Robbery downtown?"

"Yes, he's a sergeant over at Central."

"Tom, I know this is thin, but I think you should shanghai Cantrill and get him assigned to your task force. We could sort through the cases using as the criteria those with 2-11s (robberies) preceding them in the general vicinity. Cantrill's good and it wouldn't hurt to have the liaison."

"I'm desperate enough to try it, Mike. I know Cantrill and you're right, he's forgotten more about robbery than I'll ever know. Let's dig up what we can tomorrow morning on the cases, and I'll try to get him to come over for a look-see sometime after lunch."

"Sounds good to me, Tom. I'll see you in the morning."

Later that night when she fell asleep with her head on his chest, Lynette Stewart felt as if everything was getting back to normal. In reality, the fuse to the powder keg was still burning.

CHAPTER TWENTY-FOUR

The short-barreled shotgun rested on the front seat, within easy reach of the driver. The driver did not pay it any attention as he was focused on the people in and around the old brick building. The building was across the street from Pershing Square and within its walls housed several diamond importers.

The people that had caught his eye were two white males that appeared to be in their forties. They looked dirty and were wearing navy pea coats which were unbuttoned and they kept their hands in the coat pockets. They could have easily mistaken for street people, but the driver had noticed a "look" about them. It was their eyes. Their eyes darted about scanning their environment. The driver kept his eyes riveted on the front doors of the building and the two persons until the driver of the car behind him honked the horn as the traffic light changed.

Sgt. Cantrill drove the unmarked sheriff's car through the intersection. He had noticed two men that looked out of place and he was going to swing around and watch them for a few minutes. An old robbery investigator, Mike Cantrill knew that the approaching holiday season would bring additional crimes and there had begun a series of "smash and grabs" at various jewelers. Cantrill had been returning from his weekly luncheon with his mother at the Bonaventure Hotel in downtown Los Angeles when he spotted the two.

Since the park is within the city limits, Cantrill was debating over having his dispatcher try and get a black and white from LAPD to shake the two strangers down, when he heard the dispatcher call him.

"Robert 177. 10-19 and see the W-C." (Return to the station and report to the watch commander).

"Robert 177 copied. Enroute."

Cantrill watched for another minute as the two men moved slowly away from the diamond store and well into the park. He locked the shotgun in its rack and headed for the station as he wondered what his lieutenant wanted to see him about. He and the lieutenant had already spoken about the smash and grabs, revising the work schedules for the upcoming holidays, and shift rotation of the detectives in January.

Just as smoothly as he maneuvered the unit through the heavy downtown traffic, Cantrill shifted his thoughts. Lunch with his mother had been normal. Julia Cantrill had asked about the children, and then almost grudgingly, asked about his wife, Karen. His mother commented that he looked tired and asked about his health. They spoke of Washington politics and the state's economy. They discussed the stock market, his stock investments, her upcoming travel plans, and the theater. And she paid the check. She always paid the check.

Years before, Mike had tried to pay in advance and once even tried to bribe the maitre d'. It didn't work. His mother's old money had very effectively bought loyalty. The luncheon meetings were an established routine going back to the days when Mike had moved out to be on his own and joined the Los Angeles Sheriff's Department. Back then, even his father would occasionally break away from the hospital and join them. It seemed like such a long time ago. Doctor William Cantrill had died of a brain aneurysm back in 1984.

Michael had been adopted by the Cantrills while the young Doctor Cantrill was completing his residency in Chicago. Shortly thereafter, the Cantrill family moved to Southern California. Young Michael had a natural inclination for math and he developed his business sense by reading the Wall Street Journal and the business section of the Los Angeles Times. Soon, he was investing money saved from birthday gifts and his job at the grocery store after school into the stock market. It was under the watchful eyes of his parents and he had to report to them, but Mike started gradually making small profits and he would reinvest it into the market. His stock market investment was a practice that he continued as an adult. Mike could routinely make as much in a year in the market and his other investments as his job with the sheriff's department paid him. "Salary including the benefits percentage", he would say when asked by his parents.

Mike Cantrill smiled as he thought about his career choice. He knew that his mother had hoped that he would become an investment broker and settle down with that snobbish socialite, Gwendolyn Taylor. Before thinking too much about Gwendolyn, Mike forced himself back to the present, double-checked the shotgun lock, and accelerated onto the freeway and the station where his lieutenant was waiting.

At about the same time, Paul Paslosky stopped his rental car in front of small house on a quiet Dallas street. He had been enroute to the West Coast, but decided to make a lay over in Dallas. What he didn't tell Mike was that he intended to stop in Dallas to double-check on Mike's initial findings.

Once in town, Paul found things just as Mike had described. While trying to track down any other possible characters in Mike's story, he stopped at the Chamber of Commerce. It was there, that Paul was given the name of a woman who still lived in town and had actually worked on the centennial issue of the book that Mike had found with the marshal's picture.

Kathryn Tucker Wallace was a spry, eighty-three year old widow, who graciously agreed to meet with Paul after his phone call. Paul found a thoroughly charming and lively character when he walked up towards her front porch; the same front porch of the small house on the quiet street. Mrs. Wallace met him at the front door and invited Paul into her house. Paul found the old home to exude the same quiet, elegance as that of the owner. He felt like an old friend by the time he was ushered to the parlor, where there were molasses cookies and lemonade waiting.

"Well, young man what brings you from New York to visit with me? Your phone call sounded urgent and I must confess that I found it to be quite intriguing."

"Mrs. Wallace, I'll try to be succinct."

"Please, sir, call me Kate. No one has referred to me as Mrs. Wallace since Eisenhower was president."

"Very well, Kate. As I said on the phone, I'm a psychiatrist from New York. Recently, I received a phone call from an old friend who told an incredible tale about a dream he is continuing to have that troubles him. On a recent visit to Dallas, he sent back pictures to me that compelled me to check on his information. Once in town, I learned that you were possibly the only living person that had worked on the town's centennial yearbook. If that is the case, I would like to ask you a question."

"My goodness! That was a long time ago, and yes, I do believe that I am the last of the original planners for the yearbook. Though, I must admit that I fail to see what that has to do with your friend. Surely, neither one of you could have been born when I was working on that book."

Paul was listening to Mrs. Wallace while he helped himself to a cookie. "Basically, I have come to ask if you remember anything about a photograph that was used in the book; specifically, this photograph." Paul retrieved the fax copy of the photograph of Marshal Forsythe from his briefcase and handed it to Mrs. Wallace. He helped himself to another cookie as he sipped lemonade.

Mrs. Wallace studied the copy for just a minute as she adjusted the glasses on her nose. "This is a very poor facsimile, young man. Fortunately, I have a better one." Standing up, she walked over to the curio cabinet on the other end of the room. From it, she took out a framed 5x7 photograph and handed it to Paul.

He almost choked on the cookie as he stared at it. In his hand, Paul was holding the original photo of Marshal Forsythe and Amanda Weaver taken on a Saturday morning over a hundred years ago, just as Mike had described in his dream. Amanda Weaver was even prettier than he had imagined. Both the marshal and Amanda were smiling and holding onto each other; it was apparent that they had been in love.

"I cannot fathom why your friend was taken with the picture, but that man in it holds a special place in my family. You see the man, the marshal, rescued my mother when she was just a little girl..."

"You mean your mother was Melissa Peterson?" Paul interrupted.

"Why yes, but how did you know that?" Paul quickly retold Mike's tale about the marshal as best he could remember. Mrs. Wallace stared in disbelief at Paul's knowledge of her mother's rescue and the subsequent tragic death of the marshal and the newspaperwoman.

Mrs. Wallace filled in the rest of the story. The doctor and his wife had adopted her mother shortly afterwards. The photograph was discovered after the marshal's death. Melissa was too young to remember much about the man, but she loved him as only a child could. The photograph was given to Melissa as a present when it finally turned up. Mrs. Wallace even had the marshal's Winchester rifle and Colt revolver. According to her mother, the marshal's wife had taken only his Sharps rifle with her when she claimed his body.

Melissa grew up, married, and had four children. Mrs. Wallace's oldest brother had been named for the marshal. Mrs. Wallace was the youngest and last remaining child. She said that all of the children knew the story of the marshal and the amazing rescue he accomplished by heart after having been told it by their mother and other townsfolk over the years. Mrs. Wallace said it was only fitting and natural for her to include the picture in the yearbook. She knew that the woman in it wasn't the marshal's wife, but to have listed her as his girlfriend would have been scandalous at the time since most people in town had thought the two were having an affair anyway.

"Mother died in 1962, remembering very little of the man, due no doubt to her young age at the time of her rescue. I can hear mother even now as she told about the feel of the marshal's rough whiskers when he held her tightly. She also remembered the smell and feel of his black coat that she hung onto on the ride back to town. Occasionally, mother would refer to the marshal as her knight in shining armor. His death was very traumatic for mother. She remembered the doctor's wife telling her that the marshal had to go to heaven. She even recalled meeting the marshal's wife when she came for his body. She used to say she remembered the pretty lady crying as she hugged her at the train depot."

From his wallet, Paul pulled a picture and handed it and the framed photo to Mrs. Wallace. "That is my friend and his wife. It was taken six years ago when they came to New York for my wife's funeral."

Mrs. Wallace stared in awe at Mike's face. In addition to it being the same person, she noticed that the scar was the same and it was the same smile as that of the marshal's.

"There must be some mistake or something."

"It's something, but I don't know if it's a mistake. The man in my photograph saved my life during the Vietnam War. Up to a few days ago, I was a little worried for my friend. Now, I'm afraid that he's right and in trouble. He has been haunted by a recurring dream, and is troubled, because he cannot understand any of this. Until this month, my friend had never been in Texas. Yet, he told me the same tale that you have concerning not only your mother's rescue, but little known, and early details of the marshal's life."

"Are you saying that your friend is really the marshal?", asked Mrs. Wallace, who was now visibly disturbed.

"I'm no longer sure of what to think, but if I were to believe in reincarnation, this is as good a place as any to start. You see, my friend is a cop in Los Angeles, and I'm on my way to visit him next. He called me two days ago asking for my help."

Mrs. Wallace was standing up by now and wringing her hands together. Paul started to get up to comfort her, but she began walking back to the curio cabinet. This time she pulled out another photograph and handed it to Paul.

"That's my mother and father on their wedding day in 1901. Take it and give it to your friend."

Paul could see that she had tears in her eyes.

Mrs. Wallace continued, "If he's the marshal, tell him that Melissa loved him and never forgot him; and tell him I said, 'Thank you' for saving my mother."

CHAPTER TWENTY-FIVE

"Oh, Michael!" Lynette cried out as she opened her gift and saw the anniversary diamond ring. "This is too much; you shouldn't have!" She quickly slipped on the ring and was admiring it and the gold necklace that she had already been given and put around her neck.

They both had been getting ready for work, when Mike decided not to wait any longer to hand out anniversary gifts. Lynette pulled out two packages from under their bed; one small and the other, large. "I'm afraid, I didn't spend very much money on your gifts, but you wouldn't tell me what you wanted. I hope you like them."

"Honey, anything you give me will be just fine. I just want you to be happy", Mike said as he started opening the small package. Inside, he found his old snub-nosed revolver in an ankle holster. Examining it, Mike saw that the old .357 magnum Smith & Wesson with a two and half inch barrel had new glow-in-the-dark sights for night shooting. It was already loaded with department ammunition.

"I hope you don't mind, Mike, but since you've worked Vice, you carry that Italian gun. I came across your old revolver and had that gunsmith in Riverside put the new sights on. Your old partner, Gary, suggested the ankle holster. I thought this would keep you safe if you carried it as a back up. You used to shoot it all the time. You used to say `It's not how many bullets you have, it's accuracy that counts'. Go ahead and put it on."

As Mike adjusted the velcro strap, he said, "This should do it. Yeah, I guess this isn't a bad fit. I just never thought to carry this old gun once I got my nine-millimeter." Leaving it on his ankle, Mike opened the second gift and found a thin, lightweight bulletproof vest.

"Before you say anything, Michael Albert, I paid dearly for that little thing! Since you've worked undercover, you've never worn a vest except on a raid. I want you safe and sound and I'm hoping that these will do the trick. Promise me that you'll give them a try. Your last shooting was just too close. Please, promise me", she implored.

"Ok, Ok! I'll give it a try, but I'm sure going to be the butt of a multitude of jokes from the guys. Real vice cops just don't wear bulletproof vests."

"Real vice cops don't have me to come home to, you nut. What do you say Mr. Stewart, to being made late for work? After eighteen years, I bet I can still get your heart to skip a beat."

Mike's response was to grab Lynette and growl in her ear as he pushed her back onto the bed.

Michael and Lynette wouldn't have been so thrilled, if they knew the series of events and persons moving into position while they made love in their bedroom: Dr. Paslosky was finishing his last cup of coffee on the plane before final descent into Los Angeles, Carl Andrews was loading his sawed-off shotgun in his motel room, Sgt. Cantrill was discussing the killings with Lt. Delaney, and Megan Reilly was reviewing police logs at the news desk at the <u>Los Angeles Times</u>.

Chapter Twenty-six

Megan Reilly was an experienced staff reporter for the <u>Los Angeles Times</u>. She had covered the police beat early in her career in Chicago, Sacramento, and now in Los Angeles. Megan had an infectious smile; it seemed to naturally go with her red hair and green eyes. She was twice divorced, 37 years old, and she was the spitting image of Amanda Weaver.

She was also the image found in Carl Andrews' dreams.

Megan had been having dreams of her own, lately, and none of them were pleasant. She chalked most of them up to having too many glasses of chardonnay in the evening; and spending too many nights alone since her last divorce. Still, on those lonely nights, she would liked to have met the dark-haired stranger in her dreams. Other nights, she woke up screaming after seeing herself struggle with a strange man, and then shot through the back by the handsome stranger and dying on a grassy slope. At times, she could smell and feel the wet grass. Sometimes the dreams were so vivid and disturbing, that she had considered going to a psychiatrist.

This morning she was going through the press releases by the sheriff's department as she was looking for any more prostitute killings. There seemed to have been an unusual number of them, lately. She thought she may be onto a story, but every time she called the vice unit, she felt as if she was being given the runaround.

Picking up a phone, she called Peter Teyachaya, who has worked the city desk for years. "Pete, this is Megan. I'd like to make a deal with you. If you still know someone over at the sheriff's department vice unit, I could be talked into buying you lunch today."

"Would this include two gin and tonics and my choice of places?"

"You don't even care that you're taking advantage of a poor, vulnerable young lady, do you?" There was silence at the other end of the phone. "Ok, drinks and your choice of restaurants."

"Lady, break out the plastic. We've got a deal. I'll meet you out front at 11:45".

CHAPTER TWENTY-SEVEN

 As Megan Reilly was gathering her purse and coat before leaving for lunch, the sheriff's department was about to get its first break in the string of robberies and killings. They were also about to get two more victims. Carl Andrews was just walking into a liquor store on Hawthorne Boulevard in Lawndale. Inside, he shot the Asian clerk just for drill. But this time, he broke open the double-barreled shotgun and pulled out the empty shell and reloaded. Then he emptied the cash register of the $197.00 and took two pint bottles of Old Grand Dad whiskey before leaving in the car taken from the drug dealer.

The empty shotgun shell had his fingerprints on it and he left it on the floor of the liquor store. This time, the sheriff's department had a solid clue. Before the day would be over, detectives would have his name. Unfortunately, it would not be in time to save the hooker working at Aviation and 116th St.

Mike Stewart and Mike Cantrill were sitting in a sheriff's helicopter as it raced them from downtown LA to the scene in the South Bay where the latest prostitute victim had been found. As the helicopter's blades steadily beat the air, their sound and vibrations whisked Mike Stewart back to early 1968.

He was sitting in a Huey gunship with Paul Paslosky. They were flying out of Camp Bu Prang with the II CTZ Mike Force. Mike met Paul in jump school. Paul was a natural athlete and took to parachuting, like the proverbial duck to water. Mike was better on the land at survival techniques. Mike gave Paul some pointers on qualifying with the government .45 pistol while at the range. Just before a night jump, Paul was telling jokes to take the edge off of Mike's nervousness. They formed an immediate friendship.

1968 would mark the end of their tour in Vietnam. This particular mission would end before it got started, as they were inserted into the wrong landing zone. The helicopter landed within spitting distance to one of Charley's camps. Immediately, a furious firefight ensued. The helicopter was disabled, leaving the crew to fight and run for their lives. Disoriented and outnumbered, it was incredible that any of them made it out alive. For Mike and Paul, this mission would culminate in the longest and toughest forty-three hours of their lives. It would forever forge the bond between them.

The sun was beginning to set on the sheriff's helicopter as it sped across the Los Angeles skyline. But Mike's mind was racing faster than the twirling blades on the helicopter.

Those fiery eyes of his were mesmerized as he traveled back across to the Texas prairie at night on horseback. The moon was yellow and sitting low in the night sky. Robert had been tracking a gang of three killers in the Indian Territory and his progress was slower than originally anticipated. That was the reason for traveling at night. That and the fact that he was hoping to catch them unawares.

The night air was chilly and it would get colder before he would stop for the night. A lone wolf baying at the moon was his only nighttime companion. The steady rocking of his body in the saddle would have lulled him to sleep, if it hadn't had been for that constant leather creaking sound and the occasional snorting of his horse. Mike could hear, see, and smell everything in his world that had long since passed him by.

"Mike! Hey, Mike! Are you ok? Mike, are you air sick?" Cantrill was calling out to Stewart. Finally, when Cantrill shook his shoulder, Mike's journey was interrupted, and he found himself in the sheriff's helicopter.

"Yeah, I'm ok. Sorry, I was just lost in thought", Stewart replied. He looked at Cantrill's face, which was now smiling as he looked back out the window.

He remembered the last time that he worked with Cantrill in Robbery. They both were part of the surveillance team at the bank that day. From information obtained by a crime pattern analyst, he and Cantrill selected the bank as a likely candidate for the robber that they had nicknamed "Smelly" for his bad breath that the victim tellers always described.

Cantrill had spotted "Smelly" as he started walking across the bank's parking lot. They split up and cut "Smelly" off from the bank's entrance. They tried to take him into custody quickly and peacefully, but "Smelly" was packing two pistols and wasn't about to go along with their plans. It was he who opened up with his pistols sending noontime strollers ducking for cover. Mike remembered that Cantrill kept his cool when the shooting started. According to the shooting team's report, the episode lasted less than two minutes. During that time, though, twenty-three shots were exchanged by "Smelly", Cantrill, and himself.

He liked Cantrill a great deal. "Why do friends lose touch with one another?" Mike thought to himself. He leaned forward, closed his eyes, and rubbed his temples. Mike was tired, and he could not understand his dreams anymore, nor did he want to dream anymore.

Soon, the nightmares would end.

CHAPTER TWENTY-EIGHT

Lynette had picked up Paul from the airport. Mike had forgotten to tell her that Paul was coming for a visit. Paul told Lyn that he had to consult with a colleague and on the spur of the moment, planned the trip out to California. Lyn had planned a quiet dinner for her and Mike, but now found herself sitting across the table from Paul. Her evening plans had been ruined when Mike called from the office to say there had been another victim found, and he and Mike Cantrill would have to follow up on it.

"Paul, is everything all right?" asked Lyn as she returned from the kitchen where she had placed their dirty dinner dishes in the dishwasher.

"Of course. I haven't eaten a meal like this since Rebecca and I used to go out every weekend." He could say her name, now, without feeling the hurt.

"I'm not talking about the food. I'm referring to you and Mike."

"We're fine. Why do you ask?"

"Because you keep staring at me, and you been asking questions about Mike all night."

"I'm sorry for the staring; I wasn't aware of it. It's just been so long since I've seen you. I apologize."

Instead of calling him a liar, Lyn walked over and sat next to Paul. "Mike's fine, you'll see for yourself; whenever he comes home. I know you're worried about him, too. I overheard the tail end of his conversation with you when he phoned you last month." Paul could see in her eyes that she wasn't as sure as she sounded. He felt that she was trying to convince herself, as much as reassure him.

"I know Mike's fine. He killed several times during the war, but war is different than having to kill someone as part of doing your job at home. He just needed to be reassured that he's ok, and I just needed to be reassured that my old pardner is safe and sound. I thought I'd check on him as long as I was in town." Paul patted her hand, and said, "Now, where's this fine California brandy Mike keeps teasing me with?"

Lyn stood up and walked over to the cabinet just off the dining room. Paul didn't even try and avert his eyes. He watched Lyn's hips walking away from him. Over the years, he felt like a pervert, but he couldn't help but notice Lyn. Lyn never flirted or flaunted herself. It wasn't in the manner in which she walked or talked. It wasn't the way that she dressed or conducted herself. Paul found her to be a lady at all times, but there was something about her. Something that just exuded a fiery passion that even a writer would have been hard pressed to described.

Lyn gathered the brandy and the glasses. She and Paul moved to the study where Lyn kicked off her shoes and Paul loosened his tie. They spent the rest of the evening in the study talking about medicine and the sorry state of California's politics and economy.

Mike's anniversary dinner consisted of four cups of coffee and half a burger. He spent it with Cantrill, a dead street hooker, and a dozen sheriff's personnel. This killing had been the same as all of the others: a lone street-walker whose throat had been cut and her body dumped in an alley off a main street. He and Cantrill hurried back to the helicopter after they received word that the Robbery team in Lawndale had a name of a possible suspect.

It was almost 11:00 PM when they arrived back at the office. Once inside, they entered into a briefing that Lt. Delaney was conducting. Prior to concluding, Delaney told them that the press was camping in the lobby for a story. He told them that he would read from a prepared press release; otherwise, they were to continue to avoid the press until they could check further on this Andrews character. Delaney was working on getting a picture of Andrews shipped over to the unit.

As Mike was walking out of the office towards the coffee vending machine in the interior hallway, he heard the on-duty patrol sergeant call out, "Stewart, there's a woman out here asking for you by name. Says she knows you from Vice."

"So does just about every female, except for Mother Teresa", he mumbled out loud as he walked through the door to the lobby.

CHAPTER TWENTY-NINE

 As Lt. Delaney was finishing his prepared statement to the press and answering, or rather, evading questions from the reporters, Carl Andrews was driving through Marina Del Rey. Like any predator, he was watching the sights and sounds of the night. His gaze was on those people out in his world.

Andrews had spent most of the evening sitting in bars. He knew he would have to find a place to spend the night, but for some reason, he could not resist the urge to drive around looking into the ocean front establishments for something; anything, he couldn't explain it himself.

Just in case he found prey, he was armed. In addition to the switchblade knife he carried, he had his shotgun. Andrews had cut back the shotgun so it would be concealable under his coat. He affixed leather bootlaces to the chopped stock and trigger guard, and looped the ends around his right shoulder. In this fashion, the shotgun hung down under his arm while being carried without the use of his hands, but was instantly available in the event he decided to use it.

Andrews continued to drive around for almost an hour after leaving the last bar. Finally, he stopped for the night at a motel in the Venice area.

Megan Reilly was listening, but only half-heartedly, since Delaney wasn't really giving out any new information. She was really watching the side door, off from the sergeant's office. The lunch with Peter Teyachaya hadn't been that expensive, and he did give her the name of an old vice cop — Michael Stewart.

When Mike walked through the door, Megan nearly choked on her breath mint. She knew that face, scar, and eyes, but they belonged in her dream. Mike stopped completely once he saw Megan. Before he could say anything, Megan walked over to him and asked if he were Michael Stewart. Mike nodded in the affirmative, and asked, "Mandy?"

It was the same voice as the stranger in her dream. "My name's Megan Reilly. I'm a reporter for the <u>Los Angeles Times</u>. I got your name from a colleague who said you worked Vice. Is there some place we can talk away from this crowd?"

Mike escorted her through the hallways to a room normally used for interviews or interrogations. When he closed the door, there was only silence as they both stared at each other in disbelief.

Megan was the first to speak. "Do you know me? Back there (pointing towards the front lobby), you called me Mandy." She wanted desperately to ask him he were the marshal. Megan wanted to scream for she thought that she must be losing her mind. She only had bad dreams, lately; and dreams don't become reality. She needed a drink. She decided to play it cool and professional. She had worked too hard to get this far in her career. She had no intentions about blowing it because of some stupid dreams.

Mike wanted to ask Megan the same questions, but he didn't want a reporter thinking he was drunk or that some insane detective was working on Delaney's task force. His heart was pounding as fast as his mind was racing for answers. "No, I thought you were another reporter that I thought I knew.", he lied.

"I'll get right to the point, Detective Stewart. I'm interested in the rash of street prostitute killings that recently began. I want to know if there's a connection between them. Do we have another `Jack the Ripper' out there or what?"

"Lt. Delaney prepared the press release. I think you should direct these questions to him."

"Give me a break!" Megan interrupted. "Delaney's evading questions and creating more questions in the minds of the reporters. Why a task force? I heard Sergeant Cantrill from Robbery is here tonight. Why? Why are you here from Vice? What are the both of you doing on a murder investigation of a street prostitute? Come on! I've been onto something for weeks now, but every time I'd call Vice, I was shut off. I need some answers."

Megan noticed that Stewart's eyes never left her as she spoke. The stare was intense, and you could see the wheels turning in his head as she talked. Megan had to admit that she was observing everything about him as well.

He dressed well for a cop. No Levi's, polyester, or anything cheap. Sometimes the guys in Vice dressed too flashy, in three-piece suits, diamond rings, etc. Stewart was neat and in style. She thought that he was probably married, or at least living with a woman who had good taste and who bought, and picked out his wardrobe. He was cleaned up, as well. She had known too many vice cops who grew beards, let their hair grow long, and in general ended up looking like street people. Stewart's coat was slightly wrinkled in the back and at the armpits, and he had more than a five o'clock shadow on his face, but she figured that he had been at work on the case for hours.

Mike had been at work for almost fourteen hours, now. He was definitely tired, and he knew he should have been home long ago. He did not mean to disrupt Lyn's anniversary plans, and he certainly didn't want a fight on his hands when he got home. Seeing Megan caused him to forget everything, momentarily. He didn't know if he should be relieved or frightened about having the girl in his dreams take on flesh and bone. He had to admit that she was every bit as beautiful as he pictured. Mike needed to go home and have a drink and sort through this.

"I can't tell you anything other than the press release information, unless I talk to Delaney, first. If, you're really interested in this story, let me talk to him about working with the press, and I'll call you tomorrow. Do you have a business card?"

"I have a card, but do you have any information? How do I know that you will call me tomorrow?" Megan fired back.

"You came looking for me, remember? I'm dead tired and I need to get home. I promise to call you tomorrow regardless of Delaney's decision. If you knew me better, you'd know that I can be trusted." He smiled and his eyes lit up, and Megan instantly felt comfortable. Why not, she had seen his smile and fiery eyes before when she was the object of his attentions long ago.

Megan gave him her card, after she wrote her home phone number on the back. "I'll look forward to hearing from you tomorrow, then, Detective Stewart." Megan said as she walked out of the room.

As he watched her walk down the hallway, Mike felt a rush of tremendous excitement and gut-gripping fear.

CHAPTER THIRTY

"Jesus H. Christ!" Megan exclaimed out loud as she kicked off her high heel shoes as she walked into her apartment. She continued walking straight to the refrigerator, where she removed a bottle of California chardonnay. She grabbed a glass as she went into the living room and sat down. Megan didn't slow down until she poured herself a full glass and swallowed almost half of it. She refilled the glass and sipped from it as she pressed the cold bottle to her forehead.

As she sat on the couch, she repeatedly told herself that it was only a dream; and she had to get a grip on reality. Megan tried to remember when and how her dream began. She thought it was around the time that she met her first husband. The dream first came in short, fleeting glimpses; then later, the fragmented pieces seemed to flow together. By the time of her second marriage, she could visualize the whole sequence.

She thought back to meeting Stewart and shaking his hand when they met. It was the same person in her dream; the same scar, voice, the fiery eyes. She even felt relieved and comfortable when he smiled and promised to call her tomorrow. Megan was beginning to feel the effects of the wine. She started thinking that she was falling for a man in her dreams.

She shook her head to clear it. Megan thought back to her childhood. She could clearly remember growing up in the state capitol, the yearly school outings to the different government buildings and offices, the summers spent on the American River, and all the trips made into San Francisco.

Megan reviewed and re-played her memories of her life up to this point just as fast as she could screen print copies on the computer at work. They were real; her life was crystal clear and stood out even better than her dreams. The dreams had always been frightening, but they seemed hazy and unfocused; maybe too much like her adult life.

"That's it, lady. You've got to get yourself a boyfriend. You're too young and there's just too many hormones running around loose", she thought to herself as she emptied the glass. Megan refilled the glass as she leaned back into the couch.

Still, she could not explain why Stewart had called her by the name in her dream, unless there was something to it. She was still thinking about that connection as she fell asleep, holding her wine glass. Too bad for her, though, as Megan would once again dream the entire dream before she would awaken herself by spilling the wine on her lap.

It was after 1 AM, by the time that Mike quietly walked into his bedroom. He gently kissed Lyn as she lay in the bed.

"Boy, did you ever miss out on a good time", she said sleepily at Mike without opening her eyes.

"I'm sorry, angel, really I am. I came back just as fast as I could."

Lyn turned on the lamp on her nightstand and propped herself up on the pillows.

He really was sorry, as he noticed the long, black satin nightgown with the lace front Lyn was wearing. She bought it for herself years ago and told him it was his birthday gift from her. Mike figured she could melt an iceberg in that outfit.

"Did you forget to tell me that Paul was suppose to visit?" she whispered. "Because, he's in the guest room. He called me from the airport", Lyn said as she began to sit up.

"Oh my God! I completely forgot about Paul."

"I thought I heard him moving around earlier. Why don't you check on him and see if he's awake, but don't be too long. Do you have to go in the morning?"

"Yes, but not until 10."

Mike found Paul standing at the bottom of the stairs, wearing his bathrobe and holding out the bottle of brandy and two coffee cups. Mike hugged him and they both adjourned to the den. While Mike was excited to see Paul, he was just too tired to do much else but sit in his favorite chair. Paul handed him the cup with a healthy shot of brandy in it. Mike was the first to speak.

"I found Amanda. She a reporter for the <u>Los Angeles Times</u>, and her name is Megan Reilly", he said as he handed Paul her business card.

"Don't go jumping to conclusions just because somebody looks familiar", Paul said, trying to sound professional.

"You didn't see the way she just about fainted when she first saw me. I'm telling you, Paul, this is real!"

"Well, good buddy, then I guess I can show you something that I picked up in Dallas."

"Dallas?! What were you doing in Dallas?" Mike asked.

"I was originally going to come out here and suggest that you undergo hypnotherapy with a specialist that I know. I was hoping to learn the truth behind your story, but at the last minute I decided to stop in Dallas. I was there earlier this week. I just had to verify what you saw; or what you thought you saw."

From his briefcase, Paul pulled out the picture that Mrs. Wallace had given him and handed it to Mike.

"Who's this?" Mike asked.

"That is little Melissa Peterson grown up on her wedding day in 1901. The same Melissa Peterson that Marshal Forsythe saved in 1886. I got the picture from her daughter, who is still alive in Dallas. It was her daughter that put the copy of the picture of the marshal and Amanda in the city's centennial yearbook. I know because I saw that original photograph in her house." He looked at Mike, who had long since stop making sense of Paul's words, as his mouth was agape in shock or disbelief. Mike drained his cup, and Paul poured another shot from the brandy bottle.

"Melissa's daughter, Mrs. Kathryn Wallace, gave me that picture after I told her your story. She said that if you are the marshal, that I was to tell you that Melissa never forgot you and that her daughter said thanks for saving her mother." Mike stared at the picture and felt a tremendous rush of a warm sensation throughout his body. He couldn't tell if it was the brandy or what. With all that had happened to him today, he couldn't sort out any of his feelings.

"Mike, I've been doing a great deal of thinking on this. I no longer think that a hypnotherapist is needed. I cannot find one medical or scientific explanation for the information in your dreams that apparently has occurred. I did not use to believe in reincarnation, but I do not know what to believe or think since your dream apparently checks out. I agree with you that you could not have dreamed this up by yourself. I'm beginning to become worried for you, myself."

"What do you mean `worried for me'?"

"I don't mean to frighten you, but I just want to throw this out for what it's worth. If you are the marshal, and I'm beginning to think your really are, and you and Amanda have been brought back to find and kill Cooper; then what if Amanda was the only wrong person to have died that day, back in 1886?"

"According to your story, if she hadn't called out to you, then you would have walked into the trap that had been set for you. What if you were all supposed to die that day, except for Amanda? She would not have been there that day if you hadn't fallen in love with her. Even without you pulling the trigger, you're the one responsible for her death, when you stop and analyze the situation. What if to fix this, you still have to die, but she doesn't?"

"Or worse, what if after this is over and you've accomplished what you were brought back for, you and her cease to exist in this time?" Watching Mike's mouth agape, Paul could see this was the first time that he had thought about these possibilities.

CHAPTER THIRTY-ONE

"Megan, it's Mike Stewart. I'm calling you back as I said I would. I already tried your work number." Mike was talking to Megan's answering machine. "Call me when you get in. I'm at ..."

"Hold on, I'm here", Megan practically shouted as she attempted to turn off the machine after picking up the receiver. "I was in the shower. I was going to go into work after lunch."

"If you'd like, I could meet you for lunch and we could talk. I have something to show you that you might be interested in." Sometimes, cops knew just what to say to reporters to keep their interest.

"What did Delaney have to say?"

"We can talk at lunch. What kind of food do you prefer?"

"Chinese, but..."

"Good. Why don't you meet me in Chinatown? Can you make it by noon?" "I'll be there, but this had better be worth it."

"Oh, you'll love the food."

"Don't be a smart ass, mister. I'm not talking about lunch; there's a story I want, remember?"

"How could I forget? I'll see you at twelve. Bye."

As she hung up the phone, Megan wanted to be upset with Stewart for trying to play games, but she couldn't. There was just something about him that she found — warm and friendly — familiar.

Mike was at his desk when he placed the call. Having put the phone receiver down, his interest was directed fully towards the photograph on his desk. There was a picture of Carl Andrews. It was a mug shot from his last time in the "joint". For Mike it was an old familiar face; it was the man the marshal knew as G.W. Cooper. Mike was feeling a terrible sense of dread and urgency as he placed the photo in the folder that he would take with him to lunch.

The Task Force office was really jumping. With his name and the statistical information known about Andrews, the investigators were re-looking at all the murders and robberies to see if any could be linked to him. The evidence was beginning to add up against him. Shortly, Andrews would be the prime suspect with warrants out for his arrest.

Meanwhile, Andrews was on the move. He had left the motel and driven for a short time along the beach area. He didn't stop or see anyone, other than the usual joggers and skateboarders. After driving aimlessly around for over an hour, Andrews decided to have lunch at a hamburger stand on Hawthorne Boulevard.

At about the same time, Mike was standing in the center of Chinatown waiting for Megan. When she showed up, Mike watched intensely as Megan walked towards him with that purposeful, rapid walk he had seen before in another time. "Hello, Detective Stewart!", Megan said as she approached him.

"Hi. Are you hungry?"

"I'm always hungry." she shot back.

"Good, let's walk over here. I think you'll love the food. My old partner and I ate here one day after following a bookmaker inside. Ever since, I've tried to hit it up a couple of times a month."

Megan saw that he held a large manila envelope in his hands. She caught herself reaching for his arm as she started walking with him. As they entered the restaurant, he automatically grabbed her hand as it was dark and there was a small step down that she couldn't see. Mike asked the waiter for a booth. He didn't let go of her until they were seated, and she made no attempt at pulling her hand away.

After ordering lunch, Megan was the first to speak. "Ok, detective. What information do you have? Or should I say, what information will you let me have?" she said as she placed the cloth napkin on her lap.

"Are you always this direct?" Mike asked.

"Contrary to what you may think, it's still difficult to be a woman in the business world. I've spent a great deal of time to show others that I'm capable, not cutesy. Being direct saves time and confusion. It's also what I learned from men."

"Sit back and relax. Why don't you call me Mike and may I call you Megan?"

"It's ok with me. But what about the story..."

"Let's eat, then talk." he interrupted.

It didn't take long for the experienced investigator to get Megan talking about herself while they waited for their meals. He learned that her parents were still living in Sacramento. That's where she went to school. She moved to Chicago to be with her future husband, who was studying medicine in the Midwest. She eventually landed a job with the <u>Chicago Sun</u>. The demands of medical school proved too much for them to overcome, and they split up before the two-year mark. After her divorce, she moved back to Sacramento, and was hired by the <u>Sacramento Bee</u>. Megan met, fell in love with, and married a computer engineer working for the Department of Motor Vehicles. After a few years, that relationship fell apart, and Megan headed for the glittering lights of Los Angeles. She was currently living in an apartment in Westchester, not far from the beach.

During lunch, Megan helped herself to a few different items off Mike's plate as she talked. "She is really hungry!", Mike thought to himself. He had to laugh at her, as she was a completely free spirit. Megan felt as if she were having lunch with an old friend; she felt comfortable and safe. She was having so much fun; she almost forgot it wasn't a date.

As the plates were cleared and they refilled their teacups, Mike placed the manila envelope on the table. His eyes were always ablaze, but Megan's were filled with questions and anticipation. "What do you want to know about the case?" Mike asked her.

"What do you mean? I want to know everything there is to know about it. Aren't you going to caution me or ask for some favor in return? Are you new at dealing with reporters?"

"Well, I do have one favor to ask of you."

"I knew there had to be a catch. Ok, what is it?"

In a voice that sounded quiet and ominous at the same time, Mike said, "Promise me that you won't leave until I have finished."

Megan felt her stomach begin to tighten and she began to lose that comfortable feeling she had with him. She looked hard at Mike's stare as she answered, "Ok."

Mike began by telling Megan his theories behind the case. The hooker killings were only part of a pattern established by the killer. Each of the killings concluded a robbery that had occurred; usually a robbery in which there had been gun play. It was suspected that due to the exactness of each of the killings, they were dealing with only one person. The killer was stabbing through the heart and then cutting the throats of the victims. The Task Force was established to draw upon the expertise of the various skills needed in this case; primarily robbery and vice, in addition to the regular homicide detectives. That's why he and Cantrill were at the station the night before. Megan was writing down details and interrupting with questions; throughout the tale. Even she was taken back by the trail of violence that the killer was leaving across the county.

A possible suspect was named after the discovery of the discarded shotgun shell at the Lawndale robbery and killing. There had been fingerprints on the shell. This in turn was the basis for the press release and the news conference.

"Who is the suspect and do you have his picture in that envelope?" Megan asked Mike.

"Yes, I do, but first I want to ask you a couple of questions. Have you ever seen me before? "

"No!" Megan quickly lied. Her stomach was beginning to tighten up and she could feel her heart pounding in her head and throat.

"You should have seen your face when you first saw me. You looked as if you'd seen a ghost. I think you do know me and that's why I need to ask if you are troubled by a reoccurring dream that you can't make sense out of?"

"Mike, you're beginning to frighten me." Megan looked around the restaurant wondering if the restaurant served wine, she could use a drink. "Why can't I just see the picture?" She was trying to sound impatient, but her voice was just a little too high-pitched.

Mike undid the clasp on the envelope, reached in and handed the mug shot photo of Carl Andrews to Megan. It was the picture of the same man in her dream; the man that she struggled with. Megan gasped out loud, closed her eyes, and placed a hand over her mouth. "No, this can't be happening!", she cried out to herself. When she opened her eyes, Mike was staring right through her; yet, she wasn't afraid of him. Megan wanted to run to the ladies' room, but she didn't think that Mike would let her leave.

"The Task Force is in the process of reviewing the various cases and the physical evidence to ascertain how many of the total can be traced to Andrews." Mike held Megan's hand as he said, "I've seen this man before, and I've seen you as well; both in my reoccurring dream."

Megan was beginning to lose her composure. Her lips were beginning to tremble and she really wanted to run, but she was riveted by Mike's eyes just as steadily as if his hands held her.

"I recently was in Dallas, Texas and found this.", he said as he reached into the envelope again. He pushed the fax copy of the photograph of the marshal and Amanda Weaver.

Megan looked hysterical; "No! No! No!" she cried out. She started to sob, heavily now. "This isn't real; it's not happening. It's only a dream," she cried out softly. Mike got up and slid onto her side of the booth, where he grabbed Megan and pulled her towards him. He held onto her tightly while she sobbed into the lapel of his jacket.

"You do have dreams about another life in another time, don't you, Megan?" Mike said as he held onto her.

Megan nodded yes; without taking her face off his jacket.

"And you have seen me before as well as the face of the Carl Andrews?" Again Megan nodded yes.

"I don't think it's possible for two people who have never met before to have the same dream. I think that for us, the dream represents events that really happened. I believe that I have additional proof. Look at one more thing."

From the envelope, Mike pulled the photo given to him by Paul the night before. "This is the little girl the marshal saved; grown up on her wedding day in 1901. My friend found her daughter still alive and she confirmed that her mother had been saved in 1886 Texas by a marshal, who was later killed along with a newspaperwoman; the two people in the first photo I showed you. It's us, Megan."

Wiping her eyes as she continued looking at the photograph of Melissa, Megan asked, "What does all of this mean, then?" There was child-like plea to her voice that pierced his soul.

"I'm not sure. There's no script to read from, but I think the wrong persons died tragically that day in 1886 Texas. That's why we've all been brought back." Mike held both her hands as they faced each other. "I honestly believe that you and I are Amanda Weaver and Robert Forsythe and we were brought back across time to find and kill the man who calls himself Carl Andrews.

Andrews is an outlaw named G.W. Cooper who represents an evil force that continues to prey upon and kill people across two different centuries. I should have killed him in 1886 Texas, but along the way, I met and fell in love with you. I dragged you into the conflict, and I subsequently got us both killed. For whatever reason, I believe that we've all been given another opportunity to set the books straight."

"Michael, I don't feel well. I've got to leave!"

Mike tried to hold onto her, but when Megan pulled back Mike let her leave. They were beginning to cause enough of a disturbance as it were. Mike watched as Megan ran out of the restaurant. He was flooded with over a hundred years worth of doubts, worry, excitement, and fear. Megan wasn't the only one feeling sick.

After paying the bill, Mike went back to the office. He tried several times to call Megan at her office before being told she called in sick. He settled for leaving a message on her answering machine at her apartment. For Mike, the rest of the day was a blur; as only his body was present in the office.

CHAPTER THIRTY-TWO

❖❖ "Why you stupid, fucking bitch!" Carl Andrews exclaimed out loud; driving around the corner of the industrial complex in the city of El Segundo. It was after the normal lunch hour, but there was enough of a crowd walking to and from the local eateries.

It was outside one of those establishments that Andrews had seen a very pretty, and young, office worker. He had tried to pick her up by offering her a ride, but she had wisely ignored him. Andrews was pulling around the corner to try again; and if he failed again, he was prepared to use force to pull this girl into his car.

As he swung his car wide around the intersection, Andrews rolled through a stop sign. Unfortunately, an El Segundo Police motorcycle officer observed this, and started after Andrews with his lights activated and the siren blaring. Andrews immediately decided to run for it, rather than stop for the ticket. He couldn't outrun the motor officer and subsequently, Andrews had to stop on Douglas just south of Imperial Highway.

Officer Leland Carter approached the old Toyota, still thinking it was a routine traffic stop. When he walked up even with the trunk of the car, Officer Carter saw Andrews opening the door. Before he could say or do anything else, Officer Carter was hit in the chest with a blast from a 12-gauge shotgun and was knocked to the ground by the impact. Fortunately, Carter was wearing his bullet-proof vest, so he was alive, but unconscious.

Andrews closed the driver's door and putting the car into gear, he sped eastbound onto Imperial Highway and into the heavy traffic. He knew he had to get out of the area as fast, yet as inconspicuous, as possible. Andrews lit a cigarette. He appeared very cool; only sweat beads along his hairline gave an indication of any emotion. He knew that within minutes other cops would be all over the scene. Andrews also knew that he had to get rid of the drug dealer's car, as he had seen the officer using the radio as he got off his motorcycle. He was sure that the cop had called in the car's license plate number.

As he inhaled deeply on the cigarette, Andrews's heart was racing as fast as the traffic sped past while escape plans were going through his mind. As the car weaved through traffic and then slowed somewhat to merge with it, Andrews' heart slowed to a steady rhythm and stopped pounding in his ears. His thoughts slowed as well as he started to relax. The nicotine combined with the increasing distance between him and the shooting scene acted as a sedative on Andrews' frayed nerves.

It didn't take long for his criminal brain to formulate an escape plan that incorporated the ditching of the car. Andrews drove northbound to Century Blvd.; where he drove back westbound and then south on Aviation. He was looking for one of those parking lots where he could catch a shuttle bus to LAX. Almost immediately, Andrews came upon one, parked the stolen car and took the ride into the airport. From there, he boarded a city bus into the downtown area. It was clever; as it would take two days before detectives would find the car.

At about the time of the shooting, Mike Stewart was on the phone with Megan. She had called him hoping that he would have Lt. Delaney's permission for him to divulge the story to the press. Delaney had agreed provided that Stewart obtained Megan's cooperation in exchange for an exclusive on the case. Megan had readily agreed. She wanted to end the call, but Mike continued to talk and press her.

"We need to talk...about us; this thing, Megan."

"Mike, I don't know what to think, right now. I have a story to work on. I'm really busy."

"You still don't understand it; you and I are the keys to this thing. I think I know when we can best find him."

"What do you mean?"

"Let's talk about this face-to-face."

"I can't right now."

"Come on; you're stalling. We have to talk and you'd have to meet with me anyway, if you're going to work on this story for your exclusive."

Before Megan could answer, Mike Cantrill interrupted the conversation. "Mike, come on; we've got to go! There's been a shooting in El Segundo."

"What's your radio designator, Mike?" Megan quickly asked upon hearing Cantrill's voice.

"I'm Admin 32 and Cantrill is Robert 177."

"Ok. Be careful! I'll call you later."

"Thanks, Megan. Bye."

Within minutes of the shooting, the police radio frequencies were filled with the vehicle information obtained from the license plate called in by Officer Carter. Cantrill had heard one of the broadcasts.

"So, why do we have to go to El Segundo, Mike?" Stewart asked as he followed Cantrill outside.

Cantrill was smiling as they continued to rapidly walk to their car. "Because, there's been a motor officer shot by a WMA (white, male adult) who was driving an old, beat up Toyota sedan. The registered owner is Robert Martinez, AKA `Bobby Boy' Martinez."

"I still don't get the connection, Michael."

"I know `Bobby Boy', or I used to. He used to deal coke in the South Bay area, out of his car. He was found dead in an alley last Saturday by some Lomita Station deputies. The same day that Libby Thompson was found and the morning after the woman in Rancho P.V. was found. Like the women, `Bobby Boy' was killed with a knife. And one of the Rancho victim's neighbors remembered seeing an older car the night of the murder. I didn't make the connection until now when I heard the radio broadcasts from `Gundo."

"It's a long shot, but I think you're right." Stewart said as he climbed into the unmarked car. "According to State Parole's briefing to Delaney, Andrews didn't have any wheels. Get us to `Gundo, pardner!'"

CHAPTER THIRTY-THREE

The shooting scene was still chaotic by the time that Stewart and Cantrill arrived. After a quick briefing by the on-scene supervisor and the shooting team investigators, they were enroute to Robert F. Kennedy Hospital where the wounded officer had been taken.

Inside the hospital, both Mikes were on the phone; Cantrill to keep Lt. Delaney posted, and Stewart to Megan. Megan knew their whereabouts since she had been monitoring the police scanner and had heard them at the shooting scene and the hospital.

"The officer is still unconscious and is undergoing surgery for a few shotgun pellets that missed his bullet-proof vest and struck his shoulder. We should be able to be among the first to talk with him and show the mug shot of Andrews. So far, the El Segundo 'brass' has been cooperative." The speaker was Cantrill.

"All right. Keep me posted on any developments or any further movements you two make. Were there any witnesses to this?"

"We don't think so, sir. We'll check on the bus routes later, to see if any may have been in the area about the same time. Our main objective is to verify that the shooter was Andrews. If that's the case, Mike and I are concerned about the fact that this will force Andrews to abandon the car. And right now, it's about the only tangible connection to Andrews that we had."

"Stay with it, Mike. I'm sending another detective team to either assist or relieve you, depending upon the situation when they get there. What about that reporter for the <u>Times</u>? Did Stewart ever make contact with her?"

"Yes, he did. He's on the phone with her right now. We'll keep you posted, L-T. Bye."

"Mike, I spoke with my editor and he said I could use the paper's helicopter. I can be in Hawthorne in less than fifteen minutes.", Megan was telling Mike Stewart.

"There's no rush. The officer's still in surgery. We probably won't be able to talk with him until late this evening. Cantrill and I are pretty sure that the shooter had to be Andrews. If it was, our next task will be to find him before he's abandoned the car. I'm just not sure what his next move will be. But it's early; we still have time to find him."

"What do you mean `it's early'? Michael, what else haven't you told me?"

"It's November 5th." he let it slip without thinking. "Look, I have to go, Cantrill's coming back from the doctor's station and we need to talk."

"Ok, but I'm still headed for Hawthorne's airport."

"Ok, lady. I'll look forward to seeing you. Be careful."

As Megan was replacing the phone receiver, her normally cute mouth was pouting. "What did he mean by early?" she thought to herself. She called the helipad and told the pilot she was enroute upstairs. As Megan grabbed her purse and laptop computer, she suddenly realized what Mike had meant. He knew when they had died! A sense of dread rushed over her in the next heartbeat, as she realized that it may mean when they were to die again. Climbing the stairs to the helipad, Megan felt the tears beginning to well up and she felt her face get hot. She hadn't felt good about anything since meeting Stewart. She wished she had never heard or seen him — in either life!

CHAPTER THIRTY-FOUR

While she asked questions of the pilot to kill time and she put on a brave smile for those around her, Megan Reilly wasn't really that tough. Her stomach was tightened and she wished she could close her eyes and wake up from some weird dream. Instead, the brisk autumn air whipped right through her dress and the short jacket that she was wearing, as she stepped off the helicopter. After making a quick phone call to her office, Megan took a cab to the hospital.

Stewart made a call to his house and found the message that Lyn left saying that she and Paul would be at her hospital. She had been called in unexpectedly and had taken Paul with her. At least, he would not have to worry about making excuses again for being late.

Stewart found Cantrill at the nurses' station. He was speaking to one of the nursing administrators on the relaying of medical information for the detectives and for denying it to any inquiries by the media and anyone asking questions over the phone.

As Stewart walked up to Cantrill, Cantrill was the first to speak. "We've got the hospital covered. I'm thinking that Andrews must have abandoned the car by now. We should be looking at his alternatives and options. Where will he go after he abandons the car and then what is our best guess on how he gets there? I feel so helpless just sitting here waiting for him to make the next move."

"Pardner, I'm afraid that's what he does best, after killing, is to move. We're better and tougher than he is though and we'll get him. I just hope that it's soon."

Stewart was desperately holding onto the belief that he could catch up with Andrews <u>before</u> November 16th and break the cycle of events. To his way of thinking, Stewart was not in control of his actions, but rather, he felt as if he were trapped on a runaway locomotive called destiny. Straightening up and letting out a deep breath, Stewart said, "Come on, pardner, let's get some coffee. I think it'll be a long night."

In the dining room at the hospital, Stewart was looking at and twirling the hot, dark liquid in his cup. He was almost mesmerized. Stewart closed his eyes and in an instant, he was transported back. In his mind's eye, he was thirty-seven years old and he was leaning against a small tree forty-five yards from a small campfire. The smell of the coffee in the pot was slowly driving him crazy. The night was pitch black away from the fire and the night air was frigid as it whipped across the plains with a vengeance. His Winchester rifle was propped between his knees as the barrel's metal was like touching ice. The marshal was huddled in the cold dark because for the past two days and nights, someone had been trailing him. His bedroll was stuffed with his horse blanket and some grass and branches until it resembled the general shape of a man. He had only his long coat and Stetson for protection against the night.

He was drowsy and his head kept falling back. With each jerk back, it would awaken him until the frigid air would again lull him to close his eyes. The howling wind had silenced the approaching riders. The blast from the shotgun startled the marshal so badly that he almost jerked the trigger of his rifle. He really had wanted to scream in frightened reflex. The scattergun's pellets tore the blanket next to the fire in two. The screaming riders hit the edge of the campfire's glow like lightening bolts ripping a lone tree asunder. The two of them fired some six-gun rounds into the blanket parts, as they dismounted.

Before they realized their error, the marshal fired his Winchester with the speed and skill required of a man living in pursuit of other men; men whose willingness to use violence was as ingrained as breathing. With a wolf-like approach, the marshal kicked their guns away as he headed for the fire and the coffee pot. He drank from the pot, while keeping one outstretched hand over the fire.

The dead consisted of a renegade Indian called "Bird Who Walks" and a horse thief by the name of Arlo Decker. Both were robbers and murderers and had been wanted for at least two murders on Federal land in the Oklahoma Territory. Marshal Forsythe had two "John Doe" warrants for their arrest. Apparently, they thought the lone rider was some Eastern "greenhorn" that would prove easy pickings. They were dead wrong!

"Hey, Stewart! Are you expecting a reporter here?" The speaker was an El Segundo sergeant.

"Thank God, for interruptions!" Stewart thought to himself as he was jarred from another disturbing daydream.

CHAPTER THIRTY-FIVE

The noise was just too loud for the average person to comprehend anything. The police radios were squawking, the P.A. system blared way too much, phones were ringing, nurses were shouting over the other noise, and Megan could see a tall woman sobbing quietly at the far end of the corridor. She was surrounded by several officers.

The sick, sterile smell of a hospital was not erased by the autumn breeze that shot through the automatic doors each time they opened. Megan was flooded with relief as soon as she saw Mike walking towards her. She ran to meet him and he hugged her, just for a moment, before escorting her into the unoccupied nurses' lounge.

Megan looked at Michael for a long second. He was actually standing there grinning at her. "You, nut!". Megan was almost smiling.

"I didn't think you knew me that well." Mike replied.

"Michael, what kind of a world do you live in? You look as if you almost enjoy it."

"I'm living life to the fullest. I'm getting paid for doing a job that I really love and at which I am very good. I didn't know what I was missing until I realized you were not a part of that world."

In a darker corner of that world, Carl Andrews was lurking. He had gotten off the bus in the Inglewood area. He was definitely lost and without a game plan. As Andrews walked along the city streets, he came upon the parking lot at Daniel Freeman Hospital. While watching the comings and goings of the patients and the staff, Andrews decided to wait until dark and steal a car. He also needed money.

Andrews just decided to kill another victim. To his way of thinking, he would be easy prey in a reported stolen car. So, it would be smarter to rob and kill the owner. From a nearby doughnut shop, Andrews obtained coffee and a few "sinkers". He went back to the hospital to wait; another game of cat and mouse had begun. With practice honed over two life times, Andrews was good at laying in wait for unsuspecting humans.

Actually, in his more lucid moments, Andrews would have acknowledged that it was far easier to kill in this century than the last one. There were definitely more victims to chose from, they rarely were found with sidearms for self-protection, they were so reluctant to immediately use violence to resolve conflicts; in fact, he found them to actively avoid confrontation, and the current modes of transportation were varied and all were much faster than horseback.

Hidden from the streetlight's glare in the shadows of a tree, Andrews held his coffee cup with both hands to keep warm. Tree branches rustled against each other in the cool night wind. He would have trembled from something other than the night air, if he knew that the marshal with the rifle was alive and still hunting.

Inside the hospital, Paul accompanied Lyn as she checked her patients. He was having a good time; it was so seldom in New York that he actually made hospital calls; let alone rounds. He was thoroughly enjoying himself as he was given a tour of the hospital and introduced to the staff by Lynette. Paul fell right into the routine and was soon answering questions from both staff and patients.

As Paul watched Lynette, he soon realized why any man would have fallen in love with her. She was genuinely warm and comforting; yet possessing a confidence borne of knowledge and expertise. She also exuded a sensuality that simmered just below the boiling point beneath her creamy skin that could not be contained in her surgical scrub gown and pants that she wore as her uniform. The kind of sensuality that would make an experienced and worldly man shed little sweat beads that gathered momentum as they rolled down the small of his back just thinking of her.

Large sweat beads were rolling off Andrews face and down his neck as he followed and moved with Kathleen Hathaway. If the action had been recorded on film, one would have felt as if he was watching one of the great cats stalking their prey. Kathleen Hathaway was 33 years old, a registered nurse at Daniel Freeman, and a single parent of a four-year-old girl. Kathie's husband, Jim, had been a Navy pilot killed in a carrier training accident almost three years earlier. Tonight, Kathie's little girl would be orphaned.

Kathleen had left the hospital in a hurry. Being preoccupied with other thoughts, she did not really take notice of her surroundings as she walked towards her car. She did not have her keys out and she was concentrating on her purse's contents as she stood at the car door. Andrews was directly behind her and crouched low so neither his reflection would be seen off the glass or his breathing felt. He selected her not for the type of car, but because she fit a pattern that screamed "victim" to those that hunt. About now is when a great cat's hind leg muscles would flex; just before the jump, and the kill.

As the car door was opened, Kathleen was practically dragged into it with the forward motion of Andrews' lunge. In about the length of time for a heartbeat, they were both in the car and out of sight. The knife's edge was actually cutting Kathie's chin as Andrews held her down on the front car seat. "Don't scream! I need your car and your money. Just do as I say, don't look at me, and if you give me a real good blowjob, I'll let you go."

Kathleen's shock was beginning to wear off just as she realized that the knife held to her chin was cutting her. She contained her fear long enough so she did not struggle against the blade. Her assailant's words were almost as horrifying as the guttural sound of his voice. Kathleen could smell his sweat and her own fear as she felt his rough fingers holding onto her hair.

A sickening silence lasting an eternity passed before Kathleen heard her assailant grunt, "Did you hear me, lady?!" He released the tension on her neck enough for her to whisper, "Yes." Kathie wasn't trying to sound brave. She was afraid that if she opened her mouth too much, her heart would jump out. She was also trying to ascertain if the push into the car combined with Andrews' weight had broken any of her ribs.

Andrews smiled as he felt Kathleen relax and begin to breathe almost normally. He only wanted her cooperation long enough so he could drive away and kill her outside the car so there would not be a bloodstain on the upholstery for all to see. Andrews would dump Kathleen's body inside a boarded up house along the construction route of the Century Freeway.

As the shiny wheels of Kathleen's Volvo sedan spun towards the parking lot exit, Paul Paslosky looked out and saw it drive onto the street. Paul was in the hospital dining room with Lyn and two other hospital employees. From his vantage point, Paul would have seen the assault on Kathleen had he looked out the window just 64 seconds sooner. The fuse to the powder keg was burning white hot and rapidly.

CHAPTER THIRTY-SIX

 Mike stared at the back of Megan's head while he watched her type on the laptop computer on the cafeteria table. He longed to caress her hair, but knew better than to interrupt her; and also because Cantrill was in the room answering her questions.

Mike turned and noted the mannerisms of his partner, now. Mike Cantrill was leaning slightly forward in his chair with his hands clasped together. It looked as if Cantrill were trying desperately to hear the question, so he could answer it correctly. Stewart smiled and he thought back over the years as he remembered how he and all the police applicants appeared during their oral board assessments; nervous, but trying to look relaxed and confident, and not as if they were about to puke, pass out, or both.

Stewart could not ascertain if Cantrill was genuinely nervous around reporters or just this one; or did Cantrill sense Megan and Mike's mutual attraction? Now he wished that Megan had not touched his hand for so long when he was setting up her computer in the lounge. Mike was certain that Cantrill had noticed.

Cantrill was filling in the details and concerns of the Robbery Detail as it pertained to this particular murder investigation. Megan was typing almost as fast as he was speaking. Megan looked at Cantrill as she typed. He was Stewart's age, but appeared younger to her. Megan chalked it up to the college professor-style glasses and the sweater vests he wore. He was quieter than Stewart, but based on the brief work history, just as deadly. Cantrill's career with the department centered almost exclusively in Robbery and there had been too many close calls. Both his personnel file and body attested to that fact.

By the time that Megan was through with the interview, she learned that Cantrill had a degree in mathematics from Cal State Long Beach. He and Stewart actually met years before. Stewart called Cantrill after he found out about his college degree when the vice team needed some quick study in the area of odds and probabilities. They hit it off and stayed in touch over the years.

Stewart kept busy by talking with his relief team sent over by Delaney. He has them working with the El Segundo Police going over the route for possible witnesses. They should be checking in at anytime. Stewart checked his watch for the umpteenth time today, when one of the doctors in the surgery team entered the room.

Officer Carter was in the intensive care unit. The surgery had been successful and there were no surprises encountered during the operation. The doctor said that Carter should be coming out of the anesthesia shortly. He would allow Mrs. Carter and two others in his room for just five minutes. He would send a nurse for them as soon as it was time.

Stewart rested his head against a wall while he listened to Megan and Cantrill continue talking after the doctor left. He closed his eyes and thought what a waste of time this afternoon had been. He was almost certain that Andrews was the assailant and if that were true, he had probably killed again as part of his getaway and or out of excitement.

Mike thought back to that time and he wished he had continued to shoot from horseback, just maybe, he would have hit Cooper. Then, how different things would have been. What ever happened to Debbie? What had become of the children? He started talking aloud to himself and let slip an expletive. Mike appeared startled and then embarrassed. He quickly left the room and walked out and into the night air.

"Mike's venting. It's just the job, the stress. Sometimes, I want to scream and run away over something I cannot resolve in my mind", Cantrill said as Megan looked after Mike.

As she started to get up, Cantrill grabbed her hand and gently tugged on it while motioning back towards the chair, saying, "He has to think something over right now. I know this is difficult for you, but Mike needs to be alone with his thoughts. He'll be back. He'll probably apologize and come in carrying coffee. You'll see." Cantrill quickly released her hand and Megan sat down.

Megan gave it less than a minute before she stood up to follow after Stewart. Turning, she gave Cantrill a look that shouted 'I'm ok! Please mind your own business!" as she walked out.

This time Cantrill only smiled as he watched her leave.

Megan found Mike outside in the doctors' parking lot. He was staring into the night sky. The wind was blowing its frigid breath across the open lot. Mike noticed Megan, but did not say anything. Megan watched him intently for just a moment before she spoke. She appeared to be searching for something and could not find it.

"Mike", she uttered softly as she started to approach him, testing the volume of her voice against the wind as well as his reaction. "I'm afraid." She almost put her arms out for him, but stopped herself before he turned around.

Quickly turning towards her, Mike spoke and his voice cut through the cold night air like a saber swung by a strong and determined warrior.

"Of the murders or us?"

Looking at Mike's face, Megan could see that there was a certain dark and sinister quality about him; almost as if he were covered in a cloak.

"The story is scary enough, but I guess I'm referring to us."

"I told you on a morning long ago, that you had nothing to fear as long as I'm around.", he interjected.

Megan started to cry softly as she closed their distance and grabbed Mike. "You sound so cold! I didn't do anything to you. You just slipped into my life when I thought everything was going just fine. I thought I didn't need a man in my life, and now you're back to turn my life upside down again. You're just as warm and handsome and just as sinister as I recall."

Megan hung her head down and she cried louder.

Mike took Megan by the arms and held her at arms length. Megan looked at him and saw for the first time that he had tears welling up in his eyes. She couldn't remember ever seeing anything but fire in them. As he started to speak, she saw his eyes burn anew as if tinder had just caught fire.

"I'm the same man you rejected years ago in another time. I loved you then and I love you still; God help me! I'm thinking how much I loved you then. Now you and I have been brought back across time to kill a madman and here you are undecided about us! For the very first time, I'm getting upset with you!" Mike released his grip on Megan.

Megan's tears poured out and her sobbing became louder.

"I think I've come to the conclusion that I had better concentrate on finding and killing Andrews. I've thought everything over in my mind; and it's not just us. I think that if I can't find and kill Andrews, I believe you and I will be killed again. Your tombstone in Dallas lists the date of your death as November 16th, 1886. It's now November 5th. I think that we're being brought together in a rapid secession of events just as before."

A sudden gust of wind swept through the parking lot, but it could not convey the same coldness of Mike's words as Megan listened.

He grabbed Megan by her shoulders again as he continued, "I cannot think of any reason why this is happening again. What if I can't kill Andrews in time? Do I — do we have to do this again? I don't know about you, but I can't take another lifetime of this shit! To my way of thinking, you and I cannot be anything except **DEAD** if I cannot find and kill Andrews once and for all!"

Fighting to gain control of her voice while pulling her long hair off her face, Megan said, "I thought maybe it was love that brought us back this time." There were tears running down Megan's face as she continued to speak. "A second chance to find out what might have been. I was wrong! It was hate that brought us all back! I don't know if it was your hate or Cooper's hate, but it was hate!" Tears were rolling down Megan's face. "And I'm still caught up in events that I do not control. I don't want to die again! Not like this!"

Mike felt Megan go limp in his arms as she began to wail. Mike pulled her towards him and embraced her. Tears began to roll down his face, now. He stroked her hair as he calmly whispered in her ear that he was sorry and she would be all right; he would keep her safe. He kissed her closed eyes as if he could somehow stop the torrent of tears.

In the frozen darkness, they presented a tragic picture; one that was not lost on Cantrill who stood at the hospital doorway. Across the open lot, the sound of both of them crying drifted and he knew that his partner was in serious trouble.

CHAPTER THIRTY-SEVEN

The windshield wipers were louder than the striking rain. The rainy season had begun for Southern California. Mike Stewart was slowly making his way up Sepulveda Boulevard. He was headed for Megan's apartment. It was Monday morning the 11th.

The past few days had flown by. Officer Carter had positively identified Andrews as his assailant, Andrews' car had been found, and so had the body of Kathie Hathaway. Mike's sleep was continually being interrupted by the telephone ringing. He was also arguing with Lyn more now than at any other time in their marriage. Most of the arguments had been over his not being at home for any longer than a shower and change of clothes. He was beginning to lose weight. Paul Paslosky had to return to New York on urgent business for one of his patients. Prior to leaving, Paul had warned Mike about making rash decisions to avoid the 16th. He assured Mike that he would return to Los Angeles by the evening of the 14th.

This morning Mike and Lyn had been arguing over him not going to Kathleen Hathaway's funeral today. Mike answered the phone when it interrupted the argument. Surprisingly, it had been Megan.

"Mike, its' me. Thank God you answered. I'm sorry to call you at home, but you must stop by my place before you go to work. Can you come right over?"

"Ok", was the terse and solitary reply.

Mike knew the address as he had been routinely following Megan home the past few days. He was hoping for a lead in the case and thought that maybe Andrews could also be looking for one of them. Leaving his house,

Mike called Cantrill on the car phone and established an alibi for leaving for work early. He didn't want Cantrill calling looking for him and accidentally ruining it.

Mike didn't have the faintest clue as to why Megan wanted to see him at her apartment. He was beginning to feel the stress wear him down. He and Megan were starting their final week, and Andrews' trail was ice cold. Mike, the experienced undercover cop, never noticed the male driver in the blue mid-size sedan following him.

Mike parked his car in the underground garage and took the elevator up to Megan's floor. She answered the door and appeared to be in good spirits and dressed for work. "Thanks for coming over. Would you like a cup of coffee?" Megan asked as she led him inside and closed the door.

"No thanks. What's up?"

"Are you sure? It's fresh and I made it just for you. Remember, I don't drink it."

Mike rolled his eyes up at the kitchen ceiling. "Ok, I can take a hint. Megan, could I have a cup of coffee?" Mike wanted to feel at ease, but Megan was up to something.

"Are you going to try to seduce me, or something?" Mike asked as she handed him the coffee and walked with him into the living room.

"What an overactive imagination you have this morning. If I were planning on it, I wouldn't be putting your hands around a coffee cup. Here, sit down and drink your coffee", Megan said grinning. As Mike sipped his coffee, the stranger in the blue sedan was already checking out his parked vehicle in the garage area.

"Megan, what are you up to?"

"I take it you haven't seen the early morning news on television. My boss received a phone call late last Friday night. Apparently one of the local news channels has been keeping tabs on us and the task force. They know or guessed that I have a deal for an exclusive on the case based on my movements and gossip within the bureau. They want a share of the secrets or they'll turn to the tabloid news about a story of a reporter and a vice cop."

"So much for the integrity of the fourth estate. What did your boss say? Is there anything else I should know?" Mike said as he set his coffee cup on the end table. He was as aggravated as he was tired.

Megan sat on the couch next to him while watching him closely. Mike watched her as she curled her legs under herself on the cushion.

"You're very good at hiding your emotions. I'd be willing to bet that you're boiling mad right now. You can't fool me. I remember how you were with that little girl. You're a big softy under that tight jaw and behind those fiery eyes."

"Megan, I'm just a little..." whatever was supposed to come next was swallowed in the kiss that Megan planted on Mike. It was full, wet and with complete abandonment. Megan pressed her bosom against Mike and started pushing his back onto the couch. Mike did not resist, rather it was more like helping Megan as she lay atop him. It didn't seem as if either would come up for air.

"Hey, what's this?" Megan asked as she lifted herself off his chest and tapped on Mike's bulletproof vest with her knuckles.

Mike started to get up and responded, "It's rib protection for when I'm attacked by crazy women. What was that all about?"

"I thought I'd kiss you before you see this and get mad at me. Here look at this. I taped it early this morning", she said as she walked over to her television and VCR.

The tape contained a recorded commercial from one of the local stations. On it was a preview of an upcoming live interview with Megan. Clearly visible in the background was a color photo of herself. The interview was to discuss the recent rash of murders of prostitutes. Naturally, the television reporter could not resist the temptation to make reference to Jack the Ripper. The segment concluded with the time and place of the interview. It was to be at a dumpsite of one of the victims in Hawthorne.

"You just made a target of yourself for Andrews. Have you lost your mind, woman?" Mike said as he started to get up.

"Just a minute, Michael! I know exactly what I'm doing. I talked this over with my boss. You and Cantrill can't find this guy, so I bringing him to us. Besides, there's no guarantee that he's out there looking to kill me."

"We remember enough to know what we're supposed to be doing in this time. Maybe he does as well. If he remembers anything, he must remember me trying to kill him and he you. This interview will also cancel your agreement with Lt. Delaney."

"By your calculations, we'll both be dead by Saturday anyway if you can't find him. What do I care about an agreement with Delaney for the exclusive if I'm dead? Remember, I'm only trying to bring him out in the open before Saturday. I trust in your abilities to get him before he has a chance to hurt me."

"That's not very smart. Remember, I missed and killed you; that's why we're all here again."

"That's another reason for the big kiss, silly. I want you to know what I'm capable of sharing with you. Don't miss this time. I don't want to wait another hundred years for the best man to come into my life." With that, Megan kissed Mike again; the type of kiss new brides give their husbands when they must be parted by circumstances for any length of time.

As Mike left Megan's apartment, he felt the intruder without seeing him. Mike was bracketed within the glass lens markings when the finger pressed the shutter release. Mike was on film by the stranger using a telephoto camera lens.

Mike looked around, but was unable to find the source of his concern. He walked quickly to his car, looking about in all directions, and ready to use force if the unseen presence materialized. Mike's sixth sense was better developed than his eyes, for the cameraman was half a block down from his location. As Mike headed for work, the intruder stayed back and waited for Megan to exit her apartment. She made an easier target than Mike; she never knew or felt the intrusion. The stranger followed her to work.

As the stranger pulled in behind Megan for the start of her journey downtown, he made quick notes on a small tape recorder. He should have been looking in his rear view mirror.

CHAPTER THIRTY-EIGHT

The eyes squinted through the light blue smoke emanating up from the cigarette stub. The puffy folds of the eyelids were almost as yellow as the nicotine-stained fingers holding the cigarette. The smoke could not hide the dirt imbedded in the pores of the skin nor the wild hairs forming the eyebrows. The eyes were fixed on the television screen playing the commercial message. The news feature replayed the upcoming interview with Los Angeles Times reporter Megan Reilly.

The blank stare of the eyes was finally broken as Andrews muttered, "You're dead meat, bitch! Dead meat, bitch!". Andrews reached over to the nightstand and grabbed the pint of whiskey. He took a long swallow of the searing liquid. Even through the smoke and whiskey, something had clicked inside Andrews' head. This was the woman in his dreams. He remembered seeing her, but it was a long time ago. Yes, bits and pieces were coming back to him now. "This was the one who caused me so much trouble. The damned marshal's woman!" he thought to himself. "Ok bitch, you're mine." he muttered as he burned the time and date into his memory.

Andrews had been staying in the same motel for the past three days. He was still driving Hathaway's Volvo sedan. He realized he would soon have to get rid of it and find another as the police would be looking for it. He was near the beach. He actually liked the lifestyle presented: easy, carefree, no questions asked, alcohol, drugs, music, good times, and good- looking women.

Stewart and Cantrill had already figured this out. They were close, but they were looking in the South Bay area of Torrance and Redondo Beach for

Andrews. He was actually in Santa Monica. Given enough time they may have eventually located him.

Mike Stewart was thinking about the time he had left until Saturday as he continued eastbound on the 10 freeway.

"Admin 32-Robert 177. Go to 3."

Stewart heard the radio traffic and knew that Cantrill was trying to contact him and telling him to switch to the car-to-car frequency. "Admin-32 on 3."

"Mike, what's your "20" (police jargon for 10-20 - your location)?"

"I'm on the 10 headed into downtown. ETA to the station is 15-20."

"Copy, back to one."

Before Stewart could figure out what Cantrill wanted, his car phone was ringing.

"Mike, it's Mike. I just wanted to know if you were within range of my car phone. I'm on a rolling Code 5 (moving surveillance) and I'm betting that my subject has a police scanner. We're in slow-moving traffic. I think we're heading to the Los Angeles Times Building downtown. I can handle the Code 5. We should be there in 20 or less. You need to meet me there."

"I copy. Does this involve Megan?"

"Yes, but I'll explain when we meet. See you there."

As Mike reset the receiver, he couldn't think of a reason why Cantrill was tailing Megan.

Mike had parked his car off the street where he could view the entrance and exit of the parking lot for the Times Building. He saw Megan's car pull in, but he did not see Cantrill following her. It took him a minute to find Cantrill's car on the street following a blue sedan.

Mike's car phone rang again. "Mike, I see you. I'm on the street behind a blue sedan driven by a WMA (white male adult). Pull in behind and join me."

"Yeah, I see you, Mike. I'll join you in a minute."

Together, they followed the sedan into Chinatown, where the driver pulled into an alley and stopped. Stewart and Cantrill followed.

The driver got out and walked back to Cantrill's car before Stewart could park and exit his car.

"Well, well. I should have guessed it would be you, Cantrill. I picked up on you following me awhile back, you stupid shit."

"Mike, meet Doug Franey", Cantrill said to Stewart. "Doug here is a dirty cop that was busted back to civilian, just missing a trip to the "joint" in the process."

Stewart saw the Doug Franey was a white male in his early forties. Franey looked like the typical aging high school jock; he was thick and muscular, his waistline was beginning to measure up to his chest, arthritis was beginning to creep into his movements, he looked just a little slow, and he had a used car salesman's grin.

Cantrill continued, "He's also a lying sack of shit. You didn't spot me until you were on Broadway; that's why you pulled off here. Doug now does window peeping for divorce lawyers, when he can find work. Who are you working for now, Doug?"

"Eat me. I don't have to tell you a thing."

"I see that you have expanded on your vocabulary since our academy days. I won't bother introducing you to my partner, since you've taken the time to photograph him and our informant."

"Yeah, informant. Right."

"Why you no good sonofabitch!" Stewart said as he grabbed Franey by the coat lapels.

"Mike, I'd throw him on the car and pat him down. Doug's been known to illegally carry a concealable handgun", Cantrill said as he opened the door to Franey's car.

"You can't do this to me you fucking jerks! You don't have a warrant. I'll get you for this, Cantrill!"

Cantrill opened the camera with the telephoto lens, but found the film had been removed. "Mike, check his pockets for a roll of film. I saw him shooting pictures of you and Megan this morning." Cantrill found the tape recorder and removed the tape. "Doug, who are you working for?"

"Go fuck yourself!"

Stewart found the film and tossed it to Cantrill. Stewart spun Franey around and said, "Look, idiot. Who are you working for? Why are you taking my picture and following me around?"

"I don't have to answer your questions. I've got you both for illegal search and seizure AND harassment."

Cantrill broke open the roll and pulled out the film exposing it to the light. "I think you should be more careful with your equipment, Doug. I think you dropped your camera and broke that expensive lens."

Upon hearing this, Franey's face turned crimson and he almost spat out the words, "I'll have your badge for this, shithead!"

Stewart watched as Cantrill closed the distance between himself and Franey. With one hand Cantrill grabbed Franey by the hair and with his other, Cantrill pulled his pistol. It happened so fast; it was almost a blur. Before Stewart could say anything, Cantrill had shoved the barrel of his pistol into Franey's mouth. Franey almost gagged on it. Mike wasn't sure, but he thought Franey had lost a tooth. Stewart quickly looked about them to see if anyone was in the alley that could witness what was happening. Fortunately, they appeared to be alone.

"Don't puke on my gun, Mister!" Cantrill said as he pulled the hammer back. "I don't need a dirty, ex-cop telling me he's going after my badge." Franey's eyes were bulging and bug-eyed as he looked over his nose at the cocked hammer on Cantrill's pistol. "You're fucking with a very dangerous person. Go ahead and tell on me. Tell them I put my pistol into your mouth and pulled the hammer back. I don't really think that they'll believe I'm crazy enough to do such a thing. But you just remember, I'm crazy enough to drop the hammer on you the next time I find you following us again. Do you read me? Don't follow us anymore! Tell your client you're off the case. Your health depends upon it! Nod your head if you understand."

Franey nodded yes and Cantrill let him go. Stewart could now clearly see blood coming from Franey's mouth.

Stewart and Cantrill watched as Franey got into his car and drove away. Stewart was the first to speak. "Thanks Mike, but how did you know I was being followed?"

"I didn't. I was actually following you. I guessed from your call this morning that you'd be at Megan's. I only followed because I thought you may need help. I spotted Franey checking out your car in the apartment's garage."

"But why...how did you know to..."

"Come on Mike. I know something's up with you and Megan. That's none of my business, but I have a gnawing suspicion that you and her know more about this case then you're telling me. And that is my business. I figured that night I saw you both crying in the hospital lot that you were in trouble. That and the fact that you're wearing a vest. I've been following you while you were following Megan home. I was worried about you. We're partners, remember? Care to tell me anything?"

"I can't just yet, but it's nothing cheap like you're thinking."

"I'm not making any value judgments, Mike. I was taking care of my partner. Beside, I would have paid good money to screw with Franey. He's trash. Though if I were you, I'd check to see if Lyn has written any checks to cash for a sizable amount."   Stewart thought back to his early days in law enforcement and how cops had that camaraderie that seems to have died these days. "Thanks, Mike. You know that you're cute enough to kiss." Stewart said jokingly.

"Don't tease me. I'm a married man. Let's get to work."

CHAPTER THIRTY-NINE

"This is Megan", she said answering her phone. The caller hung up without saying anything, though she thought she heard breathing on the line. Megan went back to work on her computer preparing for her live telecast on Wednesday night. She actually had worked the entire weekend on the project, once her boss informed her of the threats.

The phone on Megan's desk rang again. "This is Megan."

"Say, lady do you know of a cure for sore ribs?" It was Stewart.

"Maybe, but it might be illegal to discuss it over the phone. Hi, silly. Did you just try to call me a minute ago?"

"No, why?"

"Nothing. Someone just phoned and then hung up. I guess it was a wrong number."

"I'd be careful from here on out. You and I were photographed by some private investigator this morning as we left your apartment."

"Oh my god, Mike!"

"There's more. He followed you into work. Don't worry, Cantrill spotted him and took care of the film. Cantrill also asked him to stay away."

"How did Cantrill know to follow him? How did Cantrill get to my place?"

"Apparently, he's been following me. He's worried that his old partner is in trouble."

"Mike, what did you tell him?"

"Nothing. He's just that old breed of cop and he's watching over both of us. He knows something's up, but he's not pressuring me. Don't worry about him. I wanted to know if you knew anyone that would have paid to have us followed?"

"Why would I know anyone like that? Do you think that my other call is connected?"

"I don't know. Based on your TV commercial, it could be Andrews. You had better be very careful from now on. Will you please promise me that you'll call me before you leave the building this week?"

"Ok, Mike, I promise. Thanks for calling me. Tell Cantrill thanks for me."

"Not getting yourself hurt will be thanks enough for the both of us. Talk with you later."

"Look at it this way Tom. We're going nowhere with this case. We haven't seen him since he shot the cop in 'Gundo, but we think he killed that nurse over at Daniel Freeman. If this interview entices him out into the open, great. If not, I don't see where we're any worse off." Stewart was briefing Lt. Delaney on the upcoming interview with Megan. Cantrill was also present in the office.

"Why did she have to set this up without talking to you, first? Do we have control of her or not?"

"Lieutenant, I guess we don't. The other stations and papers all want to break the case. Apparently one of them has hired a P.I. to follow the three of us around. Threats were made to Reilly's boss that if they didn't share something, then they'd fabricate a story about a reporter and vice cop. She and her boss are responding to blackmail. I think we can still use them and the interview."

"All right! But I want something out of this and I don't want to have to answer questions at I.A. (Internal Affairs). For the time being, Knox and Baxter will handle the routine legwork in the South Bay. I want you two to stick with the reporter and keep her safe! Just remember that if she eats it, we can kiss our asses and careers good-bye! Those Times people have political connections! And one more thing. I know you're busy and are putting in long hours, but make sure it's all business. I've received phone calls from both your wives since this started. I've covered for you without question. Don't make me regret it."

The rest of the day passed uneventfully. The rain continued throughout the county. Mike tried unsuccessfully to get Megan to stay at a downtown hotel or with friends until the interview or Saturday. Stewart and Cantrill settled for meeting her in the garage as she prepared to leave for the night. They agreed that they would all meet at her apartment in the morning and follow her into work from now on. They left six minutes before Andrews pulled up to set up on the garage area and wait for the girl of his dreams.

CHAPTER FORTY

Neither Mike nor Megan slept well that night. The sound of the rain beat a steady cadence through the night. In their separate beds, in separate worlds, they both tossed restlessly. The night for Mike Cantrill seemed as dreadful.

Karen Cantrill's long, dark brown hair rested against the doorjamb as she stood in the doorway watching her husband. She found him sitting in the den. It was almost 2 AM. She never said anything to him, though it's unlikely he would have heard if she had spoken. The lights were off and the drapes were pulled open so he could watch the rain as it hit the patio. A glass of wine on the end table was untouched.

Karen was worried. In the twenty years that she had known him, Karen had seen Mike retreat into himself this way only three times; when his father died, when his retired partner died, and three years ago when he had a very bad cancer scare. Those dark, unblinking eyes were in direct contrast to the smiling eyes and face of that young patrol deputy who changed her car's flat tire on the Hollywood Freeway the day they met.

He hadn't been macho or brash. Mike's mannerisms made Karen feel comfortable. In those days, patrol deputies had to wear their helmets while in or out of the patrol cars. Mike took his helmet off and asked Karen to hold it for him while he changed the tire. He was genuinely friendly and talkative. The five minute job took over twenty minutes and they continued to talk after he changed the tire.

Before he left, Mike asked her out and Karen had accepted. She remembers still the anticipation of that date. Karen wasn't seeing anyone at the time nor was she looking, but she had a good feeling about Mike. He seemed honest and genuine; quiet and caring.

The date started with Mike picking Karen up at her parent's house. He took her to the Black Whale, a seafood restaurant in Venice. The place was a two-story wooden structure packed with regulars. They had wine in the bar upstairs and talked for almost an hour before they were seated at a table. Neither noticed the time; they were too busy talking and flirting with each other.

Afterwards, they went to Westwood where they saw Robert Redford and Barbra Streisand in the "The Way We Were". Following the movie, they had coffee at a quiet little spot at the marina, where they sat outside and talked until the place closed. When he took her home, Mike walked Karen to the front door. After unlocking the door, she quickly kissed him before going inside.

Karen was a tall, dark-haired beauty of American Indian descent. Her light skin color was the result of generations of marriages with non-Indians, while her facial features were a refined, but clear link to her ancestors' pasts. Karen's brown hair matched the rich color of her eyes. She usually wore her hair long and straight down, but occasionally she pulled it up. Mike always thought she looked incredibly sexy when she did.

In fact, one of Mike's favorite pictures on his desk was of Karen with her hair up and wearing a tee shirt and blue Levi shorts. It had been hot and muggy, so she put her hair up. He snapped the picture while they were on vacation at a picnic with friends and family. Karen had been scooping potato salad onto plates when she turned to look directly at Mike and smiled just before he pressed the shutter. Her entire being sparkled and looked radiant and he captured it on film. Karen had said that there was nothing sexy or glamorous about shoveling potato salad. Mike told her then that she was absolutely the most beautiful person that had ever lived and Mike always made it a point to tell Karen so even now.

Karen had bowled Michael over. She never knew to this day if it was her rich brown eyes that were the windows to a warm, loving soul; a drop-dead gorgeous body or that voice like honey being ladled out that captured Mike. But Karen knew that he was hers and she knew that he loved her and treated her as an equal. Mike was quiet and caring. He swept Karen off her feet with his gentleness.

She, in turn, fascinated him with her ability to "know and read" his heart and thoughts before he did or said anything. Long before they were married, Karen could tell if Mike was tired, worried, or preoccupied just by listening to his voice over the phone. Karen could read him like a book and she didn't have to speak to him to convey her thoughts and feelings. She knew when to leave him alone with his thoughts and when to hold him and be there for him.

For Mike, being there for him meant being with him all the time. After their first date, they were a steady item. Following their marriage, Mike never considered being anywhere without Karen. Karen took care of their children, their pets, and Mike.

Their children were easy. Mike had a habit of spoiling their three girls and Karen had to make sure that they did not take advantage of Mike's good nature and generosity. The oldest was Stephanie. Even Karen had to admit that Stephanie looked just like her. Mike also complained that she acted too much like her mother, as well. She was health conscious and concerned about the environment. Stephanie was the one that lost children and animals ran towards. She helped her mother organize the church volunteers for soup kitchen duty. And, there were always boys calling or coming over to the house.

Then there was Katie. Katie acted just like her father. She even put ketchup on the same foods he did. Katie didn't look like either of her parents, though. Her skin was creamy white; she had a full, rosebud mouth, pale blue eyes, and a laugh that should have been on a Southern belle. As she had begun to mature and fill out, it was apparent that she didn't share any of Karen's physical characteristics. Katie was also the only one of the children who wore glasses; and she first started wearing them at age fourteen, just like Michael. Karen often wondered if she were looking at the recreation of Michael's birth mother in Katie. Karen never thought too long on that subject for she would invariably end up crying over that poor, desperate soul.

Little Heather was the youngest. Ten years younger than Katie, Heather had been unplanned. At different times, one could see traits and characteristics of both her parents in Heather. She had her mother's coloring and mouth, but her father's eyes, nose, and was leaning towards his disposition. She had a little girl lisp and laugh that could melt her father's heart.

Their pets were a pair of hybrid wolves. They were a gift from Mike to Karen. Karen's heritage must have been the reason the wolves appealed to her so much. Mike had seen Karen fawn over the pups at a ranch for wolves and hybrid pups in Victorville years before. He bought two as a birthday gift for her. Karen was so happy she cried.

Karen cried again years later. She cried when she learned that he had been diagnosed with a malignant tumor. Mike was scheduled for surgery as soon as his mother could get two of the country's more prominent oncologists flown into Los Angeles. Karen handled Mike's request to have a will made. He never saw her cry after the attorney and witnesses left. Karen excused herself and cried in the upstairs bathroom of her mother-in-law's house.

The surgery had been successful, but that period of time in their lives had not been without cost. The event and accompanying stress had strained relationships within the family. Now, more than ever, Karen and Mike were trying to squeeze as much living as possible into their time together.

She hovered in the background in his professional life dutifully attending stuffy departmental functions and she was all that mattered in his personal life.

Mike helped with the housework, he attended PTA meetings, and took the girls to their ballet classes. He remembered birthdays and anniversaries. He spoiled Karen with not only gifts, but with his words spoken from his heart to hers. Karen had several boxes full of cards and poems from him; for unlike other men, Mike never stopped writing little notes after the courtship stage.

Their neighbors and their daughters never forgot the time they observed Karen and Mike slow dancing in the rain on their patio. It was a warm summer afternoon and the rain had been unexpected. Mike had been caught in the summer showers while doing the yard work. Karen had put on a Carol King album and turned up the volume when she saw Mike standing on the patio motioning her to come outside. Karen stepped out and Mike took her in his arms. Neither spoke a word to each other as they started to dance. Slowly, Karen closed her eyes and tucked Mike's hand that was holding hers against their chests. Karen's head rested on Mike's right shoulder and he rested his head against the back of hers. She was barefoot, but her feet quickly and expertly followed Mike's as they danced along the redwood decking. It was if she knew and could see where he was about to move. Everyone saw two persons, but only one movement. All the onlookers felt the warmth; as well as the magic.

Karen and Mike also danced even the fast dances with the teenagers at their daughters' high school where they chaperoned dances. Occasionally, the older of their girls - Stephanie and Katie - fussed at them for getting caught kissing and hugging in the kitchen while preparing breakfast and the coffee. If Stephanie found her parents' bedroom door closed on weekend mornings, she dutifully steered Heather away and fixed breakfast for herself and her sisters.

They did not need to speak to communicate to one another; they only had to touch one another. Karen brushed up against Mike when they were together. He would place an arm around her waist or touch her hands. Karen always placed her hand upon his heart before falling asleep at night.

It was a habit that she developed during their honeymoon. One night after a busy day of traveling, sightseeing, and lovemaking, Mike fell into a deep sleep. When Karen stirred, she couldn't see or hear him breathing. Concerned, she quickly placed her hand on Mike's chest. She instantly felt his heart beating, but there was something else. Karen could feel a force, an energy that made her feel warm and secure. She sensed something mystical that she could not define, but readily accepted and cherished about her new husband.

Karen and Mike were more than lovers; they were soul mates.

When they first met, Karen had just enrolled in the masters degree program at Cal-State Northridge for her teaching credentials. She was an art major who had the ability to craft jewelry or paint in a fashion that expressed her real spirit. Schoolwork came to an abrupt end after their first month of dating. Her fireman father had a total fit when he found out who she was dating. However, Mike had won over her parents and the rest, as they say, was history.

After they were engaged, Karen teased Mike about stopping for cute girls on the freeway. Mike responded that even the Pope would have noticed and stopped for the tall, beautiful woman in the cranberry colored sundress and sandals stranded in the early evening rush hour traffic the day they met.

Over the years, elements of his character had changed, and not always for the better. She wanted him out of Robbery; there had been too many close calls and poor Mike didn't seem the type to handle the killings any better with time and neither could she. Karen wanted him around for retirement and for their daughters' weddings.

They actually split up in 1985 after a bitter argument over his job. It was just after Mike and his partner, Hector Baldonado, were staking out liquor stores in West Hollywood that were being robbed by three men wearing ski masks and gloves and armed with pistols and a shotgun.

One night close to midnight, they spotted the trio just as they entered a store on Santa Monica Boulevard. The two detectives called it in and waited for the suspects to leave. The robbers exited the store before the arrival of the patrol units. As they approached their getaway vehicle, Hector called out for the robbers to drop their weapons. They didn't and immediately opened fire on the detectives. Only twenty-two yards separated the two groups. Hector was instantly taken out with hits in both legs by two shotgun blasts. That left Mike all alone to face the three.

In the ensuing gun battle, Mike killed them all. He had emptied both his revolvers and a bullet had torn open the left shoulder pad material of his sports coat, but he was untouched. By the time the first black and white arrived on the scene, Mike was still badly shaken. Hector was ultimately retired for medical reasons.

While the department was calling him a hero, Karen was frightened and as badly shaken up by the event as Mike had been. She wanted him to quit. He wouldn't, and they had long, painful arguments. It had been the first time in their relationship that an argument was bitter or lasted beyond bedtime.

When Mike was cleared by the department to return to work, Karen couldn't believe he was actually going back. In her frustration, she took their two daughters and stayed with her parents in the San Fernando Valley. Mike had never cried following the shooting and subsequent investigation; not even during the lengthy sessions with the department mandated sessions with a psychiatrist. He did cry the night that Karen left.

The separation lasted twelve days, fourteen hours, and 29 minutes as neither of them could stand to be apart from each other for long. Even angry with each other, hurt, and apart, they spoke almost daily over the phone. Mike spoke gently to Karen and he listened more than he talked. Karen almost purred over the phone lines to Mike. The sensuality conveyed could have aroused the dead. They talked, they did not argue or shout; they were too much in love.

Karen's mom told her so one night as Karen hung up the phone after talking with Mike. She and Mike had talked for almost an hour. They spoke of the girls, but mostly they talked about and to each other. Karen had used the phone in her parents' bedroom, as she had wanted privacy. Mike had ended their conversation by telling Karen that he loved her and to keep safe. It was all Karen could do to blurt out, "Me too!" before she started sobbing and quickly hung up the phone.

She couldn't stop the flow of tears running down her face as she just sat quietly and motionless on the bed after hanging up the phone as her mother opened the door; which had been left ajar. She broke down and cried in her mother's arms. When she stopped crying, Karen listened while her mother talked. Karen and the girls moved back into their home the next morning. It was a Friday morning while Mike was at work.

She arranged for the girls to spend the weekend with Mike's mother and was waiting for Mike when he came home. Karen had made dinner for him and she was wearing the long, emerald green nightgown she wore on their wedding night; the gown with too much lace and without the matching robe. The dinner became cold and was left untouched on the table until early Sunday morning as Mike and Karen made love that entire weekend. Until they had breakfast after church on Sunday morning, they made do with peanut butter and crackers in their room. That weekend was responsible for their youngest, Heather.

 Karen was worried about Mike, but she was secure enough to know that he would eventually confide in her. Karen did not want to be frightened, but she felt that she had good cause based on past experiences, but she didn't know why. She tried to remember his new partner's name, but didn't know him that well. She did remember his wife, the nurse, though. They spoke throughout the night when — Lyn, that was her name — came to sit with her the night Mike was stabbed in the arm and shoulder by a drunken wife when he responded to a domestic violence call.

She felt a little better and went to check on their three blonde-haired daughters. They weren't actually blonde; Mike would just tease Karen with the term. Mike jokingly said that his past was catching up with him. Their daughters all had hair the color of amber honey. All were sleeping peacefully in their beds. Long ago, she gave up trying to figure where those hair genes came from in their families. There were no blondes in her family and

Mike had jet-black hair and eyes. Their daughters were healthy and that was all that mattered to either Karen or Mike. They were raised in a caring and loving environment.

Karen went back to bed to wait for Mike. She waited to hold him and feel his heart beating against hers. She was going to make love to him and infuse his troubled soul with her fire and spirit. He never came to bed, and she ended up with tears running down her face as she drifted off to sleep. Karen cried for Mike, not herself. She knew that old Doc Cantrill would have known what to do; and the day he died, Michael lost a good friend and most-trusted confidant.

She cried the more when she thought of Michael's father. William C. Cantrill had been a wonderful person. Quiet and yet, powerful; he was rock-steady in a crisis and he was a true friend. While Michael's mother had always been reserved towards her, Karen found Dr. Cantrill to be just the opposite. He was warm and outgoing and he told Karen to call him "dad". He would laugh at his own corny jokes and Karen could tell by the way that he hugged Michael, that he genuinely loved him.

Dr. Cantrill treated Karen just as one of his own and she really loved him. In the evenings when the families got together, Karen would always sit and have coffee with her father-in-law. She would sit on the couch next to him where they talked for hours about the news as reported by the Los Angeles Times, politics, the stock market, his grandchildren, or Michael. As much as Michael reminded her of Dr. Cantrill, Karen missed him a great deal.

Another figure also roamed through the wind-driven darkness. Carl Andrews was driving the 10 and 405 freeways. He stopped several times for coffee and to watch other night travelers. He even stopped at a school playground and just sat on the swing set. It was too much like watching a creature of the night. He only needed the red eyes of the wolf as he stared into the darkness that he was so much a part.

Wednesday morning found the three tired people, comrades now, caravaning into the downtown area. At the Times Mirror Square, Mike made sure Megan got into the elevator before he and Cantrill headed into the station. She was supposed to call after she got into her office.

"Heavy date, Megan?", the speaker was Jason Richards; another reporter.

He wanted Megan's job assignments more than her. She had always declined his invitations.

"Drop dead, Jason", was her only comment as she threw her handbag on the desk. Walking into the ladies' room, she saw the effects of no sleep on her face. This case was making her look far older than her years. "God, Michael, what have you done to me?", she whispered aloud. She was restless at night due to more than just worry.

At the same time that Karen Cantrill was on the phone to Lyn Stewart to inquire what was happening to their husbands, Megan's phone rang. "This is Megan."

"I knew you were coming. You shouldn't have come back!"

The raspy voice made the hair on Megan's neck stand up. She swallowed her fear long enough to ask, "Who is this?"

"Just wanted to let you know that you're dead meat, bitch!" The caller hung up.

Mike's words to her that their only future was being dead came back to her like a brick through a plate glass window.

Before she could dial Mike's number, her phone rang again. This time it was Patsy, one of the receptionists. "Megan, there was a strange guy here looking for you a few minutes ago. He left before I could call you. I almost called security because he was kind of rough looking. Megan? Megan?"

Megan was on another line to Mike. "Mike! He's here in the building or was a minute ago!"

"Stay put in your office. Call security. I'll be there in minutes."

Their arrival caused quite a stir in the building. Within an hour, normalcy had almost been returned. Andrews' mug shot had been shown to Patsy and she confirmed that he had indeed been the visitor. No one had seen him enter or leave. Security guards were placed at all perimeter doors. Megan was a nervous wreck! Since Megan was to have the television reporters over in the late afternoon, Stewart figured they would be there well into the night. He and Cantrill would remain with her. While Cantrill called the office to brief Delaney, Stewart sat on the couch in Megan's office. Emotionally exhausted, Megan had fallen asleep on his shoulder with her arm around his neck.

Mike just knew this would end up being a long day.

CHAPTER FORTY-ONE

The reporters arriving for the pre-interview were subjected to minor delays while Stewart and Cantrill verified identities. They were hovering over her so much that during a break Megan told them both to stay out of her office unless she called for them.

They occupied their time by reviewing maps of the area for tomorrow's street interview. Megan's boss was kind enough to let them use another office for the day. Cantrill called Delaney and secured a helicopter for standby in the area. Mike asked for a flyover of the area to determine the best surveillance locations. Delaney said that he would personally see to it that afternoon.

Sometimes the hardest part and the worst part of police work is the waiting. Both Mikes stood and sat around in the office keeping an eye on Megan. Stewart drank coffee until his stomach hurt; it matched the headache he was having.

Cantrill finally remembered to clean the barrel of his pistol, so the saliva from Franey would not cause rust. He still carried the old-style revolver. Actually, he carried two pistols to be exact. Since the Department didn't allow magnums, Cantrill carried two Smith & Wesson .38 Special Model 15's with four-inch barrels. He said they were fast, lightweight, and sufficiently powerful for the tasks at hand. He carried two, because experience had taught him that the fastest reload was a second weapon. Both of his weapons had their blue-black finish marred from repeatedly being pulled from their holsters. The metal exteriors and wooden stocks had enough nicks and scratches from being dropped to attest to Mike's prowess and need to demonstrate his reload theory. Afterwards, he asked Stewart to spell him while he stretched his legs. He said he remembered seeing a coke machine somewhere on the first floor.

Left on his own, Stewart surveyed the newspaper scene. People were everywhere and phones were ringing constantly! He saw that on most desks there was a computer monitor. He thought that it was an entirely different office setup from the one he remembered Megan working at in 1886 Dallas.

As he sat at one of the desks, he noticed that most had personal pictures under the clear blotter screens. Mike remembered that Megan had no pictures or mementos anywhere in her office. Nothing, not even her diploma. As Mike was trying to decide if this had some deeper psychological meaning, he was interrupted when Megan quietly called out to him from her office door.

"I'm sorry this is taking so long. I know you must bored out of your mind. I think we're going to be here for a few more hours. Can you stay?"

Mike remembered the face of the naive newspaperwoman of so long ago. He still wanted to take care of her. "I'm sticking with you till the end. Wild horses couldn't drag me away from you this time."

Megan looked deep into those brilliant eyes of his and felt very comfortable. She stepped out of the office and closed the door behind her. She quickly, but gently pulled on his tie, bending his head towards her and kissed his lips. "Thanks. Can we have Chinese brought in for dinner tonight?" she said smiling.

"Have I ever said no to you before?" Megan shook her head no. Stewart continued, "I'll take care of it." She winked, waved, and slipped back into her office.

Mike felt his face getting hotter. He looked around him to determine if anyone had seen the kiss. He didn't see anyone paying him any attention. He quickly wiped his lips to remove any lipstick. As he replaced his handkerchief, he saw Cantrill stepping off the elevator. Cantrill was carrying a coke and tossing an apple in the air. He was also smiling one of those, `I know something you don't know' smiles.

"Say, Michael ask me what I did while I took a break."

"Judging by the size of that shit-eating grin on your face, you must have solved the case. That isn't it, is it? Andrews isn't in custody?"

"No, nothing that big. But I did solve a minor mystery on this case, though. I sat and spoke to Patsy Reynolds, the receptionist. We had a nice, friendly chat and guess whose name came up?"

"Ok, I give, who?"

"It seems that Doug Franey's known to Patsy. She has seen him and recognizes his voice on the phone when he calls for Jason Richards."

"Who the hell is Jason Richards?"

"According to Patsy, he's another reporter here; one who has the hots for Megan. Patsy said Megan has too much good sense to give him the time of day. He and Franey spoke on the phone every day last week and Franey called him this morning; *after* our visit with Franey. Maybe rejection has led to revenge."

"That's pretty deep for an aging cop who chases bank robbers."

"Yeah, but you guys in vice aren't the only ones who get feelings, or is that get groped?" Cantrill said as he tossed the apple in the air.

Stewart caught it and took a big bite out of it before handing it back to him.   "Thanks, Mike. I wanted to test the apple for hidden razor blades before I took a bite out of it myself."

"I'm glad that I brought you along on this case, lad. Now which one is Richards?"

"The young stud over there in the three hundred dollar suit", Mike said jerking his head in the direction of Richards' desk. Richards was on the phone, but he noticed the two strangers looking at him as he replaced the receiver. He felt extremely uncomfortable without knowing exactly why. He smiled a nervous smile at them and buried his face behind the computer monitor on his desk. The detectives left him alone for the time being.

Dinner was unusually quiet for three persons and friends. Megan slowly chewed small bites. She was heartsick over the possibility of this being her last days together with Stewart. She dutifully smiled whenever she caught one of the Mikes staring at her. Mike Stewart thoughtfully chewed bigger bites while he had the same thoughts; those unspoken feelings. Mike Cantrill was inhaling his food over chopsticks while trying to piece the case together and to make sense of why his old partner was possibly keeping information from him. The unspoken thoughts created a tension in the air that could be felt like a slap across their faces.

Their section of the office was empty and darkened with most of the lights turned off. Staring across the empty food cartons at Megan and Mike sitting next to each other on the couch, Cantrill was the first to stand up. He walked over to the window and looked out into the cold night air blanketing Los Angeles. As he watched the autumn air blow dark clouds across the light of the partial moon, he called them over.

As they approached the cold windowpane Cantrill said, "See the clouds being blown across the moon. Isn't it somehow haunting, yet hypnotically beautiful?"

Megan had her arm around Mike Stewart's waist. She touched Cantrill's shoulder with her other hand as she replied, "Yes it is. Similar to you and your partner's souls; quiet, dark, and yet very beautiful and noble. Thank you, Mike." She released her grip on Stewart, grabbed Cantrill's hand, and kissed it.

Awkwardly, Cantrill excused himself saying that he needed to check the garage and talk with the night watchmen. As he left, Megan and Mike were framed in the window against the night backdrop of Los Angeles.

The gusty night air shut out other night sounds from Cantrill as he descended the staircase. Primarily, it hid the pounding heartbeat of the person on the staircase above him. Cantrill's use of the stairs was completely unexpected. The dark silhouette was caught off guard and had to make a dash for the upper landing. Cantrill was somewhat flustered by Megan's conduct and he never heard the stranger, but his habit of doing the unexpected had almost been his undoing.

CHAPTER FORTY-TWO

While Cantrill was in the garage talking with two of the night watchmen, the silhouette remained on the stairwell, Mike Stewart and Megan were alone on the fourth floor, and at the same time the phone at the Stewart house was ringing and ringing and ringing.

After holding onto each other and standing at the window for several minutes, Meagan finally broke the silence. "Mike, I'm very worried about tomorrow. No, I'm worried about us and us not having enough time. There's so many things I want, need to say. I don't want to die! I'm scared", she said. "I feel as if I have been lost all these years and now you have found me. I don't want to lose you again!"

"I'm frightened, too, but not about tomorrow. I'm concerned that I may be spending the last days and hours with you; and I resent having to divide my time between you, Cantrill, and the job. Dying doesn't bother me; the thought of not being with you does."

Neither noticed the shadow of a man walking along the outer offices towards them.

"I made a mistake a long time ago and I need to correct it, and now is as good a time as any", Megan said as she looked into Mike's eyes. Her face looked radiant to Mike. "Marshal Robert Forsythe, I love you. You're just the kind of, no you are the man I need and want! I'm so sorry that I didn't say it sooner in 1886."

Tears rolled down her cheeks as she continued. "Maybe none of this would have happened or ended the way it did. I shouted it the day we died, but I don't know if you heard me. Robert, I'm sorry. I'm so sorry. Oh,

Robert!" Megan said as she grabbed and hugged Mike. She buried her face in his jacket.

"Mandy. Mandy", Stewart cried as he squeezed her against him and brushed her hair with his hands. The shadow on the wall stopped and remained motionless. "In another time I would have worn out horses to get to you. I promise I'll keep you safe this time, no matter what."

The shadow moved back along the wall in the direction that it had come.

Cantrill called out to Mike as he approached. Megan had just enough time to pull away from Mike and wipe her eyes before he came into view. Cantrill looked cold and pale as he spoke to both of them.

"The wind is really picking up out there. I think that it has spooked the guards. Surprising, there's plenty of pedestrian traffic tonight. I say we call it quits for tonight and plan on meeting for lunch to discuss the last minute plans for tomorrow's interview. How about it, Mike?"

"What has spooked the guards?" Stewart asked.

"I can't put my finger on it other than to blame it on the wind. It's noisy out there in the garage and there are enough shadows normally for the guards without having to watch out for a specific creep."

"Ok, I guess we can call it a day, but this is the last time that you'll have your car out late at night." Stewart said looking at Megan. "I would prefer that you ride with one of us until this thing is over."

"I'm too tired to argue with you guys, anymore.", Megan said as she picked up her purse and coat.

When Stewart arrived home he found Lyn sitting at the dining room table with the phone. "Mike, Paul suffered a heart attack this afternoon."

"Is he alive?" Mike interrupted.

"He's in critical but stable condition in ICU right now. I spoke with his doctor. It was his doctor, Dr. Martinez that left a message on our machine. According to Dr. Martinez, Paul told him to tell you that you must not come to check on him until after the 16th of this month. What does that mean, Michael?"

"It means that Paul knows I'm tied up on this case right now and I hope to have it wrapped up this week."

Lyn stood up as she said, "Mike, Paul's your best friend in this world. You must go and be with him, now!"

"Lyn, I can't leave just now! I must be here on Saturday, the 16th."

"I don't believe what I'm hearing! Lately, you just haven't been yourself. I don't know you any more!"

"Lyn, you don't understand!"

"You damned right I don't understand! Your best friend is in a New York hospital in critical condition and all you can think of is your damned job! Or is there more that you're not telling me, Michael?"

There was only silence in the room and in those few seconds, the entire house seemed to hold its breath in anticipation of the answer.

"There's a `redeye' out to New York from LAX at 1:15 in the morning. I'll be on it. One of the Stewarts should do the honorable thing."

"Lyn!"

"I don't want to talk to you! Just leave me alone while I pack" as she stormed out of the room and down the hallway.

CHAPTER FORTY-THREE

The sliding patio door was unlocked and opened slightly. The wind gently pushed the curtains aside. The fluttering curtains acted as a backdrop for the person's silhouette. The person was barefoot and walking silently across the room to the figure in the chair.

Mike had fallen asleep in the chair still in his work clothes and sports coat. The half-finished drink was still in his hand; his gun hand. His pistol was snapped down in the holster on his belt. Dawn was still hours away and the room's interior was dark as he had not turned on any lamps while sitting in the chair. Mike had opened the patio door earlier, but had fallen asleep without closing and locking it.

Karen leaned over and kissed Mike's forehead at the same time reaching for his glass and pulling it from his grasp. Mike Cantrill stirred slightly and though groggy, instantly knew that his neck was stiff and sore.

Closing and locking the patio door, Karen whispered, "Mike, you have to wake up and get up. It's not healthy for the girls to find you like this too often. They'll think that there is something wrong between us."

Mike opened his eyes and tried to gather his thoughts.

"Is there?" Karen asked.

"Is there what, honey?" Mike asked as he rubbed the circulation back into his neck.

"Is there something wrong between us?" she asked again as she walked back towards her husband of nineteen years. Stopping in front of him and setting the glass down on the coffee table, Karen was clearly visible from the light in the hallway. She continued, "You've been very quiet and to yourself, lately. I've come to expect you to work late any more, but you seldom shut me out the way you've been doing since you started this new case."

"You hardly touch dinner any more; enough that you're losing weight. Your pants are beginning to hang off you. Your mother has already fussed at me over it. You don't spend any time with either the girls or me, anymore. Even when you're here, you're not here. I covered for you with your mother, but I'm sure she suspects that something's not right. You come home and sit and think until you fall asleep."

Karen hesitated for just a moment before continuing. "Is it the can—", Karen stopped herself by placing a hand over her mouth. She couldn't say the word. It was an ugly word with too many painful memories for all of them.

Mike had used only eight sick days in all the years that he had been on the sheriff's department. Then, it seemed almost overnight he became sick without explanation. There were those awful tests, too many x-rays, and the different medications before the proper diagnosis was made.

It was also the only time that Karen had struck Mike in anger. It was the night before his surgery. It was in the hospital after his mother and the girls had left. Mike was depressed and he started telling Karen what to do if something went wrong during the surgery. Karen couldn't take it when Mike told her that she must authorize removing him from life support. She slapped his face twice by reflex; the type of reflex one has when having been frightened. The tears flowed down her face as Karen practically shouted at Mike.

"Stop it! Stop it! I would sooner kill myself, for without you, I would be dead on the inside! I can't add time to our relationship, and I won't deduct a minute; a heartbeat. I won't; I can't! Oh, Michael, Michael!"

The act startled and shocked them both. Karen cried in his arms. She kissed and held onto Mike. She spent the rest of the night in his room holding him in her arms. Later after the nurses gave him his evening medication and something for sleep, Karen whispered to Mike that she would be there when he awoke in the morning and he replied that he knew that and he was counting on it.

There was also the recovery period and her blowup with Michael's mother. After bringing Michael home, it seemed to Karen that his mother was constantly criticizing her. Julia Cantrill complained that the house wasn't cleaned well enough, the girls were eating too many fast food meals, they were too noisy, Mike wasn't getting enough rest, or home-cooked meals. Her list of complaints went on.

Mike told Karen and his mother that he felt better almost immediately after the surgery, but it was almost six months before Mike looked or really felt any better. Karen remembered the horrible chemotherapy treatments Mike had to endure. Mike was sick after each treatment. He said he always had a metallic taste in his mouth. He couldn't keep any food down for days following the chemotherapy. Understandably, Mike lost his appetite, and he began to lose too much weight; worrying his doctors. Julia wanted to bring in a dietitian. Karen snapped at her mother-in-law that she could take care of Mike.

Karen knew that even as a little boy, Mike had been fond of egg custard, but she had always restricted his eggs and his sweets. Switching to egg substitutes in Julia's recipe, Karen started making the custard for Mike and allowed him to eat it every day without restriction. Even sick, Mike would eat his favorite dessert. It must have been a boost to his spirit as well as his body for the chemotherapy treatments became tolerable and his weight loss stopped.

By the end of the fourth month, the worst seemed over and by the sixth month, even his mother commented that Mike was beginning to look and act like his old self. Shortly thereafter, he suggested a second honeymoon to Karen. She was ecstatic. Karen knew that this was good sign that he was on the road to recovery and she was grateful, as it had been over seven months since they had been intimate. She also welcomed the opportunity for a break from his mother.

When informed of their plans, Julia spoke privately with Karen and told her that the last thing her son needed was a tiring journey away from home just so "someone's sex life could be taken care of". That was the last straw for Karen. A few years earlier when Mike and Karen found out about Heather's pending arrival, Julia had lectured Karen about her age in relationship to childbearing. When she touched on the subject of sex, Karen interrupted her and told Julia that her and Mike's sex life was not a topic of discussion for her mother-in-law or anyone else.

Karen told Julia everything that she had wanted to say not only for the past months, but for all the past years as well. The discussion quickly deteriorated into several ugly exchanges. It lasted too long. Their relationship since that time had been one only of necessity and formality.

As Mike was formulating his reply and before he uttered a word, she hurriedly continued, "Are you ok? I can take whatever you have to say to me, just tell me something, Michael!"

Karen didn't say anything further as her voice was about to crack from the pressure of the emotions. She clenched her hands and her composure was going, as evidenced by her trembling shoulders and arms.

Without a word and a speed borne of time and experience, Mike grabbed Karen and pulled her onto his lap.

"Karen, I'm not sick anymore; not since the surgery, and there's nothing wrong between us." he said as he brushed her hair back off her face. "I've been put on a difficult case and it's very frustrating, that's all. There are so many factors to consider. I've never come across anything like this before. It's nothing that I can really talk about. Stewart and I will resolve it soon, I hope."

"I was worried that it was your health." she said as she rubbed Michael's chest with her hand. "— or something. I imaged all sorts of things, Michael." she sighed as she pressed against him.

He could see that Karen was teary-eyed. Mike heard Karen breathe in large gulps of air and felt her tremble as if she were about to cry. He felt sorry for her and he was ashamed for having made her think such thoughts. He held her tighter.

As tired as he was, Mike noticed how good Karen smelled. Karen always showered in the evenings and wore pretty nightgowns. She always smelled of perfume or powder. He could feel her heavy bosom straining against the silky material of her nightgown and pressing into his chest and he didn't feel as tired as he had moments before.

"I'm sorry, Karen. I'm just old and tired, but you and I are ok." Mike whispered softly as he patted and rubbed her shoulder and arm. He fought with his senses to stop thinking about Karen's full, matronly breasts so that he could enjoy smelling her hair. It smelled of roses and Mike knew she had opened and used a new bottle of shampoo.

Mike gently nuzzled Karen's face and throat. Karen responded by kissing Mike. She wasn't gentle. When they took a breath, Karen moved her lips along Mike's face, stopping at his ear. "Then carry me to bed and make love to me before I start to feel ugly and neglected. Hurry, I want to make noise", she said in a husky whisper.

In the darkened room, it was too difficult to tell who grabbed who first. Fortunately, the children's rooms were upstairs.

Mike Stewart was awake and would not fall asleep until after dawn. Lyn had left in a cab without saying another word to him. He felt ashamed, but not for letting Lyn leave. He wanted to go to Paul, but he knew more than anyone that he must stay and meet his fate on the 16th.

Delaney's phone call woke him up. The briefing would be held at 1500 hours at the Lennox Station. Cantrill woke him up an hour later. He wanted them, including Megan, to meet for lunch at the Italian restaurant near Megan's apartment building. Stewart agreed to the one o'clock luncheon and he would pick up Megan.

The restaurant was large and elegantly decorated. The lunch crowd was beginning to drift back to work and they had the place to themselves before their lunch was served. The three of them looked tired and haggard. It was Mike Cantrill that broke the obligatory small talk.

"I heard you two talking last night before I called out as I came back from the garage. I froze in my tracks with what I heard. Anyone else would have thought you two were crazy."

"What are you talking about, Mike?" Stewart asked, looking suddenly wide awake. Megan had put down her fork and was looking at Stewart.

Leaning forward and placing his arms on the table, Cantrill continued,

"Aside from the department and my wife, most people don't know that I was adopted. For the first seven years of my life I was raised in a Catholic orphanage in Chicago. I was left as an infant at the church probably by some young girl or housewife during the years immediately following World War II. There was no note or anything. I didn't even have a name. I was named Michael by Sister Celestine.

The aging parish priest arranged for Dr. and Mrs. Cantrill to adopt me. I think he called in a few markers to pull it off. You see, he was worried about his failing health and who would want to adopt an older child."

"Mike, I hate to interrupt, but..."

"Then don't, Mike. You see the priest's name was Father Jacob Forsythe." You could hear Stewart's heart pounding. His mouth was wide open, but he did not make a sound.

"I remember Father Jake telling stories to us kids. One of those stories was about his dad, a U.S. marshal riding the Old West." Mike stopped for a moment to emphasize the point he was going to make. "A marshal by the name of Robert Forsythe. The same name I heard Megan call you last night." Mike stopped talking when he saw the tears were rolling down Stewart's face.

Stewart almost whispered, "Jacob was my second child. He had his mother's patience and quiet charm. I always teased him that he would make a fine priest." "Holy shit!" exclaimed Cantrill. He looked at Stewart and then at Megan and back again. "This isn't possible! It can't be!"

"Did he ever say anything else about the family?"

Numb-looking and lacking any color to his face, Cantrill just sat there.

"Please, Michael, I have to know."

"He said that his brother was an Army doctor killed during a shelling attack in the first World War. His sister married a Southern boy who was a lawyer."

"What about his mother?"

"Mike, don't do this to yourself!" said Megan. She had tears running down her face as well as the men.

"Father Jake said she died of a broken heart after his dad was found murdered in Texas. When I was little, I would cry after hearing the story, myself. I felt sorry for the brave marshal killed from ambush. Father Jake said that his father was a knight without armor and the lack of armor was the only reason he got killed. He said astride a good horse and with his Winchester rifle, there wasn't anything on this earth that could have stopped his father. Now will you tell me what is going on here, Michael?"

"How do you know so much about his family, Mike?" Megan asked as she pulled Kleenex from her purse.

"I was always inquisitive and Father Jake indulged me. Stories of the Old West have always fascinated me."

"You sound as if you were his favorite", she continued.

"I was one of the oldest at the orphanage. In those years immediately following the war, people were busy giving birth to the baby boomers. Later those couples that couldn't have children preferred to adopt a baby and not a child. My adopted parents couldn't have children and they were in their late twenties at the time. I overheard Father Jake tell Dr. Cantrill that I was his favorite and that was the reason I had been left behind at the orphanage. It was the only time I ever knew him to tell a lie. Father Jake loved each of us as if we were his own, but he had no favorites. We were all loved and well cared for by Father Jake and even old, strict Sister Celestine. So you two, what's up? Or am I the crazy one?"

"You're not crazy, but you'll think that I am. I cannot explain it any other way than to say that I'm Marshal Robert Forsythe and Megan is Amanda Weaver. In 1886, I was trailing a ruthless killer in Texas by the name of G.W. Cooper. I met Amanda in Dallas and fell in love with her. On the morning of November 16th, I was ambushed by Cooper's gang. Amanda was there trying to find me as well. We had a bitter argument before I left her house looking for Cooper. It's hard to believe and harder to repeat." Mike was struggling to keep from sobbing aloud.

"Cooper shot my horse out from under me and I got hurt. Amanda struggled with Cooper to keep him from shooting me as I lay dying from my injuries. I - I tried to shoot Cooper, but instead I shot — I shot and killed Amanda!"

"Judas Priest!", Cantrill exclaimed. He just looked at both of them. Megan's head hung down and she was quietly crying. Stewart put his arm around her and gently squeezed her.

Stewart continued, "Up until this case developed, what I just told you was nothing more than a series of repeated dreams. With the killings and this Andrews being identified, I think that my dreams were memories and not dreams. Andrews is the spitting image of G.W. Cooper. I think that somehow by falling in love with Amanda and dragging her into the conflict, I screwed things up. For some reason, we've been brought back to try and fix things as they should have been in 1886. I know it sounds crazy, but I don't know what else to think."

"Over the years I had the same flashbacks that Mike was having, but I had never met him until this case. At least not in this lifetime. I tend to believe him as I cannot explain why two people who do not know each other could have the same dreams. Actually, Robert's bullet exited me and wounded Cooper, but I don't know how badly as he ran off. He knows who I am, but we don't know if he knows about Robert - I mean Mike. I purposely set up the news conference tonight in hopes of bringing him out into the open before the 16th."

Mike picked up the story now, "My fear is that if we cannot find him in time, history will repeat itself and Megan and I will be killed again on

Saturday the 16th. I really don't know how to explain it any better. I've even talked with a psychiatrist about this. I'm sorry you had to ask about this Mike, but at least I don't have to worry about lying to you any more."

"Then what is my role in this whole thing?" Cantrill asked.

"Your role? You aren't part of this. You're just a good cop who happens to be extremely intuitive and smart."

"There has to be more to this than that; I mean why am I involved?"

Megan answered for Stewart. "You're a good friend; better than most people ever get or deserve, but you must stay out of this. Mike's fate and mine are tied to Cooper, I mean Andrews. We do not want to see you get hurt, and with Andrews that is a real possibility."

Stewart interrupted at this point in the conversation. "Look, Mike, you're a good friend; just as Megan said, better than I deserve. Your only function is to help me protect Megan. No matter what happens, I must handle Andrews by myself. Do you understand?"

I understand perfectly", Mike Cantrill responded. "As a child, I thought to myself that from the description given by Father Jake, his father must have ridden faster than his guardian angel could fly. That would have accounted for his dad's death; at least in a child's mind. Maybe I'm here as your guardian angel."

Megan grabbed his hand with hers as she said, "Mike! You're not listening. Just help keep an eye out for me, so that Mike can go after Andrews."

"Mike, this isn't a kid's game. This is heart-attack serious stuff. Andrews has killed across two centuries, because of my failure to originally bring him to justice. Just don't go off the deep end on us. I screwed history up once already. Please don't compound my original mistake. I must handle this by myself. If I involve others from the department, I could get them killed. I've thought a great deal about this matter and I've come to the conclusion that this has to be a one-on-one confrontation between Andrews and myself. This isn't about some killer being chased by the Los Angeles Sheriff's Department. This is about two enemies chasing each other across time.

Don't get the wrong impression. I'm not some madman or someone with a grudge to settle. I need to end this thing once and for all. Then, I — I —I loved Megan then and I still love her today. I will gladly shout my love from the rooftops for this woman. It's just that somehow I did something wrong that day in 1886 and I don't want to make any more mistakes. I intend to find and kill Andrews and then ask this lovely lady to marry me and hope that I can make up for the tragedy and lost time. With your assistance, I believe that we can catch Andrews and put an end to this cat and mouse game across time."

"You never said anything about marriage before, Michael", said a shocked Megan.

"Maybe not in this century, but I haven't changed my thoughts or feelings about you in over a hundred years, lady. I thought that the comment you made about not having to wait another hundred years for the right guy meant you made up your mind as well. Didn't it?"

"Yes, it did. I just wasn't quite sure what you were going to do about it."

"Well now you know. Will you do me the honor of being my wife and spending the rest of this life with me, Megan?"

"Absolutely. I'll see to it that the wait was worthwhile.", she replied and kissed him.

"Between the kissing and crying, I don't think that we'll ever be allowed back in here. Why don't we eat up and get to the station, pardner?" said an embarrassed Cantrill. `

CHAPTER FORTY-FOUR

Mike Stewart and Megan Reilly spoke for several minutes in the restaurant's parking lot. She decided to ride to the station with Cantrill. They were worried about him and his attitude over his newfound information. When they were through talking, Megan kissed and hugged Mike.

Inside the unmarked unit, Megan watched Cantrill while he adjusted the mirror and made several last minute checks around his surrounding before he pulled out of the lot. "You're very careful and thorough, Mike.", she said as they drove down Manchester Boulevard.

"Behave yourself! Mike's just ahead of us.", he teased.

"Really, Mike! You must be even more cautious than normal. Andrews is as good at killing as you are at catching crooks. You're probably right; Mike does need you, but not in dealing with Andrews. He really needs you to look after me."

"Don't worry about a thing; we'll get Andrews this time."

"Mike, it's not that simple. I knew Mike from another time. Believe me when I tell you that I never felt so safe with or so afraid of a man in my life. He was awe-inspiring whether astride his horse or standing next to him on foot; you could sense the raw power in the man. I've seen him change from a loving, caring man into a dark and cold, killing machine. On that last day, I saw him kill two men in matter of seconds; all while they were shooting at him from ambush. Even if his horse hadn't have been shot out from under him, I don't know who would have won the struggle. For a few brief seconds, I fought with Andrews myself and he's very frightening. You must do as Mike and I say in this matter. Our very lives and fates are dependent upon it."

Cantrill abruptly slowed the car to a stop after pulling over to the curb. Turning to face Megan, he said, "I'm not some rookie that's going to botch an operation. I've faced the hard cases before and I'll do my share this time as well."

"Damn it, Cantrill! Aren't you listening?", Megan shouted as she hit his shoulder with her clenched fist. "As Marshal Forsythe, I doubt there were any tougher or deadlier men than Mike, but in the end, even he was killed!

Mike told me that you have a beautiful wife and three young daughters. I don't want to see them hurt any more than I want to see you hurt. Give Mike a free hand so that he can do what he must. Just protect me so Mike doesn't have to worry about me. I think that worrying about me prevented him from killing Andrews the last time. Don't you get it? I would rather die, if it means Mike can finally kill this calculating murderer and end our nightmare."

She let go of his jacket and looking down, she spoke in a very hushed and strained voice, "Maybe I should have died with Cooper and not Robert that day." Tears rolled down Megan's cheek. Before Mike could reach out his hand to touch her shoulder, Megan hit it away. Looking straight at Cantrill, she said, "You don't get it, do you?! Someone is going to die between now and Saturday. Maybe me, or Mike, or Andrews. If you get too involved or careless, maybe even you!"

"Mike wants to marry me and I want to marry him. I'm going to do everything he tells me from here on out. Mike, think for a minute! Mike killed me in the last encounter with Andrews and yet I'm willing to listen to him; can't you?"

"All right. Take it easy. I'll do as Mike says. Try not to worry so much. I really believe that this time, everything will work out ok."

"It's got to.", Megan breathed.

The rest of the drive to the station was in silence.

Everyone was waiting and ready to go at the station. Delaney would remain behind and coordinate the activities. T.J. and Baxter would handle the night scope so they had the high ground in a second story motel room. Dougherty had the back door. Two helicopters would be on the ground ready to go at a moment's notice behind some abandoned hangars on Imperial Highway. Cantrill would stick like glue to Megan once they left the station. Stewart would be set up across the street in a liquor store as the scout. There were only two businesses directly across from the location of the interview - a fast food Mexican restaurant and the liquor store. Stewart was counting on a direct approach by Andrews and he figured the liquor store would be Andrews' first choice for vantage points.

Delaney and Stewart wanted everyone set up at least two hours before the interview was to take place. Delaney's plan was simple: spot Andrews and take him into custody before he could hurt anyone. There were a total of ten black and whites scattered and hidden , as well as four more plain units. If

Andrews started to move out of the noose before it could be tightened, then the helicopters would keep him in sight until he could be boxed in.

Stewart's plan was even simpler; he was packing his Beretta nine-millimeter pistol and carrying four extra loaded magazines for it.

Cantrill and Megan would remain behind at the station awaiting the media personnel. Megan and Cantrill walked with Stewart out to his vehicle in the parking lot behind the station. "Megan, please remember what I said to do if…"

"Mike, we already went over this a dozen times." she interrupted. "Cantrill will be protecting me. The waiting is scarier than the doing. You be careful.", she said as she moved closer to kiss him.

"Aren't you afraid of someone seeing us?", Stewart asked her.

"I don't care about them. I care about us.", she responded just before kissing Mike. "Don't miss this time, marshal.", she whispered in his ear after the kiss.

As he opened the door to his unit, Stewart turned to Cantrill and said, "I've entrusted Megan to you Mike. No matter what happens, keep her safe."

"I will. I won't let either of you down. I know we haven't really spoken about the specifics, but I wanted to remind you to be careful about any shootings tonight, Mike."

"What do you mean?"

"If you get into a shooting with Andrews and miss or don't kill him outright, IA (Internal Affairs) will have you on ice until the SRB (shooting review board). It means that you won't be around for the 16th!"

"I hadn't thought of that". He hadn't and the now the realization of missing Andrews hit Mike like cold water in the face. "Thanks, Mike. I'll see you out there", Stewart said.

A slight, but steady rain began to fall on Megan and Cantrill as they watched Stewart drive out of the lot.

CHAPTER FORTY-FIVE

Lyn sat in the private hospital room. It had been a struggle for her to see him since she was not family. Lyn had bullied her way into the intensive care unit and past the nurses. She had first been coy and then pleading with Paul's doctors to let her into his room.

Paul was still asleep. Apparently she missed seeing him when he first came to from surgery. Watching him as he lay on the bed, Lyn thought he looked so much older, tired, and helpless. Paul was receiving oxygen and an IV was hooked to his right arm in addition to the monitors affixed to him.

The remnants of tears had dried along their paths on her face. Lyn sat thinking hundreds of thoughts a minute. She was thinking about Mike, as well as Paul. She still could not believe that Mike would not go to Paul's side during this time. What was wrong? What was he doing? As she sat there in the room, Lyn looked down at the floor at her suitcases. After leaving the airport she had taken a taxi directly to the hospital. She had no idea where to stay in the city. She had only been to New York once and that was to bury Paul's wife.

At least there wouldn't be another funeral on this trip. Lyn had read Paul's chart after talking briefly with his doctor. His condition was critical, but stable. The recovery period would be long and difficult knowing Paul's lifestyle, but his prognosis was good. She used the bathroom in the room to clean up and fix her makeup.

"I can't properly apply any makeup if you're going to keep on squinting, Love." The speaker was a makeup artist that the studio sent along.

"It's that glare from the lights. I didn't realize until now how hot and bright they are.", Megan replied.

"Don't you have any lights for the parking lot?", Stewart was asking the owner of the liquor store at the same time.

"The fixtures are there, but the kids, pimps, and hookers keep breaking the bulbs out. The cops never gave a shit before now.", replied the store owner, without even bothering to look at Stewart.

Stewart shot a glance back at him. An older white male; probably bought into the store and the neighborhood before it went to seed. No sense in getting mad with him, especially since he was right. No one in the criminal justice system could care less about such vandalism today. Stewart went back to looking out the side window.

The interview was less than fifteen minutes away and the radio communication was quiet except for regular radio checks and an occasional comment among the detectives. No one on the perimeter had seen anything unusual enough to report. Megan was through with the last minute briefing and walked over to Cantrill, who was straining to hear anything from his radio earpiece over the noise from the television crew and equipment.

He led her to a chair near the edge of the lighting and knelt along side her. "It's very difficult to clearly hear over all of this noise. I don't want to overreact, but I'm damn sure not going to wait if I can't make something out." Instinctively, Mike placed his hand on the revolver on his hip. "Once you're in front of the camera, you're out of my reach. I need you to listen to your surroundings as much as to the TV reporter."

"I will." answered Megan. "How's Mike?"

"He's fine. So far, there's nothing to report. Everything's going to work out, so smile."

"All right.", replied Megan breaking into a smile.

Cantrill realized how cute and impish Megan looked when she smiled. He understood how Stewart could have been smitten.

The live broadcast was under way and still no one had anything to report. Delaney sent one of the copters up to take a quick look around. He also wanted to have one up in the event any trouble broke out for the ground units. The camera crews created some commotion; enough for drivers to slow down as they passed by. The activity across the street was actually good business for the liquor storeowner. Knox and Baxter were reporting steady car activity in and out of the store's parking lot. Stewart's attention was being divided between the customers in the store and those in the lot.

He missed the driver of the non-descript VW "bug" stolen earlier in the day from a lot at Santa Monica City College. The driver didn't miss seeing Stewart inside the store. Andrews' heart may have skipped a beat upon seeing his enemy from so long ago, but he retained control of himself and the car long enough to leave without bringing any attention to himself. As Andrews pulled back out onto the street, he caught just a glance of Cantrill standing on the edge of the lights.

As he drove away deeper into Hawthorne, he recognized Cantrill as the cop he almost ran into on the stairwell. He figured that the marshal must still be a cop, too if he was keeping such company. Andrews didn't stop until he was deep into downtown L.A. He needed more time to plan his next move. It had been a long time since he felt as the hunted and he was a little more than worried. While not completely unexpected under the circumstances, seeing his old enemy was unnerving to say the least.

Andrews finally stopped the car in the back parking lot of a tavern. The lot was not illuminated by any lights. In the cold night air, he sat and shivered while he lit a Camel cigarette. He took a long drag off the cigarette and sucked the thick smoke deep into his lungs as thoughts raced through Andrews' mind.

Sitting in the cold quiet, Andrews' puffed more slowly on the second cigarette. He checked his shotgun to make sure it was loaded and then he left the car and hurried into the tavern. He sat at the closet barstool to the door and ordered a bourbon; which he gulped. Picking up his refilled shot glass, Andrews sat down at a booth. He had to try and think this chain of events through.

Meanwhile, the interview was over and the television crew was just about ready to depart. Cantrill had long since whisked Megan up to the motel room where Knox and Baxter had been stationed. Stewart was the last one in. Knox was on the phone with Delaney. Delaney called it a night with the instruction that they all meet downtown tomorrow morning at nine.

As Megan, Stewart, and Cantrill walked out to their cars it was Megan who said, "I don't know whether to be glad or cry because he didn't show."

"It was a gamble and it didn't work. I guess there's truth to the saying that you can't change history.", Stewart answered.

"We still have two more days until the 16th. Maybe something will break between now and then. You know more this time than last. I think we still can change things." The speaker was Cantrill.

"Mike, you must be the last boy scout, or something.", Stewart said to Cantrill.

"No. I just don't think that we're whipped, yet, that's all. Do you two want to get something to eat?"

"Thanks", answered Megan, "but I just want to get out of these high heels and into a hot shower."

"Ok, I'll see you two downtown in the morning." Cantrill said as he got into his car and headed for his home in Redondo Beach.

Both Megan and Mike were quiet on the drive back to her apartment. As they walked up to her apartment, Megan asked, "Would you like to stay for a drink?" "Yes." was Mike's only reply.

It was quiet at the Cantrill house. Michael had returned home to find everyone in their beds. He had gone straight to his bedroom. Now in the night, the only light was from the digital alarm clock with its luminous numbers. The only sounds were of Michael's breathing and with his head on her chest, he could hear Karen's heart beating.

"Karen, can I ask you a question?" Michael's voice was a cushioned whisper.

Karen stopped stroking his hair, but didn't move as she said, "Michael Cantrill, you are something else. You wake me up from a sound sleep to make love to me without a word, and now you ask permission to ask a question. What is your question, silly?"

From the dark came the words, "What do you think of reincarnation?"

Karen moved to sit up jarring Mike off her. She reached across the pillows, turned on the lamp, and pulled the sheet up to cover herself. "Is this what's been bothering you on this new case?", she asked.

"I don't have any hard facts, but there appears to be some events that cannot be readily explained. I'm sorting events and statements in my head and I'm confused. You're not Catholic and are not operating under certain religious constraints. I would like to hear your thoughts on this."

Mike watched Karen's big brown eyes as they silently studied him. When she spoke, Mike noticed that her voice was as soft and smooth as the skin on her bare shoulders looked.

"Maybe you should sort things out through your heart as well as your head. I believe as my ancestors did that all creatures and things of this world have a soul or spirit that cannot be destroyed and I believe that God is a loving, just, and merciful father."

"But do you believe in reincarnation?"

"I don't believe in people coming back as cats and dogs, if that's what you mean."

"No, that's not what I meant. I guess I'm talking about the person. Can the dead come back again?"

"I'll tell you something that I have never told anyone before. My grandmother, Mattie Dillinger died four years before I met you. I really loved that sweet woman. She was full of life and she was very intelligent. She was very special to me. Well, anyway, I remember it was the first night that I came home from the hospital with Stephanie. You had fallen asleep on the chair in the den and I was asleep on the bed when I smelled lilacs. The smell is what woke me. When I opened my eyes, I saw Grandma Mattie standing over the baby's bassinet in our room! She turned to look in my direction and she smiled and she was gone! She never said a word. Even after she disappeared, I could smell the lilacs and that's when I remembered that she always wore lilac water.

There's more. I saw Grandma Mattie on the first night that we brought Katie and Heather home. To tell the truth, I was waiting up for her on each of those subsequent times. One second she wasn't there and the next, she was. It happened so fast, if you blinked, you would have missed it. She always appeared after you were asleep and she was always standing over the bassinet as if she were checking on our babies.

I cannot explain it other than I believe that God allowed my grandmother to come and check on each of her great-grandchildren. I believe that she always was seen in our home and not at the hospital, for this is the place where her memory is kept alive. This is the place where she is loved."

"Is love what brings them back?"

"I don't think so, otherwise all the world's loved ones would be seen all the time and this type of incident would be commonplace. I'm not sure how to explain it, but I think that love must be a part of the whole or the crossing wouldn't be possible."

"Why didn't you tell me this before?"

"I didn't know what you'd think of it or even if you would believe me."

"Well, if it's any comfort, I believe. I really believe. Now will you turn out the light and come over here? I think I need a hug."

As Karen snuggled next to Mike she was worried; she could feel the violence and she was sure that her husband was involved. She was almost afraid to speak, but decided to anyway since she was more afraid of not speaking.

"Mike, I think there's going to be trouble over this case that you're working on."

"Karen, we're chasing a wanton killer. He robs people and he kills afterwards just for the sheer pleasure it brings him. I don't think that anyone on the team believes that this will end peacefully. He's been doing this for quite some time. I have the feeling that Stewart and I are being guided or pushed to a conclusion with him; almost as if this were meant to be."

"Is this person the one you were referring to about reincarnation?"

"Well, he's a part of it, but we can talk about it later."

Mike had his head propped up on the headboard with one of the large pillows and Karen had been resting with her head on his chest. Now she turned and sat up looking directly at Mike.

"Will there be a later for us, Michael?" Mike couldn't see in the dark that her eyes were brimming with tears. "You've never done what you did tonight. We always talk and kiss before we make love. Were you in a hurry or are you desperate?" Without waiting for an answer, Karen continued, "I'm frightened for you, Michael and I'm scared for myself and our daughters. I can feel violence."

"Karen, it's..."

"When you talk of destiny, that's how I feel about us.", Karen interrupted. She was wound up and not about to stop. "I've always thought that my flat tire and your passing in the patrol car were the results of divine intervention. We were meant to be together. There are eight million people in this county and I know that God had to take a hand in the matter if we were ever going to meet.

When I think of you, I never dwell on the fact that since we've been married, you've killed five men. I'm saddened only because I know what it has done to such a gentle and kind person. I know that the man I love is wiser, more understanding, and more compassionate than his years. The man I love is a good provider and father to my babies. Michael, I love you for all the little things that you do for and because of us. Like when we found out I was pregnant with Stephanie, you bought me a Volvo station wagon and made me stop driving my Camaro or the fact that since I've known you, you've never gotten to eat one of the cherries that come in drinks or on top of desserts, because you've always given them to me or the girls.

You're quiet, yet strong and dependable. You don't suffer from any male macho stereotypes. I've sent you to the store late at night for girl things and you've never said a word. You just take one of the dogs with you and leave the other one here to guard us girls. I watch you with your mother. You're respectful towards her, but you never let her walk over you with her pushy ways." She paused only long enough to catch her breath. "I know that you will love me and stay with me long after I'm old and wrinkled. A lot of women don't have that kind of commitment or security. I think you're special and your heart is true, just as is my love for you, Michael Cantrill. I would do anything to keep you. Don't get caught up with or do anything that interferes with my plans for us."

Mike reached for and grabbed Karen, pulling her to his chest. "And I love only you, Karen Lynn.", he said kissing her forehead. "I don't know if it was God or not that brought us together, but I thank him every day for sending you to me. Without you, I would have been lost and only partially complete and never known it. Please don't be afraid, my love. I'm sorry that I haven't been as attentive as I should have been. These past weeks seem as if they have dragged by for me and I feel just as uncertain and adrift like those horrible ten months when I was sick. I know I should have confided in you sooner and I'm sorry ..."

Karen interrupted Mike by placing her hand on his mouth as she sat up. "Michael, quit apologizing. There's no ledger listing debits and credits between us. As far as your illness, you never have to mention that again, unless you want to talk about it. It was a terrible time for all of us. The girls think you're magic, because there isn't a bank robber or disease you can't beat.

I know there nothing magical about you. I know your fears and I know mine. I thought I was going to lose you. I still worry about you. That's why I watch your diet and always check on you while you're sleeping. You know, my mother was right about you from the very beginning."

"What did Eve say?"

"She said that she could tell you were an honorable and loving man. She also told me that she saw great strength and hurt in your eyes. When I asked her if you had been hurt or would hurt others, mom only said, 'Both'. I was puzzled, but before I could ask another question, she hugged me and whispered in my ear. She said, 'Marry him quickly, Karen. He's the one you've been waiting for. He will make you happy and he will need you every bit as much as he loves you."

Karen's voice was soft and reassuring as she continued. "Michael, I like you as much as I love you. I will always be here for you. As far as talking goes, you talk to me with your heart and I listen with mine." In the darkened room, Karen searched for Mike's face with her soft hands. Finding his lips, Karen gently kissed Mike before settling back down with her head on his chest.

"I'm a very lucky man. Maybe we're both a little on edge. I think my partner is in more danger than I am. I'm planning on being around for quite some time to come. Why, I'll even wake you up again for some loving very soon, if you like."

"I'd like that just fine.", was all that Karen said.

In the quiet dark, Mike felt Karen's hot breath on his skin as she placed quick, little kisses on his chest and stomach. He also wiped away the tears filling his eyes.

Stewart was lost in his thoughts. Inside the apartment, Megan told Mike to get the drinks while she wiped the rest of the theatrical makeup off her face. She returned to find that Mike had poured her a glass of wine, but he was drinking scotch. Mike turned and looked at her as Megan entered the room. In addition to having scrubbed her face, he saw that she had quickly changed into jeans and a sweatshirt.

Grabbing her wine glass, Megan sat down on the couch next to Mike. He was looking into his glass and he seemed at least a million miles away. She stroked the back of his hair; an act so natural that it gave the impression they had been together for ages.

"It's almost funny how things work out.", Mike said still looking into his glass. "Getting another chance to catch a killer and finding my son helped raise my partner."

"I also got another chance with you.", Megan replied. It was a more a purr than words. Mike continued looking into his glass while swirling the amber liquid; its residue clinging to the sides of the heavy crystal.

"I'm glad. Though no telling what we might have had. You were just so uncompromising.", Mike said as he turned to face her.

"Oh, Michael! I know and I'm sorry." Megan's voice was rising and there was a slight urgency to it.

"There's nothing to be sorry over.", Mike interrupted. His voice held a quiet calm. "We can't undo what's been done. I just wanted to share my life with you then and I still do. The last time, I saw it as you wrote words such as life and wings, but I was the one who lived and flew."

"I was frightened and I still am."

"Then come and stand behind me. I'm strong enough for both of us."

"I believe you are.", Megan replied. She made up her mind.

She set her glass down and put her arms around Mike's waist and squeezed so hard he grunted. Releasing her grip on Mike, Megan moved so that their faces were practically touching.

"I won't wait to find out our fate on Saturday. Stay the night with me, Michael! Stay with me these next two days, please! I won't ask anything of you until the 17th."

"We may not make it till then."

"Then all the more reason to make the most of our time together. We've both been waiting too long." she punctuated her sentence by kissing Mike and unbuttoning his shirt. They made love like newlyweds until just before dawn.

CHAPTER FORTY-SIX

The sun had been up for almost two hours when he first crossed over the small ridge in the North central plains of Texas. As he rode over the top of the ridge, Robert saw a small band of ten Comanche warriors on horseback. He could see that they were all wearing war paint. He had surprised them as well. They spotted him at the same time and started shooting. Robert quickly fired two shots with his revolver and two warriors fell off their ponies with a crashing thud that was lost in the echoing of shots and war whoops.

The plains in late September 1879 were lush and just beginning to show a glint of the colder weather to come. Marshal Forsythe didn't notice as he spurred his horse back over the direction in which he had come. For the past week he had been trailing whiskey peddlers. All that was forgotten as he rode like one of the devilish whirlwinds that cut over the country on a late autumn afternoon.

They had been less than fifty yards apart when Robert had dropped the two braves. Now he and the Indians were separated by more than a hundred. The nine-year old quarter horse mare named Bea was slow building up her speed, but from past experiences Robert knew she could run with the best of them. She'd have to now!

A rifle shot rang out past the right side of his head. Robert turned around in the saddle and emptied his .44 revolver at the pursuing riders. Like the old cavalry man that he was, Robert reloaded on the gallop and holstered his weapon. He turned his attention to out riding his opponents. One hundred and forty-five yards!

His backside was set back firmly onto the saddle and his weight evenly distributed over the mare's back. The balls of his feet were braced on the centerpiece of the stirrups and his hands held the reins firmly. He leaned slightly forward; more to keep a lower target profile. As his head was closer to the horse's head, Robert could clearly hear the loud sounds made as she took in powerful breaths of air. With his legs hugging the horse's side, he could feel each breath and exhale. Two hundred yards! Robert knew that less than two miles up ahead was a small river that possibly held safety in the sparse grove of trees beyond it. He shouted encouragement to the horse. Bea's breathing became more raspy-sounding that Robert knew was from the strain of continued running. The Indians continued to ride directly into the dust kicked up by Robert's horse; screaming and shooting the entire time. Robert continued to strike Bea's flanks with the reins to drive her on at a faster speed. Two hundred and fifty yards!

As Robert caught sight of the line of trees, he was over three hundred and fifty yards in front of his pursuers. He was over four hundred yards ahead when he and Bea hit the edge of the near side of the river. At the horse's speed when she hit a soft spot in the wet sand, she lost her balance sending Robert over her head and off to the right side. Robert heard Bea's right front leg snap while he tumbled over her head.

When Robert regained his footing, he saw the wide-eyed look of total panic and pain on Bea's face. Robert shot her in the face with his pistol and ended her suffering before she could cry out again. Across the flat Texas plains, Robert could see that the Indians had closed the gap to almost three hundred and fifty yards. Robert raced to the saddle and pulled out his Sharps and Winchester rifles, and propped the Winchester against his dead horse. Three hundred yards!

Robert shoved a cigar-sized .45 cartridge into the chamber and fired the first shot from the big Sharps. The second rider from the lead on the right side was shoved backwards and off his pony. Seven Indians and two hundred and fifty yards!

White gunsmoke and hot brass were ejected from the rifle before it could be reloaded. On the second shot, the lead rider and pony skidded onto the hard, dry plains. Two hundred yards!

With his third shot, another Indian was killed and Robert dropped the Sharps and grabbed the Winchester. Working the lever-action, the Winchester barked as smoking empty brass cases were dropping onto Robert's hat and clothing. One hundred yards! Robert took cover behind his dead horse.

Two Comanche rifle shots hit the carcass of the once proud quarter horse raised on the Texas prairie. Two more smashed into Robert's fifty-two dollar saddle. Robert continued to work the rifle's lever. The Indians drove onward. The Winchester was empty. Robert pulled his Colt pistol and started to shout as he stood up to face the oncoming threat. He could feel the water spray from the river on his face as he stepped back.

"Michael! Michael, wake up! You're having a nightmare!", shouted Megan as she leaned over him shaking his shoulders. The water spray on his face had been from her wet hair. Megan had just stepped from the shower when she heard him screaming. Mike opened his eyes and stopped his shouting. Mike grabbed Megan and she noticed he was shaking.

"They're not dreams, are they? They're memories, huh?" Megan said as she kissed his face. Mike only nodded his head yes. She held him as she sat on the bed and gently rocked him while whispering to him that he was safe and all right.

Megan fixed Mike breakfast while he got ready for work. When he came into the kitchen, he saw her still in her robe. "You'll be late for work."

"I'm not going in today or tomorrow. I already called my editor and told him I needed a few days off." she said as she poured and handed him a cup of coffee. "It'll give me time to clean house and get a few groceries in the house. It's been a long time since I've had company around here. Besides," she said with an impish grin, "I've got to get to the store; you used the last of those things that I had in the night stand."

"Well it's been a long time since I was referred to as company. And thanks for the opportunity to use `those things'."

"No, thank you." Megan said as she put her arms around his neck and kissed him.

As they stood in the kitchen, Mike said, "I'm thinking that if you're going to stay home, maybe I should stay and keep an eye on you."

"I'll be perfectly safe. No one's followed you here, except Cantrill. Check in at work and see if there's been any new developments, but you can come home early if you like. I'll be rested.", she said with a wink.

Downtown the task force commander was frustrated, worried, and bordering on hostile. "Why don't you two explain to me again just what last night's game of that reporter bought us."

"Nothing, Lieutenant. And that's just what we had going into this week." It was Cantrill taking the heat on this one.

"Since the `Gundo' shooting, we think that he killed that nurse from Daniel Freeman, but we can't prove it. There's been eighteen killings in the county area and seventy-eight robberies. We haven't even looked at ten-8-51's (stolen autos)."

"For all you guys know the idiot could be riding around on horseback."

"Sir, for all any of us knows, he could be arrested for some other offense or dead. That's just the problem; we don't know a whole lot about this character and his habits."

Even T.J. Knox, Delaney's shadow, spoke in the group's behalf. "Look, L-T, we've been beating the bushes for this guy since the Lawndale killing. We may have turned the heat up enough between us and the TV spot to scare him out of the area or drive him underground for awhile. The news girl's not a whore and that's what he's been after since he came to our attention. Since we haven't had a street whore killed since the nurse killing, I tend to believe that he's locked up, gone, or dead."

"That Rancho PV victim wasn't a whore either, but she's just as dead! And we know that Andrews did that one!" fired back Delaney.

It was Stewart's turn, now. "Tom, I'd like to put my two cents into this. Except for the downtown grocery store 211 and the killing of the street hooker that we believe was the first since his release from the joint, Andrews has been striking in the South Bay area. Since the El Segundo incident, we've been in relatively close contact with the local PDs. Andrews' picture is plastered throughout the South Bay and we haven't had him turn up either dead or in custody. Therefore, I think he's hiding, or he's having good luck or us bad.

So far, he's struck within the South Bay region and we've been looking at all their homicides and robberies. But we haven't been checking all their ten-8-51s or 4-5-9s (burglaries). Andrews could be jogging in place so to speak and we aren't aware of him."

Delaney was now sitting down at his desk with a fresh cup of coffee. "Ok, I'm sorry for blowing up at you guys. We've been stymied and I was just blowing off steam for having the division commander take a piece of my hide last night. Ok, I'm open for suggestions. And before we begin on that subject, where is that reporter?"

"She's at her apartment. She's taking a four day weekend. I think she'll be ok. Without Andrews making news for her, she has nothing to do either.", said Stewart. "I suggest we continue to turn up the heat in the South Bay area a little longer. If he's still out there, he has to surface. We just need to spread a little money around. The types of people and areas that he hangs around are very susceptible to a little flash money." he added.

"All right then men, let's get down to business and hammer out a program for our friend."

CHAPTER FORTY-SEVEN

Megan was feeling pretty good about everything as she pushed the grocery cart down the aisle. In fact, she felt like a new bride, especially when she stopped at the pharmacy section. When she was waited on by the regular clerk, Megan actually blushed.

"Megan, is there anything you want to tell me?", as she rang up the sale of the dozen condoms, instead of the usual three-pack.

"I can't talk right now, Carrie. I'll tell you everything later. Bye", Megan replied blushing. It had been a long time since she blushed when purchasing contraceptives.

Everything was going along fine as she left the grocery store, but as she left the cleaners, her troubles began anew. Andrews was driving along the beach area when he spotted a couple of motorcycle officers working radar on the main drag, so he pulled onto a secondary artery. He almost missed her as he drove by, but she had parked her car on the street instead of the parking lot and she had to walk back to it and into his line of vision.

Andrews swung around the corner and back through an alley. He saw her driving through the intersection in her black Honda Prelude as he reentered the street. The only good luck that Megan had was that the light at the intersection turned red behind her causing Andrews to be left back. He noticed that she pulled off onto a residential street up ahead, but he was unable to find her once he made it through the intersection. After spending over fifteen minutes circling the main traffic arteries without seeing her car, he felt confident that she lived within the residential section bordered by those arteries.

At the same time, Stewart and Cantrill were having lunch at Marie Calendar's as they reviewed their game plan. "I don't care what Delaney has for a plan of action. I really feel that no matter what we do, Andrews won't surface again until Saturday.", said Stewart.

"I'm not going to debate it with you, Mike, but I think we must still keep our guard up", replied Cantrill.

"I'm all for that; we'll probably both do that by our nature. I was just thinking of kicking back today and tomorrow with Megan; resting up so to speak for Saturday's fight."

"If you want to leave early, I'll cover for you with Delaney, but what about Lyn?"

"Lyn and I had an argument the other night. My old Army buddy, the doctor in New York, had a heart attack. I wanted to go and see him, but that would mean that I would miss the 16th. Anyway, Lyn left to see him. I don't know if she's coming back."

"I'm sorry, Mike." Is there's anything else that I can do".

"No, you've already done more than anyone could expect and more than I can repay.", interrupted Stewart. "I think I will take you up on that offer of leaving early a little later; after we're through checking a couple of things. But first, what kind of pie are we having for dessert?" Cantrill couldn't help but notice Stewart's eyes were ablaze.

They spent the rest of their time together checking different places, mostly bars. Stewart stopped and talked with a couple of street hookers that he had previously arrested. They showed everyone Andrews' picture. No one had seen him. Stewart slipped some money to two of the barmaids that he knew were taking bets in the bars. He told them that he would overlook their betting action if they would just call him if they saw Andrews. To the street hookers, he offered them his business cards in case they were picked up. While everyone assured them that they would call in the event they saw Andrews, they both knew they were playing mighty long odds.

Andrews also spent the afternoon driving around burning up gas. He was driving through the residential area that he had seen Megan drive into. While he didn't linger at any one place for fear of a resident calling the police for a suspicious person, he was cruising in a rather systematic basis. Fortunately, Megan's apartment complex had an enclosed garage and living area that was not readily visible from the street. Unfortunately, she was about to leave the complex and go back to the store. As she was leaving her apartment, Megan ran into her neighbor, Sandie Jeffers.

Sandie and her husband Tom were a few years older than Megan and rented the apartment next to Megan's. Sandie and Megan hit it off right away. Sandie would regularly invite Megan over for dinner during the month. She and Tom would also include her for holiday gatherings. The girls gossiped like sisters instead of neighbors.

"Megan, hi."

"Hi, Sandie."

"It's seldom that I ever see you out in the daytime with your schedule. What have you been up to lately?"

"Nothing much. I'm taking the rest of the week off on vacation. I already went to the market once today, but a recipe I'm making for dinner calls for a can of chicken broth and I don't have any. I seldom cook for myself, anymore", she explained.

"There's no need for you to run to the store again. I have a can of soup that I can part with. This wouldn't have anything to do with that good-looking stranger I saw leave your apartment this morning, would it?" she asked as she led Megan into her apartment.

"I wouldn't call him a stranger", Megan replied with a devilish grin.

"Megan, get in here and tell me all about it."

Over diet cokes, the girls talked while Andrews drove past their complex.

When Cantrill dropped Stewart at his vehicle, it was late in the afternoon. Stewart told Cantrill that he would be in the office at the regular time in the morning. On the way to Megan's, Mike stopped and purchased roses from one of the young Mexican boys hawking them alongside the major intersections. At the apartment complex, Mike parked in the garage area and walked up the stairs. He did notice the woman looking at him through the opened blinds of the apartment next to Megan's. He smiled a slightly nervous smile as he waited for Megan to open the door.

Mike noticed that Megan looked out the window before opening the door and he was grateful that she remembered his advice, even if it meant being under Sandie's scrutiny a little longer. Megan hugged and kissed him as he stood in the doorway. Mike gave her the flowers when they came up for air and he closed the door behind him.

"The flowers are a nice touch. It's been a long time since a man's brought me any. Well, can you smell dinner?" she said after taking and smelling the bouquet.

"I'm not thinking about dinner right now", Mike replied as he stared at her.

"Silly, first dinner, then dessert", Megan laughed.

"Then let's eat." Mike said as he grabbed her around the waist and walked into the kitchen.

The digital alarm clock read 2:18 AM when Megan turned over in bed. Mike wasn't there and she sat up and listened. She and Mike had gone to bed immediately after dinner. They both fell asleep after making love and talking. Megan put on her robe as she got out of bed and walked into the living room where the lights were on. She found Mike sitting on the couch. Next to him, she saw his bulletproof vest and pistol. He was running his hands through his hair as his head was bent down.

"Mike, were you having nightmares, again?" she asked.

Looking up at her, Mike smiled and said, "No, angel. I woke up and couldn't get back to sleep. That's all. Rather than wake you, I thought I'd come out here and think."

Sitting down next to him, Megan stroked his hair momentarily before saying, "I love you."

"God, I love hearing those words. I love you too, lady."

"Hold me. Just hold me and don't say anything." Megan pleaded.

He did and they stayed there for hours.

CHAPTER FORTY-EIGHT

The intermittent rains that had been falling throughout the Los Angeles area had stopped on the morning of the 15th. The sun was out, things were beginning to look much brighter than they had been, and Mike Stewart was feeling almost confident as he drove to work. He decided to stop for coffee at a 7-11 before hitting the freeway. Megan didn't make breakfast for him this morning. She did make love to him on the couch before he carried her back to bed where he covered her up and left her a note.

As Stewart walked into the store, he heard a voice call out, "Mike, get me a cup, too." It was Cantrill shouting from his car as he pulled into the lot. Stewart started walking to meet Cantrill as he left his car.

"Your wife's going to get jealous if you don't stop following me, Michael."

Grinning, Cantrill replied, "What can I say? I find you habit-forming, honey."

Inside the store, Stewart poured the coffee and said, "Seriously, Mike! Don't you think you're carrying this surveillance thing to an extreme?"

"No. I try not to waste my time foolishly. I'd rather be safe than sorry. It's no big deal. We only have one more day left to worry about."

They continued the discussion as they stood outside the store on the walkway drinking their coffee. "I can't help but think that since we haven't heard from him for so many days, just maybe something has happened to him." said Stewart. "Then my mind tells me that history cannot be changed and he's going to pop up in the next forty hours."

"We're together on this, no matter what happens. It's not as if you're running away or avoiding him. You haven't found him and he hasn't found you or Megan. I hope the 16th passes without incident. I'll feel better because if it passes without incident, you'll settle down and maybe we can catch him without involving Megan."

"I hope you're right. Until I figure out what to do next, why don't we get to work?"

Andrews was also up and moving around. He bought coffee at one of the numerous non-descript places that line any boardwalk along the ocean. Right now, he was in Santa Monica. He had spent the night in his car parked along the ocean front north of the city limits. Lighting his third cigarette, Andrews was trying to formulate a search plan for Megan. He decided that today was the day he would find her and that damned marshal and settle all accounts!

When Megan woke up she found the note folded on her nightstand. Sitting up in bed she read it, *"Good morning, angel. Please stay in the house this morning. I'll call you later. I'm planning on leaving before lunch so that we can have the rest of the day together. What do you think? Maybe dinner out and a quick night on the town. Say, do you have any dessert left? Love, Mike."* Megan smiled, folded the note back and placed it on the nightstand, and proceeded into the shower.

It was just before noon in New York and Lyn had just opened the door to Paul's room. She had returned from the nurses' lounge and locker room where she had taken a shower and changed her clothes. She was surprised to find him awake.

"I already talked to the duty nurse. She told me that you arrived by yourself. I'm glad that Mike didn't come."

Lyn thought Paul sounded weak and tired. Walking completely into the room before talking, Lyn sounded upset and angry.

"I just don't understand either of you! How could you be grateful that your friend did not come to see you at this time? Can someone explain to me what's going on here?"

"It's not what you think, Lyn. Come and sit here on the bed and I'll try and explain it."

Megan was sitting at the kitchen table with the phone waiting for Mike's call. Always practical sometimes to the exclusion of her own emotions, she was writing and sorting through several papers. Before her were the sparse paper documents verifying her existence. She had written and placed a letter with instructions to Sandie in case she and Mike didn't make it through tomorrow in a small envelope. In a larger manila envelope, Megan had placed her rent agreement and receipts, the pink slip and keys for her 1987 Prelude, her savings account passbook, and a short letter to her mother explaining about the new love in her life. She figured that her father would know what to do with the rest of the documents and could settle her meager estate.

She wasn't expecting anyone, so the knock on the door of her apartment startled Megan. She waited for half a second at the table just in case it was Mike and he would call out to her. Thoughts raced by at lightening speed as she realized she had not given Mike a key to the apartment. Except for her husbands, she had never allowed any man to stay over or live in, necessitating a key. As the seconds ticked by in silence, she walked very quietly to the window and was relieved to see Sandie. She opened the door almost gratefully. She had been concerned on how to approach Sandie and she didn't want to just leave the envelopes on the table to be picked up by the police.

"Good morning, Megan.", Sandie said as she entered the apartment.

"Hi, Sandie. I was thinking about calling you or stopping by this morning."

"I was going out to the beauty salon and then to the grocery store. I thought that I'd stop by and ask if you wanted me to pick up anything that you might need for the weekend?"

"I don't need anything from the store, but I did want to ask a favor of you. I want you to keep these papers for me over the weekend.", she said as she walked over to the table and handed her the manila envelope and the letter size envelope with Sandie's name on it.

"Megan, what is it? Are you in trouble? I knew something was up with that guy. He's married isn't he?"

"Mike's not the problem', she interrupted.

"I knew something was different about him", Sandie continued. "He's cute, but there's something dangerous about him. You can see it in his eyes."

"Sandie, Mike's a cop. He and I are going out tonight and there's just some guy that's been causing him and I trouble; serious trouble. I cannot explain it any better to you. I need you to promise me that you'll see that my parents get that big envelope in case anything happens to me." Tears were beginning to well up in Megan's eyes as she spoke.

"I don't like this at all, Megan. I don't think that I should ..."

"I'm a big girl, Sandie." Megan interrupted. "I'm not asking your permission to date Mike. I am asking a good friend to hold onto some important papers for me. It's only temporary, but if something were to happen, I don't want to burden my folks with having to sort through my things. So will you or won't you do as I ask?"

"I'll do it for you only because you're asking me, but I don't like this at all, Megan. And I don't think that I like your new friend, if he's causing so much trouble in your life."

Megan started to cry, but only out of relief. "Mike has asked me to marry him and I have accepted, Sandie. We just need to clear up a few things and he has this one guy to take care of before we can proceed. I think that everything will be all right by the end of this weekend."

"Men can be such scum. There are not that many worth our tears. They're certainly good for bringing us trouble, though" she said hugging Megan.

"You aren't telling me anything new, Sandie. Me, trouble, and men go back a long, *long* time." Megan said as she started laughing through the tears at her own joke.

Chapter Forty-nine

Mike Stewart pulled into the driveway at his house. He wanted to stop by for a change of clothes and to check for any phone messages. So far, he had not heard from Lyn or anything more on Paul's condition. He and Cantrill had talked Delaney into giving them the rest of the day off for an early weekend. They had both put in more than enough time.

As he got out of the car, his neighbor came out of her house and called out to him. "Mike, where have you and Lyn been hiding yourselves?"

"I've been tied up on a big case lately, Mrs. Newland. Lyn's visiting a sick friend in New York. Is something wrong?"

"I don't think so. It's just that Dennis and I haven't seen you two around. I think there was a car in your driveway last night. I heard a car's engine and then I thought I heard a car door shut. It drove off before we got a look at it or the driver. Dennis called the police and they came out and took a look around, but didn't find anything out of the ordinary. One of the officers left me a card in case there was something wrong."

Mike didn't say anything as he ran to the back door and entered the house. He looked throughout the house, but didn't find anything amiss. The doors were still locked and it didn't look as if anything had been disturbed since he was last in it. The answering machine was still on, but there were no messages. He walked back over to Mrs. Newland's house. He thanked her for the information and asked if she remembered the time. She thought it was between 11 and 12 midnight. She handed Mike the business card of the Manhattan Beach officer in case he thought they could shed more light on the incident. Mike thanked her and went back to his house.

Mike called Megan from his house. He hurried over to her apartment where she had made lunch for them. Mike tried to keep the conversation upbeat and Megan deliberately avoided any mention of what was on the agenda for tomorrow. They ate lunch while looking over the Times in preparation for their night out.

Later, as they were dressing, Megan made a point to call and ask Sandie for a pair of earrings. Megan didn't need them, but she wanted to introduce her to Mike. Megan disliked the thought of Sandie harboring any ill will towards him. Their meeting was cordial and almost pleasant. Megan had told Mike that she wanted him to make a good impression on her friend. She thought he had, but sensed that Sandie was holding back just slightly. As Mike held the car door open for her as they left the apartment she said, "I don't want to be out too late. Can you bring me home early enough so that I can spend some quiet time with you to myself?"

"My sentiments exactly, my love."

At about the same time, the phone was ringing at Stewart's house. Before the phone answering machine could pick it up on the sixth ring, the phone stopped ringing. Lynette placed the phone receiver back in its cradle. She was at Paul's apartment. He had given her the key after they were through talking. Lyn thought he was delirious at first. She still found it hard to believe. She wanted to talk to Mike, but he wasn't home.

Lyn poured herself a glass of wine; a large glass of wine. Sitting on the couch, she was trying to sort through the flood of thoughts that kept her wide-awake; despite her lack of sleep. Incredible as the story was that Paul told her about Mike, she was shocked further when he told her how he felt towards her; how much her coming to see him meant. Paul had said that he had always found her to be sensual and sexy as well as intelligent. He also felt that he cared deeply for her; the same type of caring that she must have had for him to travel all this way. Lyn really wanted to talk to Mike. Where was he? Who was he?!

It was just before 8 o'clock that same evening when the phone rang at the Cantrill household. Karen was in the study making a pastel drawing of the mountains outside Demming, New Mexico captured on a photograph that Mike had taken years before. She and Mike had traveled throughout the Southwest on their honeymoon. A native Californian, the Southwest was an area that Karen had always wanted to see. Mike indulged her and she took very good care of him in return.

Karen was paying more attention to Mike, who was also in the study reading the newspaper. Heather, bathed and in her nightgown, had climbed into her father's lap and he was reading out loud to her from the business section of the Times. Karen was thinking back to that afternoon. Mike had actually come home early from work, for a change. He parked his unit on the street as Heather had been drawing with chalk on the driveway, under the watchful gaze of the two wolf dogs and Karen.

Mike exited the car and waited momentarily for Heather to say something to him. When she didn't, he called out, "Hey, Ruffle Britches!" It was Mike's nickname for her because of the style of lace-trimmed underpants worn and exposed by the short little dresses that Karen placed on her baby. "You know the next time it rains, you'll lose your pretty drawings."

"Yeth, daddy." was Heather's reply without looking up from her artwork.

Before Karen could walk out of the house to greet Mike, Katie had run past her with a book in her hand. Karen saw that she ran straight for her father with tears in her eyes. Katie explained that she didn't understand her math homework; it was the metric system, and there was going to be quiz on Monday.

Karen watched as Mike took a piece of chalk from Heather and drew a graduating scale on the driveway. She saw that he knelt on his hands and knees on the driveway softly explaining as he drew, while Heather took advantage of the situation and sat on Mike's back. Karen smiled as she listened and in three minutes, Mike had explained the metric system using the scale. Then Mike took Katie's book and asked her a question. She didn't get the first one, but after Mike explained how the scale applied, Katie got the answer for the next problem and the third. She was elated, she hugged her father, and came running back into the house. Mike took off his sports coat and continued drawing with chalk on the driveway with Heather as easily as he could use the blued steel revolver on his belt. Karen thought to herself the entire time walking out to greet Mike, why would such a gentle, educated man do what he did for a living.

Dinner that night had been fun; more fun than it had in weeks. Everyone was there as Stephanie postponed her Friday night date to Saturday. Karen had asked her to since Mike had come home early she thought they could treat it as a special occasion. All seemed in a good mood and the conversation was animated. After dinner, Karen pulled her chair next to Mike's as their girls cleared away the plates. They held hands and Karen rested her head on Mike's shoulder.

She was feeling good and started thinking that maybe she had been wrong about her feelings last night. Maybe, everything would work out ok. When Mike asked what was for dessert, Stephanie and Katie threw oranges at him from the kitchen. Karen barely ducked in time. Mike said he was going to buy some sugar stock as that would be as close as Karen was going to let him come to refined sugar in his diet.

As she watched him now, Karen couldn't believe how much she loved him and how much she was attracted to him. She was anxiously awaiting the girls' bedtimes. That's when Stephanie came in and announced the phone was for Mike.

"You won't be on the phone too long will you daddy? I'm expecting ..."

"Some boy to call", he finished the sentence for her. "Don't worry, Princess. I will not be responsible for your social demise at the tender age of 17."

"Good. Then I won't have to plan on being an old maid and living with you and mom for the rest of our lives", Stephanie fired back as she smiled and kissed the top of his head before she picked up Heather off his lap and danced with her down the hall towards the kitchen.

"The spitting image of her mom. She's going to melt some unsuspecting boy's heart some day", he thought to himself as he walked down the hallway and reached for the phone.

"Hello."

"Mike, it's TJ. I've been trying to get through to Stewart, but all I get is his answering machine. Do you know where he is?"

"He was planning on having dinner out tonight. What's up, TJ."

"One of his street hookers was trying to get a message to him. It was Cindy or Sheila or something".

"Never mind the name. What was the message?"

"Quote. Check out the green Buick sedan cruising Sepulveda and Manchester at 7:15. Unquote. Is this related to our case or is this strictly a vice thing? She was calling in on Stewart's vice number, but the night detectives forwarded it to me."

"I'm not sure, yet." Mike lied. He knew that Big Cindy was one of the street hookers that Stewart had stopped and given his business card to along with a warning about the psycho that was prowling the streets. "When did the call come in?"

"Vice forwarded the call to me at 1932 hours tonight."

"I'll continue trying to get in touch with Mike and relay the message. Thanks, TJ."

Mike hung up and immediately dialed Megan's home phone number. From the location given, Mike knew that Andrews had been right on top of Megan's apartment complex. As it rang for the fifth time, Mike whispered, "Pick up the phone, dammit!"

"Hello." It was Megan.

"Megan, it's Mike Cantrill. Is Mike there?" Megan was surprised that Cantrill had actually called her apartment looking for Mike, but she quickly handed the phone to Stewart. "Mike, I don't care if I'm interrupting anything or not. Big Cindy phoned in and said Andrews was seen in the vicinity of Sepulveda and Manchester less than an hour ago. Her exact word was cruising."

"Holy shit! Megan and I were out at dinner. We came in that way, but we just now came in."

"Were you in your unit?"

"Yes, but ..."

"Did you park in Megan's garage area?"

"Yes".

"Sit tight! I'm leaving here enroute to your location in five minutes. Bye."

"Steph, who was on the phone for dad?" asked Karen, walking into the kitchen where she saw that all the girls were making popcorn in the microwave.

"It was dad's work."

"Water or juice, but no sodas, ladies." Karen instinctively replied as she walked out of the kitchen and down the hallway towards the master bedroom.

"Mike, who was that ...", Karen asked as she walked into their bedroom. She stopped in her tracks when she saw that Mike was putting extra bullets into his coat pocket.

"I've got to go out for a while, honey. That was Sgt. Knox on the phone. The suspect on our case was seen not far from here. I'm enroute to pick up Stewart. I don't think that I'll be too long."

She continued to stand there as Mike sat on the bed and changed his shoes. As he stood up putting on his pistol, she blurted out with, "You didn't forget that your mother is planning on coming over for Sunday dinner?"

He walked over and grabbed her shoulders and said, "No, I didn't forget about mom. Karen, I know you're worried about me, but don't. I'm ok. My partner needs my help, tonight."

Karen had hung her head, but raised it and looked directly at Mike. "I feel like such an idiot. I want to ask you questions or fuss at you for your work schedule, but I'm trying hard to be supportive. I want to scream, but instead I ask about Sunday dinner. I didn't want or know how to tell you that I sense something isn't right. ".

"It's ok, angel." Mike said as he hugged her.

"Mike, I have a bad feeling about tonight. Please be careful!"

"I know you're worried. I worry about me some of the time, too. I know that you wanted to be assured that I'll be around on Sunday. I think you handle everything between us very well and you've done a great job raising our girls."

Karen had placed her head on his shoulder and Mike stroked her hair as he leaned towards her ear and whispered, "Just remember when you get really nervous or worried, that I'll always come home to you Karen; just for you. Always."

Karen picked her head up and looked directly into his eyes. Neither spoke another word. Mike kissed her and Karen kissed him back. She kissed him as if she was trying to share the flame and fire that stirred from her soul.

CHAPTER FIFTY

As Mike put the phone down, he told Megan, "Cantrill's on his way over here. You and I need to change clothes fast. Andrews was seen cruising near here less than an hour ago."

"I don't understand. What do you guys mean 'cruising'?"

"I'm not sure, either. One of the street hookers I know called it in. Were you followed home or close to home, recently?"

"No. I didn't go out, except the one time for the groceries and the cleaners. I didn't see anyone behind me and I haven't moved the car from the garage since", Megan replied as she followed Mike into the bedroom.

As they changed clothes, Mike told Megan that Cantrill was still sitting on her apartment each morning. He also told her about his neighbors hearing a car in his driveway the other night. This news sent a shiver down Megan's spine as she said, "Mike, I'm really frightened."

"I'm very concerned too, but I want to check with Cantrill when he shows up. It may very well be that he was checking my house before going home."

The knock on the door was clear and sharp and accompanied by Cantrill's voice. They quickly let him in.

"What's the story, Mike?" the speaker was Stewart.

Cantrill repeated Big Cindy's message. "She could only be talking about Andrews. This is too close for comfort. Could you two have been followed?"

"We don't think so, at least not tonight. Megan was out at the store yesterday, but she didn't see Andrews or anyone else. That reminds me. Did you stop and check out my house the other night around midnight?"

"Yeah, that was me. I've been trying to cover all the bases just in case. Come on! Let's get going. We'll take my unit."

Once outside, they began looking for Big Cindy. It didn't take long as she always hung out near the main roads surrounding LAX. They found her and one of her friends smoking near La Tijera, just off Sepulveda. Her friend, LaWanda, started walking off once she saw the unmarked unit.

"Come on back girl! It's just the sheriffs; not the pole-leases." Cindy said as she walked over to Stewart who was sitting on the front passenger side.

"I see you gots my call, Mr. Stewart." Looking at Megan in the back seat she said, "Girl, what's they got you for? You bees looking too tiny to cause any trouble."

"She's too tiny to squeeze a pimple!", announced LaWanda as she joined Cindy. Megan felt her ears getting hot while the two street hookers laughed. As Big Cindy's pendulous breasts and enormous middle shook, it was easy to see that no other nickname would have sufficed.

"Cindy, darling. Tell me some more about this dude that you called me over."   "Mr. Stewart you told me to call ifen I was to see him and eyes seen him and eyes called you. What's that worth to you sheriffs?"

"Cindy, I already gave you a `get out of jail card'. Don't hold me up for anymore. You see my partner over here", pointing towards Cantrill, "works Robbery."

Leaning and looking into the car Cindy said to Cantrill, "Honey, you better bees carrying a gun. You don't look so tough. Hell, I seen scarier paper boys!"

"Girlfriend!" LaWanda squealed and slapped Cindy's back and both the girls started laughing again. This time, Cantrill and Stewart also started to smile and laugh.

Stewart handed Cindy two twenty-dollar bills that she took and placed in her purse. "All I seen was the white guy in the picture you showed me." Cindy said. Collecting her thoughts and looking serious, Cindy leaned into the car even further before continuing her story. "Eyes waiting to cross Manchester and eyes seen him driving by real slow like. Eyes seen him looking every which way, you know? Just like some cop on a stakeout."

"When was that Cindy?" Cantrill asked.

"7:15 just like I called it in. Eyes seen the time on the sign for the time and temp, that's how I know. And I called yore number on the card from the pay phone at the gas station."

"Have you seen him since then?" Megan asked.

"Not really, child. You sees LaWanda and mees been busy with a couple of high school kids riding around in a limo. We's just got left off a couple of minutes ago ourselves."

"Cindy, I thought you knew better than to go after that `too young to know better' stuff?", interrupted Stewart.

"Yeah, right. Don't you know that wees in a recession? Besides, what's that in the back of yore car, Mr. Sheriff?"

"I'm serious, Cindy. Maybe you two should call it quits for tonight."

"You white boys shore do want that bad ass. Wha'd he do?"

"That guy we're looking for is nothing but trouble with a capital T. Besides, it's going to rain again," replied Stewart.

"Cindy, can you tell us anything else about the car other than a green Buick?" asked Cantrill.

"Nope, `cepting that there's a big long crack on the windshield. That's all eyes seen."

"Ok ladies. Thanks for your help", said Stewart as he motioned for Cantrill to drive away.

"What do you suppose he's looking for Mike?" asked Cantrill as he pulled back onto Sepulveda Boulevard.

"I'm not sure. Maybe he was just looking for a hooker."

"Then why didn't he pick up Big Cindy?" interrupted Megan.

"I don't think she's his type. While some of his victims have been black, they were all tall and leggy." replied Stewart.

"Cindy just looks like too much woman and too much trouble for him." interjected Cantrill.

"All you wimps say that", fired back Stewart, mimicking Big Cindy.

Even Megan managed a smile as she said, "Can you two stop acting like little boys long enough to figure out what's we're going to do next?"

"I guess we should just start driving along the same streets and see what develops. What do you think, Mike?" responded Cantrill.

"Yeah. Let's check out all the gas stations and fast foods stops along the main arteries until we come up with a better plan." said Stewart.

"You think he's looking for us. That's why he's out driving around so close to my apartment," said a nervous Megan.

"I think if he knew where you were, he'd kick in doors to get to you. I honestly don't know what he's up to, but it's possible that he's just cruising for a hooker or maybe to rob another liquor store." replied her Mike.

Megan sat back on the seat trying to figure out if he was lying so she wouldn't worry.

"Father Chris, the phone is for you." It was Mrs. Kollar, the rectory's housekeeper.

"Thanks, Marie. I'll take it in the study."

Walking into the room and picking up the phone receiver, Chris Stewart answered, "This is Father Chris."

"Chris, it's me, Lynette." Before Chris could say anything else, Lyn broke down and started crying. She cried, she rambled on about Mike and then Paul, and she continued crying. Chris stood alone in the rectory's study. His heart was pounding in time with Lynette's sobs. His worse fears had become reality.

Taking several deep breaths while Lyn cried, he finally sat down in one of the larger chairs; one with an ottoman. Chris had the feeling that this would be a long conversation and maybe, a long night.

CHAPTER FIFTY-ONE

Surprisingly, the time did not seem to drag by as they drove through the night scene. As they checked the main arteries and secondary streets, residential areas, and the convenience stores they did not see any sign of Andrews. Outside an all-night doughnut store, both Mikes talked and drank coffee while Megan used the bathroom.

"It's 11:45 Mike and we haven't even seen a green Buick. Just in case this guy is looking for you two, why don't you both go to your house and spend the weekend there?" asked Cantrill.

"I'm not sure if and when Lyn could show up.", said Stewart, almost shouting above the regular traffic noise on a Friday night in the Los Angeles. "Besides, I don't think that I want to chance having Mrs. Newland see me bring another woman home after I told her that Lyn was out of town."

Looking about before he spoke again, Cantrill could smell the ocean on the wind that also carried the scent of more rain. Speaking in more hushed tones, Cantrill asked, "Speaking of Lyn, what are you going to do about the two of you."

Stewart looked as if he had just taken a punch to his solar plexus. "I'm not sure. I guess that I'll have to call her in New York. I'm just going to wait and see how this thing ends between today and tomorrow. Straightening up and stretching, Stewart continued, "I have no idea how I'm going to tell her. She'll never understand. Hell, I don't understand!"

By this time, Megan exited the shop and started walking to rejoin them. She only watched as they finished their coffee.

Cantrill asked, "Are any of our activities mirroring the activities of the night before the last time this happened?"

"No. Megan and I were at her house and I'm not sure what Cooper and his men were up to the night before. This time we have you and Andrews is by himself."

"Last time it happened shortly after sunrise. It's getting late. Why don't we go home, Michael?" said Megan.

"Why don't you both stay at my house tonight?" offered Cantrill.

"Thanks, Mike, but I'd rather spend the night with Mike at my place. Why don't we just plan on meeting first thing in the morning and seeing what develops then?" she replied.

"Lyn, if you're asking if this even possible; I used to think that I had the answers, but I don't think so anymore. I can tell you that I know that Michael Stewart is real. I was seven when he was born. I changed many of his dirty diapers and I blessed him before he shipped out for Vietnam. Mike's real. You and Paul are real. I can't say the same for his story. I think that Mike's been under too much stress, lately."

"But Paul says the same thing as Mike. This would account for the way Mike's been acting. I had been thinking to myself, lately, that he just hasn't been himself. Maybe, he never was who we thought."

"Lyn, you're not thinking clearly. Look, you're tired and distraught. I think that ..."

"I think I'm making perfect sense", Lynette interrupted. "

"No you're not!" Chris practically shouted across the fiber optics. "There's no such thing as reincarnation. I don't believe in it and the Church does not believe it and you shouldn't be talking of such matters, Lynette!"

"Then just what am I suppose to be talking about?!" Lyn shouted back. I'm told that my husband is acting as if he's the reincarnation of a dead marshal. A psychiatrist is telling me that he believes that Mike is not really the Mike that we thought he was. I'm being told that there is another woman in this whole thing and that Mike and the woman could be killed in the next two days if they can't find and kill a madman that's eluded them for over a century! If they live, Paul thinks that they'll pick up with their lives where they left off a century ago. Tell me Chris, just what am I suppose to think, to say, and to do about this? I really want to know!"

There was only silence from the other end as Father Chris had no idea what to think or say.

CHAPTER FIFTY-TWO

It was midnight and Karen was peering out the living room window from behind the heavy drapes. The neighborhood street was quiet, the girls were asleep in their beds, and the animals brought in as Karen had smelled the rain in the air. She had tried watching television, but settled on reading a book after the girls went to bed. She was waiting for Mike. She had not changed clothes as she had put off taking her shower. She was concerned about Mike and she just couldn't get comfortable. As she looked out the window, she was hoping to see Mike's car turning onto their street. But there was nothing; nothing but the dark and the quiet.

The upper levels of the hospital were also quiet at that time of the morning. It was three AM and snow flurries were falling in New York. Lyn remembered the bitter cold wind just as she was about to exit the cab. Living in California did not prepare her or her wardrobe for the eastern winters. She had gone back to the hospital in answer to Paul's phone call. Lyn had hung the phone up after talking with Chris for almost two hours.

She was just finishing the bottle of wine when Paul called. The muscat canelli was just sweet enough and she knew that she was feeling too good considering the circumstances; she had to be drunk. Paul told her that it was the 16th and he thought they should be together for any incoming calls from Los Angeles.

Lyn had been there since midnight. She had tried to silence Paul several times, but he kept talking to her in a voice just above a whisper. He talked of the first time that he met Mike. He talked about the war. He talked of

Rebecca. He talked of Mike's dreams and their implications. Paul spoke of his hopes and dreams. Paul talked, he laughed, and he cried.

So did Lyn. She didn't know if she was crying for Paul, Mike, or herself. She just held onto Paul and cried. Paul quietly held onto Lynette. It was quiet in the upper floors of the hospital at that time of the night. It seemed as if Lyn and Paul were all alone. Snow was falling outside, but the room was warm and comforting. Lyn looked at Paul's hand that she was holding. She placed a quick kiss on it and then without thinking about it, she kissed him. Paul smiled weakly and said that he loved her. Lyn only smiled and held Paul to her chest.

Twenty-eight hundred miles to the west, a life and death struggle was unfolding.

A light rain had begun to fall on Los Angeles again as Cantrill pulled the unmarked sheriff's unit into the garage area of Megan's complex.

"Are you sure you'll be ok? You know that you're both welcome at my place. I'm sure Karen won't mind and the girls will think that it's an early Christmas what with all the noise and excitement at night. Please reconsider for your safety."

"Thanks buddy, but I think we should stay here. We're probably safe until the morning. Besides, if this is the last day, she and I have a great deal to discuss. The last time, we left too much unsaid."

Megan squeezed Cantrill's hand as she exited the car and said, "Thank you, Michael. When you come in the morning, bring coffee and I won't have to get up so early to fix some for Mike."

"You can count on me Megan. I'll see both of you at eight in the morning", Cantrill said before he drove out of the garage.

They stood in silence in the dimly lit garage watching Mike drive away.

"Let me check on the mail, Mike. It'll only take a minute." Megan said as they left the garage and proceeded along the darkened corridor which led into the complex. Mike released his grip on Megan's hand as she turned towards the mailboxes off the side of the pool. He slowed his walk and turned his head for just a split second as he scanned the walkways of the second and third floors of the complex.

When Mike heard the clatter of keys as they hit the sidewalk, his heart almost stopped. He would have looked frozen in time if he hadn't moved for his pistol in its shoulder holster.

Before his head made the turn back to Megan's direction, he heard a gruff voice; one that he hadn't heard in over a hundred years. "Don't even try it, marshal. It's over and you lost. Toss your gun into the pool!" It was Andrews!

Mike finished turning his head and saw that Andrews had gripped Megan by her face with his hand covering her mouth. He saw the sawed off shotgun pointed directly at him. He also saw that Megan's eyes reflected total terror.

"I said into the pool, copper or somebody's going to get dead!"

As Mike tossed his pistol into the pool, his heart sank as fast as the pistol's weight carried it to the bottom. Mike fought the searing rage within himself as he desperately tried to devise a plan that would save him and Megan, but all that he could think of was the fact that Andrews had the upper hand and he was going to win — again!

The splash the pistol made only momentarily drowned out Andrews' words. "Just your bad luck, eh? I saw your wife the other day driving that black Honda Prelude. I just kept driving around and looking into garages and guess what? I found it parked in the corner of this garage. Too bad they put your names on the mailboxes, huh sweetie?" he said turning to face Megan. "Say marshal! Did you ever wonder how we all came back?" Mike saw that Andrews was grinning. "Come on over this way; out of the light. Even drunk I thought about it and us." Mike watched helplessly while Andrews pulled back on Megan's face; back into the direction that he wanted them to follow. Back into the edges of darkness where Mike knew that Andrews would kill him.

Mike started to move forward as he said, "Yeah, I've often wondered about it." Mike was gauging the distance between them and the distance to the darkness and slowed his pace once that he saw Andrews was listening to him. "Did you ever think it through?" Mike asked.

"Naw! But it sure is enough to make you get religion if you think long enough about it." Andrews still had that grin on his face.

"Long thoughts — that pretty much leaves you out!" Mike fired back.

Andrews stopped walking and that grin finally disappeared. "Whose got the drop on who if you're so goddamn smart? You lose! Again! I'm going to kill you, but this time I just wanted you to know that me and the missus are going to get better acquainted."

At this time, the front light came on at Sandie's apartment and her door started to open. When Andrews' took his eyes off of Mike, Mike dove for cover back into the corridor leading into the garage area. To his surprise, Andrews never fired, but apparently ran off.

As Mike struggled getting his backup gun out of the ankle holster, he heard two quick shots fired almost together. One was a shotgun and the other a pistol! "Sonofabitch!" was uttered in a deep voice. Megan screamed! There followed four quick pistol shots. Mike raced out into the courtyard and out through the walkway leading to the street. Nothing! Mike stopped to catch his breath. He was trying to suck in the air while trying to stay quiet enough so that he could hear over his racing heart.

The street was heavily tree-lined and their foliage blocked out much of the light from the meager street lamps. The wind accompanying the rain made for an eerie setting and made hearing and seeing difficult. If it hadn't have been for the muffled cry of pain, Mike would not have seen him.

Farther down on the sidewalk he saw Cantrill half sitting up trying to stop the blood flow from the gaping wound on his upper left leg.

Rushing to his side, Stewart knelt down to help Mike, who was losing a tremendous amount of blood. In the middle of Cantrill's leg, between the knee and hip, was a ragged hole torn into the flesh. Stewart practically ripped off his sports coat and placed it around Cantrill. He then knelt and pried Cantrill's hands off the wound so that he could get a better look. Almost simultaneously, Cantrill started to explain what had happened.

"I saw a green Buick with a cracked windshield parked on the street as I drove out and I suspected it was his. The engine was warm and not hot, so I figured he was waiting." Mike was talking almost as fast as he was bleeding. "I started moving towards the complex, but I wasn't prepared to bump into him with him carrying Megan off here on the sidewalk." Mike said as he watched Stewart take off his belt and tighten it around the wound.

"Shit, that hurts! Boy, that son of bitch was lucky!" Mike screamed through clinched teeth as Stewart pulled on the belt, but at least the blood loss slowed.

Lights were coming on in the houses surrounding the complex and dogs were barking. Stewart stood up and cupped his hands around his mouth. "It's the Sheriff's Department. Someone call the police and we need an ambulance!" shouted Stewart at the top of his lungs.

"Mike, I'm sure I hit him. He faltered for a split second after I fired. I fired the rest of my rounds low into the ground as I went down, because he started to walk up on me and I wanted to scare him off and not hit Megan. He ran back towards the alley between those two houses." Cantrill said pointing with the barrel of his pistol.

Tightening the belt more almost stopped the blood flow. As Stewart looked around, he didn't see or hear them. Turning his attention back to Cantrill, Mike looked directly into his eyes and said, "I can't stay and you can't go, Mike! I don't leave my partners behind, but I've got to go after Megan! The police will be here any minute now."

Stewart stood up as an elderly man in pajamas, slippers, and holding an umbrella started walking over to them. "We're cops! My partner needs an ambulance!" Stewart said to him.

"My wife already called the police. Can I help?" the elderly man replied.

"Just stay with my partner!"

"That old revolver's a nice touch, but I bet you didn't bring extra ammo for it." Cantrill grunted as he held out his hand with several loose .38 special rounds. As Stewart took the ammunition, Cantrill shouted, "Go on, get!" while he opened the cylinder of his revolver with his bloodied hands and tried reloading it from the loose rounds in his jacket pocket.

Stewart quietly moved towards the shadows that Mike had pointed out. Cantrill, meanwhile, fell over on his right side and cried aloud in pain.

Without trying to right himself, he continued to reload his pistol. Mike was badly hurt and while the movements caused further pain, he felt that if he didn't do something he would pass out and he was afraid that if he lost consciousness he wouldn't wake up again.

Stewart sprinted between the houses that Cantrill had pointed to and stopped in the backyards to listen. Lights were coming on everywhere and he could hear men's and women's voices. Even the pool lights came on at one of the houses he was standing between. The owners were having landscaping work performed and the fence was down. He couldn't see into the alley yet, but figured with so many lights coming on, it would be a matter of time before they would light up Megan and Andrews.

Stewart almost felt the sound before he heard it. It could have been the rain hitting an empty garbage can, but it could have been something brushing against it. He turned and headed towards the alley, but down back towards the apartment complex. He thought he may intercept whatever or whoever made the noise.

The alley was still dark as Mike surveyed the scene. Nothing! No footsteps, no muffled screaming, nothing! The seconds seemed as hours as Mike stood in a darkened corner and listened. His heartbeats pounded in his head as he struggled to hear above the noise the neighborhood was making as it was being dragged awake. Peering into the alley revealed nothing. Mike was beginning to panic. He was afraid to wait any longer for fear that he misjudged and Andrews was making his escape at the other end of the alley.

Mike started walking rapidly up the sloping alleyway. In the distance, he could make out the faint sounds of a police siren. It sure felt comforting! He crossed over towards the darker side of the alley with its bush and vine-covered exterior. It started to rain harder now and as it pelted him, he was forced to struggled all the more to see as well as to hear. As he again passed the house with the pool, he saw the shadow along the other side of the alley move. He pointed his pistol at it just as Megan came into view!

Mike could see that behind her hid Andrews. He was holding a knife to her throat; in fact the blade had cut the skin and a small trickle of blood was glistening in the dark. It ran along the right side of her stretched neck and spilled onto her sweater. Andrews' shotgun was pointed at Stewart. Mike could barely make out Andrews' outline. It appeared that he was crouched behind Megan and deliberately shielding his head from Mike's view.

"Drop the gun or the girl dies right here!"

"Don't Mike! He reloaded!"

"Shut up, bitch!"

It was the first that he heard from Megan since this began. Mike couldn't make out enough of Andrews to risk a shot in the darkness. He dropped his snub-nosed revolver onto the alley.

"You can't beat me. You never could. Now you're going to die again, shithead!".

Andrews pushed Megan out in front of him and into enough light so that Mike got a good look at him. Andrews motioned for Mike to walk over into the alley and away from the shadows that he realized he had been standing in. As Mike moved, so too did Andrews. Mike saw a broadening crimson stain on the right side of Andrews' shirt. Cantrill had hit him, but it wasn't a fatal wound. Mike figured that Cantrill had aimed wide trying to avoid hitting Megan by accident.

Mike continued to move until Andrews told him to stop. Mike was gauging the distance between them. Too far to try and make a grab for him or the shotgun. He was hoping that his bulletproof vest would protect him long enough for him to reach the barrels or Andrews. The sound of the sirens was growing louder, but Mike knew they'd never arrive in time to help him.

Andrews pushed the barrels out further and Mike started to brace himself for the noise and impact when he heard, "Hey, asshole!" It was Cantrill's voice!

Looking over Andrews' shoulder, Stewart could see Cantrill. He had hobbled in between the houses and was behind and slightly off to the side of Andrews. Unfortunately, he was also silhouetted against the backyard lights.

Andrews turned to fire at Cantrill. As he did so, Megan started to push against his hand with the knife and Andrews lost his balance as his feet collided with Megan's. Andrews and Cantrill fired again at the same time. Megan screamed as she felt and heard Cantrill's bullet fly past her left ear. This time he had aimed to kill, but hadn't anticipated Andrews' losing his balance. Andrews fired both barrels as he lost his balance. Cantrill's bullet missed, but both shotgun charges hit Cantrill and he fell backwards.

Stewart was moving for his pistol as soon as Andrews had shifted positions to fire at Cantrill. By the time he retrieved it, he saw Megan moving away from Andrews. He fired from a kneeling position and hit Andrews high in the back a split second after he fired at Cantrill. Andrews spun around to face Stewart. Stewart stood up and fired two more times hitting Andrews squarely in the chest. Andrews hit the ground hard falling face up. Andrews was trying to say something as he lay on the ground. Stewart fired once more, striking him in the forehead. It was 12:19 AM on the morning of November the 16th. The long nightmare was over!

"Michael! Help!"

It was Megan. He heard the splash of water. Stewart looked over the landscaping material and saw Cantrill floating face down in the pool that had been illuminated by its lights. Blood was billowing out from his body. The impact from both shotgun blasts had knocked him into the pool. The splash was from Megan who had jumped into the pool and was trying to hold Cantrill's head up out of the water. Racing over to the edge of the pool,

Stewart grabbed Mike's arms and pulled him out. Laying him down on his side, Mike went back and with one strong arm, swept Megan from the pool.

Mike rolled Cantrill onto his back as he heard the screeching of brakes and the slamming of car doors. Megan was kneeling across from Mike and shivering. He could see that her lips were turning blue from the cold water and she was crying.

"Is — is he dead?" she whimpered.

"I thought I heard him breathe as I laid him down." Pulling at his shirt, Mike found that Cantrill had been wearing a bulletproof vest, as well. The vest was peppered with shotgun pellets. By this time, an LAPD officer was running up with his gun drawn.

"We're LASD! My partner's been shot and I need an ambulance right now!" Stewart shouted. "There's a dead suspect up in the alley," he added pointing. Looking over Stewart's shoulder, the officer saw Cantrill and said that an ambulance was already on the way.

As the officer ran up the yard to where Stewart had pointed, Mike had Megan pull on the belt around Cantrill's leg wound while he took off his vest and checked for pellet wounds or other injuries. He found several pellet wounds on his upper arms. Fortunately, the shot size was relatively small and the pellets had not penetrated too deeply past the skin.

Meanwhile Megan pulled so tightly on the belt around Cantrill's leg, the metal buckle was digging into the skin. Still the blood ebbed freely from the torn flesh.

"Oh Mike, the bleeding's not stopping!" She looked at Cantrill's still form and his shallow breathing. "He looks really bad!" Megan cried as she pulled on the belt and continued shaking from the cold and crying out of fear and frustration.

Stewart didn't have the time or free hand to hold her as he was pressing Cantrill's femoral artery against the leg bone in a desperate attempt to keep his guardian angel alive. He looked at Megan over Cantrill's limp body and saw her close her eyes and she continued crying.

The first of several sheriff's units started arriving by the time the paramedics had Cantrill stabilized for the trip to the hospital. The paramedics had hurried as Cantrill's vital signs were not good and he never regained consciousness. The patrol sergeant told Stewart that sheriff's Homicide and Internal Affairs investigators were enroute and he was staying put. Stewart had Megan ride to the hospital with Cantrill. He knew that the department would send a black and white for Cantrill's wife, drive her Code 3 to the hospital, and he wanted someone there when she arrived and Stewart wanted Megan to have a doctor check on that cut to her throat.

CHAPTER FIFTY-THREE

It was almost eleven in the morning by the time that Internal Affairs investigators drove Stewart to the hospital. On the fourth floor outside the intensive care unit, Stewart found Megan. She was sitting next to Karen Cantrill and saw Mike at the same time and started running for him.

"Oh Mike! They just took Mike out of surgery and the doctors think he's going to be all right!"

As he hugged Megan, Mike could see Karen and her father standing up. They approached Megan and Mike. Mike met them half way and took Karen's hands in his.

"I'm sorry Mike got hurt, Mrs. Cantrill, but he saved both our lives this morning."

"I know. Megan told me all about it."

Shaken and with a tear-stained countenance, Mike thought that Karen looked very frail and vulnerable. He was glad that her father was there. Looking at her father, Mike thought to himself that he was built like a short bear; thick and powerful. Mike saw that even though there was a pained expression on his face now, it was a quiet, knowing face. The kind that lit up every time he saw his daughter or his grandchildren. It was a kind face on a good person.

Karen picked her head up and straightened up to her full height as she spoke. "I think you were both very brave under the circumstances. Megan told me how you tried to stop the bleeding. I'm glad that you were there to help Michael."

"No Mrs. Cantrill, it's Megan and I that are glad Mike was there. He was smart and very brave. As for helping, Megan did the hard part."

Megan came over and put her arm around Karen's shoulders. It was a gesture meant to steady Karen more than anything else.

"Everyone's been so considerate. Mike's captain showed up along with his division commander. Even one of the assistant sheriffs stopped by and said to call him if we needed anything." Karen looked down at the floor and continued talking. "I didn't even know that he had his vest on." she said in voice that was just above a whisper. "He usually does not wear one. I'm glad you're both ok. They wouldn't let me see Michael; not even for just a second. They were prepping him for surgery in pre-op by the time they drove me here and I signed the papers."

Karen paused momentarily. She appeared physically ill. "The doctors told me that they think he'll keep — keep his leg." She turned and started crying again as her father gathered her in his strong arms and escorted her back over to the chairs in the lobby.

"Are you all right?" Stewart asked as he looked Megan over. She was wearing a surgeon's scrub shirt and there was a bandage on her throat.

"I'm ok. They even took a few x-rays, but I'm fine." she replied.

"I want to see Cantrill!" Stewart said as he started walking over to the nurses' station.

"No one except family members can visit any patient in ICU," recited the nurse without even looking up from the chart that she was reading.

"You can take your regulations and stuff 'em, Nurse Retched. I'm going to see Mike!"

"Doctor!" called the nurse, whose full attention had been shifted to the man standing in front of her.

An older man appeared from around the corner.

"Look doc, I killed the bastard that did this to my partner, and I want to see Mike now! I'm not taking no for an answer!"

Before he could answer, a voice was heard from around the corner. "Elgin, I do not care if this impetuous, young man is allowed in to see my son."

Stewart saw a well-dressed lady walk around the same corner that the doctor had come from. Apparently, he had been talking with her when Mike had interrupted. "As you wish, Julia." said the doctor. He had been doing his residency with her husband during the Korean War and all had remained good friends, even after the death of Doctor Cantrill.

She couldn't have been five feet two, but she stood ramrod straight and had the bearing of a queen. Stewart watched as she walked straight towards him. For a moment, Stewart was reminded of his mother, Clarise Forsythe. He saw the same bearing and quiet confidence that only old money can give one fortunate enough to be born into it.

"I'm Julia Cantrill, Michael's mother and you must be his partner." It wasn't a question.

"Yes ma'am. I am Michael Stewart. Your son saved my life today. I need to make sure that he's ok."

"I can assure you, Mr. Stewart that Michael will indeed survive his wounds. I would not consider otherwise. While Michael is not completely out of danger as yet, he has everything he needs. I appreciate your concern for his welfare, though. Please follow me."

Inside the unit, Stewart saw Mike laying on one of the beds. Mike almost looked as if he were resting peacefully in his own bed, except for all the monitors. His hair was combed and he was even shaved! In addition to the monitoring system, Mike was receiving oxygen and he was hooked to an IV and enough electronics to be part of a NASA program. The antiseptic's yellow-purple tint was visible around the edges of the bandages on his arms. His left leg was elevated and lower torso uncovered by the sheet. Stewart supposed that the staff needed to make regular inspections. The bandages and sutures could not hide the damaged skin, the continued draining, and the blood. His entire pelvic region looked badly bruised. Stewart thought to himself that Michael had been very lucky.

"Michael will remain unconscious for several more hours. The wound was serious requiring extensive surgery. He was just brought here. Not even Karen has seen him, yet. I wanted to have him cleaned up before she saw him. Karen is very strong and she genuinely loves Michael, but I'm afraid that this would just be too much for her right now. Michael has been hurt before, but nothing as serious as this injury."

Julia Cantrill stopped talking for just a moment. She looked as if she was bracing for a punch.

"I want to thank you for helping my son this morning, Mr. Stewart. Elgin, Dr. Pierce, said that Michael would have bled to death if you had not used your belt as a tourniquet and applied pressure to his femoral artery to stop the bleeding."

Stewart looked at Mrs. Cantrill while she spoke. Despite her rigid backbone and stern demeanor, he saw genuine love and concern for her son. Mike thought to himself that no one would have ever been able to tell that Julia Cantrill have not given birth to the young man that she was providing such care and protection. Stewart now knew where Cantrill had come by his character that refused to give up or consider defeat. He was ready to wager, though, that Mike must have taken after his father in his friendly, gentle, and warm-hearted demeanor.

"No thanks are necessary, Mrs. Cantrill. Mike saved both Megan and me this morning. We're the ones who are in his debt. He's a very special person."

"Yes, he is." replied Julia in almost a whisper as she stroked her son's hair. "Michael has always been brave. My husband showered Michael with love and attention. I loved him too, but I also tried to teach him to be strong in this oftentimes harsh world."

Julia was speaking softly; almost as if to herself. "I remember the first time that I saw him. You see my husband and I adopted him."

"Yes, I know. He told me so over lunch just the other day", replied Stewart.

Julia Cantrill stopped and stared at Stewart momentarily before speaking again. "Then, you must be very special to Michael. I don't think that he's ever told a dozen people that information."

Turning back to her son, Julia continued.

"I really didn't want to adopt when I found out that I could not have children of my own; but William, my husband, was adamant that I see the little boy in the orphanage that Father Jacob administered. Michael had been scrubbed clean and rubbed raw. His hair was combed and parted to one side. They dressed him up in a blue suit with a matching bow tie. An old, German nun by the name of Sister Celestine escorted Michael into the office. I saw then that he had a death grip on her black robes, but he dutifully followed and obeyed instructions. When Father Jacob introduced him to us, Michael walked over and shook William's hand."

She stopped to wipe away a solitary tear from her eye. "I always thought he had been acting braver than he really was, but you couldn't help but fall for the little guy. Yes, Michael's very special to me."

Mike pulled up a chair and sat down. He reached over and held his partner's hand.

"It's over. I guess you were right. I did need a guardian angel. I owe you my life — my future. Thanks for Megan and everything, buddy."

Mike watched while Mike's chest moved rhythmically.

"His full name is Michael Francis", Julia Cantrill whispered. As she continued, she raised her voice slightly. "Father Jacob said that Sister Celestine named him for the guardian archangel and a gentle saint. She thought he could use the protection and guidance of the angels and saints considering how he came to the orphanage. Father Jacob said they found him on the church's doorsteps in the middle of a January Chicago blizzard wrapped in a woman's car coat. Michael wasn't but a few hours old. He was taken to the hospital where he was baptized and given the last rites of the Catholic faith because the doctors weren't sure if he would make it through the night. After his release from the hospital, Father Jacob said that he thought Michael was destined for great things. I think Michael has certainly lived up to his namesakes."

Stewart looked over at her and saw that Julia had tears running down her cheeks.

"After we adopted Michael, Sister Celestine spoke to me in private and told me, 'You take very goot care of my boy!' She had a profound influence on Michael. She taught him to speak German, he loves listening to Wagner, prefers German beers, and even to this day when Michael is being insolent, he will mutter under his breath, 'ja, ja, ja' in a German accent."

Stewart examined the IV hook up and watched the steady drip of fluid, before standing up and leaving. He stroked Mike's arm once more before leaving.

Julia Cantrill followed Stewart out. She said, "You look strangely familiar. Have we met before, sir?"

Stewart noticed that she had dried her eyes and there were no signs of the tears on her face. Mike smiled his best charming smile and said, "No ma'am, we have never met before. Is there anything that I can do for you or Mike's family?"

"I'm fine, thank you. As for Michael's family, I'll see to any of their wants or needs. Is there anything that I can do for you, sir?"

"Yes. You can quit calling me sir and allow me access to Mike as soon as he's conscious. Everyone calls me Mike. You can too, if you like." Mike was watching the expression on Mrs. Cantrill's face. "She can take a punch well for an old lady," he thought to himself.

"All right. I'll see to it that you are notified as soon as Michael's placed into his own room, Mike."

"Good!" he thought to himself. He had learned how to handle Clarise Forsythe and it appeared to be working with Mike's mother as well. He started to turn away from her, but quickly caught himself.

Speaking directly at Julia, Stewart said, "Inside you spoke of the priest that ran the orphanage." Speaking quickly before he lost his nerve, Stewart asked, "By any chance, would you know whatever happened to him?"

"Strange that you should ask about Father Jacob." she replied looking directly into Stewart's eyes.

Stewart didn't flinch, but remained silent. Looking slightly disappointed as well as puzzled, Mrs. Cantrill continued.

"Father Jacob was very old back then. Four days after my husband and I signed the final adoption papers for Michael, Father Jacob died in his sleep. William always said thereafter, that it seemed that getting Michael adopted was his last dream or goal. William was positive that he died happy knowing that Michael had been adopted."

Stewart had been looking down at the floor as Mrs. Cantrill finished her story. He looked up and directly back into her eyes and said, "Thank you, Mrs. Cantrill. Thank you very much."

He quickly turned and headed for the waiting room. Standing alone in the hallway, Julia was certain that she had seen tears in those fiery eyes of Mr. Stewart.

Before walking out the doorway, Mike stopped and turned around and walked back to Mrs. Cantrill. He stopped and said, "There's a pretty lady out in the waiting room with a tear-stained face. She doesn't have access to her husband the way you do with all your connections and pull. Let Karen in to see Michael immediately. She needs it as much as he does."

She looked indignant over the manner in which he spoke to her, but all that Mrs. Cantrill said was, "All right."

"One more thing, Mrs. Cantrill." Mike saw that she stiffened and fixed her eyes on him. "You didn't ask, but I thought I'd give you some good advice. Few of us ever get a second chance at life. Let your stiff upper lip down and let Karen into your life. She didn't steal Michael from you; she's an enhancement to everything that he brought to your world. Life's too short! Don't let the good pass you by!" Mike stopped, as he was afraid that his voice would crack if he continued to talk.

Julia Cantrill was speechless! She just stood in the hallway intently staring at Stewart.

Deciding to make a hasty retreat, Stewart said, "I'll be seeing you around, Mrs. Cantrill and for what it's worth, I think you followed the old nun's advice perfectly." and he quickly headed for the waiting room.

Stewart found Megan still sitting with Karen, who looked a little more composed. Upon seeing Mike come into view, Megan got up and hugged him again. "Are you ready to come home mister?"

"That's all I ever wanted to do since dinner last night."

Julia entered into the waiting room almost immediately after Mike. Mike watched as she walked up to Karen and taking her hand and placing an arm around Karen's shoulders, walked with her towards the double doors that led into ICU. Stewart watched them as they walked. Just as they reached the doorway, Stewart saw Julia stop and speak rapidly to Karen, but they were too far away and he could not hear their words. He saw that Julia had stopped talking and started to stare at the floor before Karen leaned over and hugged Julia. As he watched silently, he saw the both of them crying before heading back through the doorway to Michael's room.

Megan looked at them and then at Mike before she continued, but in a whisper, "Well, stop wasting time then and take me home and to bed." "But first, I think that we both need a shower," she said wrinkling her nose.

Mike replied, "I'm not wasting time. This is the first morning in a long time that we have our whole lives ahead of us. From now on, we get to make history and not relive it."

On the elevator ride to the lobby, Mike and Megan had the elevator to themselves and they held onto each other. It was Mike who said, "I'll have to make a phone call to New York when we get home. I have to talk to both Paul and — Lyn." His voice sounded a little sad; almost a sigh from the heart. Megan placed her arms around Mike and leaned her head against his chest. The rest of the ride was in silence.

As they stepped off the elevator, they were struck by bright sunlight flooding the surroundings through the floor to ceiling windows; as well as the noise and confusion accompanying the comings and goings of a major hospital. A new day had begun. Megan and Mike just stood in the middle of the lobby. Their struggles of the past night seemed such a long time ago.

Sensing something she could not put into words, Megan put her arm around Mike's waist.

Looking up at him, she said, "I'll be there with you when you make that call to New York. I know that it may seem a little frightening, but I'm here with you and I'll never leave your side again, Robert."

She had called him Robert without thinking. Mike's smile instantly returned and he hugged and kissed Megan.

Stepping back from her, Mike said, "Ma'am, I'm Robert Forsythe. I'm a United States Deputy Marshal." He bowed and swung his arm out in a sweeping gesture.

With a slight curtsey, she replied, "I'm Amanda Weaver, sir. I don't think I've met a United States Marshal before. Will you be staying in town long?"

"For the rest of your life, lady." he said as he kissed her hand. "Across time and forever." he continued as he straightened up.

They walked out of the hospital and into a bright new day.